# CHARLOTTE MACLEOD
## The O

A SARAH K
and MAX BITTERS

"The screwball mystery is Charlotte MacLeod's cup of tea." —*Chicago Tribune*

$5.99 US / $6.99 CAN.

ISBN 0-446-40397-0

9 780446 403979

5 0 5 9 9

$\triangleright$ S EAN

## Also by Charlotte MacLeod

# CHARLOTTE MACLEOD
# The Odd Job

**THE MYSTERIOUS PRESS**

Published by Warner Books

A Time Warner Company

MYSTERIOUS PRESS EDITION

Cover illustration by Mark Hess

The Mysterious Press name and logo are registered trademarks of Warner Books, Inc.

 Mysterious Press books are published by
Warner Books, Inc.
1271 Avenue of the Americas
New York, NY 10020

Visit our web site at
http://pathfinder.com/twep

W A Time Warner Company

Printed in the United States of America

Originally published in hardcover by The Mysterious Press.
First Printed in Paperback: September, 1996

10 9 8 7 6 5 4 3 2 1

It was in 1979 that young Mrs. Sarah Kelling Kelling was spotted somewhere near the corner of Beacon and Park Streets in Boston, waiting for her bearish Cousin Dolph to open the family vault and inter the remains of even more curmudgeonly Great-uncle Frederick. Since our first meeting, Sarah and I have had a number of adventures, out of which she still emerges as a blooming young woman. As our relationship brings us closer to the end of this century, however, I find myself at serious odds with Father Time. Somehow or other, I've aged lots faster than she, as have many things about Boston itself.

The ambience within which Sarah and her entourage function keeps having to be slowed down in order to retain a credible pace among the various episodes while today's Boston gallops ahead regardless of an author's continuing dilemma. For instance, I've had to create a reasonable facsimile of the old Charles Street Jail because the new one is far too elegant for my purpose. By now there are so many discrepancies that I've given up worrying about them and console myself with reminders that my characters are not taken from flesh-and-blood models but have hatched themselves out of the ever-flowing stream of the might-have-been. They are only as real as we make them, but that needn't stop us from enjoying them.

Charlotte MacLeod

# The Odd Job

# Chapter 1

"I never meant to be a prop for a clinging vine."

Sarah Kelling Bittersohn was far too well-bred to say so out loud, but there it was. How could she have anticipated two months ago that Cousin Anne, as Cousin Percy Kelling's horticulturally minded wife was now calling herself every chance she got, would twine about her like a morning glory (family Convolvulaceae) at every opportunity?

So far, Sarah hadn't figured out whether Anne's sudden devotion sprang from Cousin Sarah's having helped her to recover a treasured painting of a small ancestress serving as a perch for a parrot two-thirds her size or from Sarah's having refrained from telling Percy the awful truth about Anne's brief encounter with a total stranger (genus: *Homo*, presumably *sapiens*) who'd been clad at the time only in a rhubarb leaf.

Sarah supposed she oughtn't to blame Anne for the fact that a self-styled gentleman farmer from whose thoroughbred cattle Anne obtained the high-grade fertilizer for her prize-winning roses had just been appointed head of trustees at the Wilkins Museum. She did blame herself for having let Anne and Percy suck her into joining them at a Sunday luncheon with the farmer and his wife.

Lala Turbot was more or less what Sarah had expected. She'd seen too many of these overdressed, over-jeweled, over-

coiffed and underbred birds in gilded cages, married for better,
more often for worse, to older men who liked to play with
dolls. Lala had run through her lady-of-the-manor act and
offered them a preprandial drink, making sure they noticed
the handsome big art books piled ever so casually on the
coffee table. Sarah also noticed the transparent shrink-wrap
in which most of them were still covered. Poor woman, one
couldn't help feeling a bit sorry for her.

Elwyn Fleesom Turbot was another cup of cappuccino.
Sarah pegged him as a product of family money and one of
the less-ivied eastern colleges, where he'd have majored in
football and date rape before joining the family business in
some relatively lofty position. At this stage in his career, he
could hardly have escaped being chairman of some board or
other. Sarah had realized that the moment she'd stepped out
of Cousin Percy's elderly but well-maintained Volvo and been
given a shrewd once-over before Turbot had committed himself to a brief but emphatic handshake. But why the Wilkins?
How was this hybrid country squire, captain of industry, and
presumed champion of the arts going to fit in with a group
of superannuated aesthetes?

For many years, those high-minded old codgers had had
little to do except meet once a month and congratulate themselves that, true to the terms of Eugenia Callista Wilkins's
last will and testament, they had kept the palazzo she'd caused
to be reared in Boston's Fenway exactly as it had been on
the day it was first opened to the public. It was a great pity
that none of the trustees had been a little younger, a little
sharper, a little less easily overborne before the awful truth
about the Wilkins Collection had blown up in their faces. By
the time the dust had settled, two people associated with the
Wilkins were dead, one in jail, and nobody eager to chair the
board. Finally the meekest of the codgers had been bullied
into taking the chair, had meekly carried his burden of office,
and meekly passed to his reward several months ago. Those
unhappy few left on the board had each declined the honor

of replacing him. Sarah had known the Wilkins was desperate for a new head of trustees; she hadn't yet learned how they'd hit upon Elwyn Fleesom Turbot, but she would.

It had been at the grand opening in 1911 that a then Mrs. Alexander Kelling—there had always been Alexanders among the Kellings—had observed with the tact and courtesy for which Kellings were ever noted that Eugenia's latest plaything looked less like an Italian palazzo than a Babylonian bordello. Some wit among the crowd had picked up the quip and by the time the reception was ended, half the guests were calling Mrs. Wilkins "the Madam."

Making the best of a bad business, Eugenia Callista Wilkins had ordered new calling cards to be engraved with the name Madam Wilkins, but had never left one on a Kelling. Thenceforth, the Kellings in turn had boycotted the museum until one fateful Sunday afternoon when Mrs. Sarah Kelling, at that time a young widow running a boardinghouse, was invited there to a concert by one of her boarders.

This was a man whom she'd met not long before her first husband's sudden, shocking demise. His name was Max Bittersohn. He was a private detective specializing in the recovery of precious objects, notably fine art and antique jewelry. He had recovered a Corot for old Thaddeus Kelling, he'd been of inestimable help to Sarah after Alexander died. He was less than ten years her senior, he was attractive in a non-Kellingish way, and he was fun to be with.

Sarah had still been only in her mid-twenties then; there hadn't been much fun in her life so far, she'd accepted Mr. Bittersohn's invitation as a chance to taste forbidden fruit. The two of them had been leaning over one of the palazzo's balconies, watching a white peacock spread its tail among the massed flowers in the enclosed courtyard below, when the oldest security guard hurtled past them and crashed to his death on the antique mosaic pavement.

Thus, either by chance or by kismet, Sarah Kelling Kelling and Max Bittersohn had become so closely involved with the bizarre situation at the Wilkins that they'd wound up inseparably entwined with each other. Of course objections were raised on both sides. Max's mother had been urging him to marry, but she hadn't bargained for a daughter-in-law from the Codfish Aristocracy. Cousin Mabel Kelling had screamed even louder and longer than the peacock when she'd learned that Sarah was perversely intent upon changing her name to Bittersohn. Sarah herself was only too glad to make the switch, she'd been a Kelling quite long enough.

Marrying Max had meant marrying his odd profession, Sarah had taken to it as avidly as the Public Gardens' ducks took to popcorn. The ongoing involvement that developed between the Bittersohns and the Wilkins was by no means their most lucrative account, but so far it had paid for their honeymoon, the furniture for their new house at Ireson's Landing, and the obstetricians' fees for their son Davy, now going on three years old and the image of his father. Thanks to Max's diligence and expertise, and Sarah's sound common sense, a goodly part of the loot from the longest-running art robbery Boston had ever known was back where the late Madam Wilkins had decreed that it must hang until her stuccoed walls should crumble to ruin and molder away in dust.

Naturally Max hadn't had the Wilkins project all to himself. Other art detectives had taken up the challenge, but sooner or later they'd dropped out of the hunt. The Wilkins Collection was too chancy a proposition, considering how long ago some of the best pieces must have been stolen and how relatively small the museum's commissions would be if anybody did succeed in getting anything back.

Max Bittersohn, a Boy Scout in his youth, had been prepared. Starting from scratch with a brand-new doctorate in fine arts, a keen mind, a hopeful disposition, and a reputation for clean dealing, he had built up not only a loyal clientele but also a widely distributed network of part-time secret agents. Most of these worked primarily for the thrill of the game. So, if the truth were told, did Max Bittersohn.

Until Sarah came into his life, Max had run his far-flung enterprise pretty much single-handed. Together, they had added to the network an inner cadre, beginning with a distant cousin of Sarah's. Brooks Kelling was an ornithologist, a photographer, a sometime entertainer at children's parties, and, at the time of his recruitment, an odd-job man at the Wilkins Museum.

Even as the Wilkins scandal was breaking all around them, Brooks had carried on a brief but tempestuous wooing, mostly by bird calls, with Sarah's most glamorous boarder, a gifted tea-leaf reader named Theonia Sorpende. Part gypsy, wholly the grande dame, Theonia Sorpende Kelling was especially effective at extracting stolen property from middle-aged gentlemen of elastic conscience and susceptible tendencies, of whom there was seldom any dearth. Theonia's methods were entirely respectable and *comme il faut*, a fact that usually dawned on her willing targets just a moment too late.

Another holdover from the boardinghouse days was Charles C. Charles, an actor generally disguised as a butler but ready to assume any other role his employers might happen to need him for at any given moment. The real mover and shaker of the household on historic Beacon Hill, though, was Mariposa, who'd been Sarah's dear friend ever since Sarah had declared her independence by firing her late mother-in-law's lazy, cantankerous, untrustworthy personal maid.*

Lately the ménage had also acquired an apprentice. Sarah's cousin Lionel's eldest son Jesse, already skilled in acts of vandalism, pillage, and assorted rogueries at the age of seventeen and a bit, was being coached to steer his talents into legitimate channels and doing quite well, all things considered.

In theory, this unlikely assemblage of free spirits ought to have been a disaster; in practice it worked astonishingly well. Like other Beacon Hill houses of the early nineteenth century, the one that Sarah Kelling had inherited was not large, but it

*The Family Vault*

was tall. Counting the finished basement where Mariposa and
Charles had their private quarters and Brooks his darkroom,
there were five levels. Brooks and Theonia, as permanent
caretakers, used the master suite. Sarah and Max reserved the
third floor for such times as they wanted a pied-à-terre in the
city, and Jesse had the attic all to himself.

The street floor had been designed for a drawing room, a
smallish library, and a gracious dining room. In the days of
coal fires and five-dollar-a-month housemaids, the kitchen
had been in the basement. With the advent of gas stoves and
electric lights, part of the dining room had been sliced off
and turned into a small but adequate kitchen.

An office could have been squeezed in somewhere, but
none was either needed or wanted. In its fledgling days, the
one-man Bittersohn Detective Agency had rented a small
office in a big building on Boston's Windy Corner at the
junction of Boylston and Tremont streets. Some previous tenant had left a battered oak desk and an old-fashioned swivel
chair; Max had never got around to changing them. He was
seldom in the office anyway; nowadays it was more apt to
be Brooks who occupied the swivel chair.

Brooks would not be in the office for the next week or so,
however; nor would Theonia be trailing her lace-and-satin
elegance down the curving staircase of the Tulip Street brownstone. The pair had taken Jesse with them on a training exercise
that would include chasing down an elephant folio of Audu-
bon's *Viviparous Quadrupeds of North America*, allegedly in
near-mint condition, and a next-to-priceless flock of duck,
goose, and snipe decoys hand-carved by the great-grandfather
of a friend of Tweeters Arbuthnot's. The big treat would
be a flight in Tweeters's seaplane to visit some auks of his
acquaintance.

Tweeters had hoped that Sarah's Aunt Emma would join
the auking party. He'd been performing tentative courtship
rituals for the past year or so, but Emma was not getting the
message. Instead, she'd kept telephoning Sarah, demanding

to know why Tweeters couldn't take his mating instincts to some far-off haunt of coot and hern.

Sarah hadn't been able to offer much in the way of cheer or counsel, she'd had enough on her hands helping Max to set up a gest of his own.

One of Max's scouts in South America had sent word of a *rancho grande* in Argentina where there was a highly touted though quite possibly chimerical opportunity to recover two charming Watteau *fêtes galantes* that were still missing from the Wilkins Collection. Finally released from a long and tedious convalescence, too much a professional to ignore even the ghost of an inkling, Max had packed his bag, kissed his wife and child, and soared off into the blue.

Sarah had rejoiced to see her husband back on the job, though she wished he hadn't had to go so far away so soon. She also wished he'd been more specific about some of the things she'd be having to cope with during his absence, including this latest brainstorm of Percy's, whatever it might be. Max had mentioned it when he'd last telephoned from Argentina Thursday night; he'd suggested that Sarah might give Percy a buzz and see if she could figure out what the hell he was talking about.

She hadn't heard from Max since then, to her regret, but she'd heard plenty from Anne, who'd been acting, no doubt, on Percy's instructions. The gist seemed to be that Anne had been unofficially delegated by Percy to wheedle Cousin Sarah into going with them on Sunday to a luncheon at the Turbots' as Max's proxy. Just why had it been so important for her to alter her plans and come all this way to eat a boring meal with boring people and stare at a pastureful of large, ruddy beasts, when she might be missing a phone call from Max? What new machination did Percy have in mind?

It stood to reason that Percy Kelling would never have let himself be dragged out of his own armchair on a peaceful post—Labor Day weekend without some more powerful incentive than a bunch of bovines. Sarah had thought at first that this visit must have something to do with the Wilkins, but that was a bit unsubtle for Percy. One thing she was sure of, Elwyn Fleesom Turbot had to be one of Percy's absolute top-ranking clients. Even his polled Herefords were purported to be so highly pedigreed that it seemed like lèse-majesté to be partaking of one.

At least Mr. Turbot claimed that the beef now on the table had come from one of his own steers. There was no way to tell, as the meat had been cut up for what Sarah assumed was meant to be boeuf bourguignon. The fancy menu was of a piece with the too obviously interior-decorated dining room; that and the drawing room in which they'd had their aperitifs were all she'd seen of the house. These were quite enough.

On the whole, Sarah would have preferred to go back outdoors and hobnob with those handsome animals she'd watched lolling in lush green pasturage with their red-brown legs tucked under their snow-white chests and their jaws moving back and forth in placid rumination. They reminded her a little of George III.

So, now that she thought of it, did Elwyn Turbot. The resemblance had been quite marked when he'd stood out beside the pasture gate, contemplating his herd. His wife, however, showed not the slightest hint of resemblance to that shy, plain, docile little Charlotte Sophia who had dutifully borne His Bucolic Majesty fifteen children, dutifully shared the dull, rural life that farmer George had preferred to the not much livelier pomp and circumstance at court, and had dutifully kept her own counsel about the then-unknown disease that had gradually and sporadically driven Britain's beloved ruler, who was also his rebellious American subjects' allegedly baneful tyrant, into madness and ultimate death.

Bereft of the cows' company, Sarah tried to amuse herself by guessing Mrs. Turbot's age. Either Lala, as the others were addressing her although that was hardly likely to be her proper name, was at least twenty years younger than her sixtyish husband, or else she knew an awfully clever plastic surgeon.

Her hostessing costume was stunning. The tight-fitting silk pants, the low-cowled satin blouse, the flowing chiffon kimono coat, all in shades of old gold and smoky amber, struck precisely the right note with her swept-back auburn mane and her greenish eyes, and must have cost old Elwyn a mint. The shoulder-length golden earrings, the heavy gold neck chains in various lengths, the armloads of golden bangles, the up-to-the-knuckles gold rings on all eight fingers and both thumbs were perhaps a bit much for a quiet day in the country, Sarah thought, but perhaps they helped to take Lala's mind off the Herefords.

If, in fact, Lala had a mind. She must have run through her entire repertoire of elevated small talk over the aperitifs. Since they'd moved to the dining room she'd done little but smile vaguely when anybody addressed a direct comment to her and keep on playing with her freight of jingling bracelets. Perhaps she'd had a drink too many, she was eating almost none of the food that a good-looking but sour-mouthed young male servitor, got up in brown denims, a floppy-sleeved home-spun shirt, and a buckskin waistcoat, was handing around with no great éclat. Sarah couldn't blame Lala for her lack of appetite; the much-touted main dish said little for the Turbot beef and still less for the Turbots' cook.

Sarah herself could turn out a tastier bourguignon with a cheap cut from the supermarket, and often had. Her sister-in-law could do it even better in half the time. Once more Sarah wondered what had possessed her to give up a chance to spend some time at the lake with Davy and her beloved in-laws for a cool reception and a so-so meal. She might have got more of Elwyn Turbot's attention if she'd been a polled Hereford.

What it would take to capture Lala's undivided attention Sarah could not imagine, unless, God forbid, she and Anne had both shown up in garb even more exotic than their hostess's. Neither Sarah's sleeveless blue silk dress with its loose-fitting jacket nor Anne's crisp, daisy-patterned shirtwaist, though both becoming and suitable to the place and the occasion, could begin to compete with all that swoosh and jingle. Whatever had possessed Anne to insist so passionately—passionately for Anne, anyway—that the Turbots were both on tiptoe to meet her interesting cousin? And why had Sarah been fool enough to capitulate?

Along with the Tulip Street brownstone, Sarah had inherited from her first husband over thirty acres of waterfront and a dilapidated wooden firetrap at Ireson's Landing on the North Shore. Now the old Kelling place was gone; in its stead had arisen a joyous, simple house that seemed to be made out of sea air and sunshine. Sarah's friend Dorothy Atwood had drawn up the plans, Max's father had supervised the building, Max's mother had sewn the curtains, Max's sister had embroidered the cushions. The Kelling family's reactions had been mixed.

Cousin Percy's voice had been loud among those who'd excoriated Max Bittersohn and all his ilk for having destroyed the ramshackle ark that not one of the whiners would have raised a finger, much less a penny, to keep in decent repair. Actually it had been Sarah herself, alone and unaided, who had hired a wrecking crew and watched in triumph while they'd razed the drafty relic to the ground and trucked it away down to the last splinter.

Sarah had told Percy time and again that the house had been hers and hers alone, and that its destruction had been all her own doing. Nevertheless, he'd been adamant that nobody of Kelling blood could have committed so flagrant an act of vandalism unless she'd been goaded into it by that tribe of Shylocks she'd been fool enough to get mixed up with.

Percy had begun to modify his tone, though, now that he'd been made to realize how highly the Bittersohn family were rated around the North Shore, and where Max in particular stood with Dun & Bradstreet. No certified public accountant in his right mind could wax too censorious over an in-law

whose income and reputation for probity were both right up
there with Percy's own.

And this despite the known facts that Cousin Max's hair
was still showing not a hint of gray, much less a bald spot,
that his doctorate had been earned at a university which was
not Harvard, and that no evidence could be found to show
he had ever joined a fraternity. Or one of the right clubs. Or
even a wrong one. The man was an enigma.

But a successful enigma. Sarah was beginning to read the
fine print. Percy must be working up to have one of his upper-
echelon assistants drop a hint into Mr. Bittersohn's ear about
advantages that could accrue should Mr. Bittersohn care to
consider transferring his accountancy business to the presti-
gious firm of Kelling, Kelling, and Kelling. This engineered
visit, taking Percy's cousin to meet one of Percy's affluent
clients, was just another case of the camel's nose and the
nomad's tent.

Naturally Percy would not come straight out and admit that
Turbot was one of his clients. Percy was chary of naming
names; but if Turbot hadn't been on Percy's books, then Percy
would not have been here today. Turbot had just been elected
to chair the Wilkins Museum Board of Trustees. Max Bittersohn still carried their carte blanche to seek out and return
as many as possible of the museum's stolen originals. Just
why these circumstances should become a tempting hook to
catch another well-heeled client didn't make a great deal of
sense to Sarah; but why else would Percy have primed his
dutiful wife to lure her into acting as bait?

Sarah saw no earthly reason why Percy couldn't have
approached Max directly. It wasn't as though the two were
strangers, they'd met often enough at Kelling family festivities
and funerals, between which there was often not much difference. It was simply that directness was not Percy's way. He
loved to plot some intricate plan of action, then turn over the
legwork to one of his trusted deputies. Since engineering these
sorties was about the only fun Percy ever allowed himself,

his reasonably well-treated staff were quite willing to fall in with his schemes, playing their parts like real old Yankee horse traders. And this despite the fact that two of them were Finnish and one was Japanese.

# Chapter 2

If Max wanted to play games with Percy, that would be up to him. All Sarah wanted was to hear his voice. Max might be trying to reach home right now, hearing her taped message on the answering machine and wondering why she wasn't around to take his call.

Well might he wonder. On Wednesday, she'd had her work schedule and her support group all lined up in perfect order. Early Thursday morning, the kind lady who obliged at Ireson's Landing had woken up with some kind of stomach bug and didn't think she'd better come to work for fear of passing it on to Davy. Normally Max's sister Miriam Rivkin, who lived nearby in Ireson Town, would have been delighted to take Davy long enough for Sarah to get some work done, but she and Ira, her husband, had rented a vacation cottage on a lake that was just too far away for a reasonable commute.

That left Sarah and her son alone at the Landing, with Mariposa and Charles holding the fort on Tulip Street. Late Friday night, Mariposa had got an urgent summons to the bedside of a cherished great-aunt who was fading fast and calling for her. The aunt was in Puerto Rico. Sarah had spent most of Saturday rushing to Boston, with Davy in the car because she'd had nobody to leave him with, getting Mariposa paid, packed, and ticketed; turning her over to Charles for delivery to the airport, then rushing back to Ireson's Landing in hope that a miracle would happen.

Miracles weren't hard to arrange in the Rivkin family. Davy's grown-up cousin Mike had offered to pick him up first thing Sunday morning, drive him out to the lake, and give him a crash course in sand castles and minnow-chasing so that Sarah could get some work done. At bedtime, Sarah had told her son a story about a minnow, given him several extra good-night kisses, sung him to sleep, packed his small duffel bag, and staggered off to her own bed. Shortly after daybreak, Mike and his girlfriend had zoomed up the drive. The girlfriend had picked up the duffel bag, Mike had slung Davy over his shoulder and carried him off gurgling with joy.

Sarah had stood waving until they were out of sight, gone back inside to get dressed, decided it wasn't worth the bother, and carried a cup of coffee out to the deck. The seagulls weren't much company but they were better than nothing.

Not a great deal better. Sarah had had a premonition that, once Mike had got Davy out to the lake, Miriam would be on the phone suggesting that he stay on a while so that Sarah could get some work done. Sarah had seen beneath the artifice. Miriam and Ira wanted Davy to themselves, she'd be lucky to pry him loose by the end of the week. A whole, long week without Max, without Davy, without Miriam and Ira, without Brooks and Theonia, without Mariposa, even without Jesse. It was a grim prospect.

But somebody had to mind the store, as Max was wont to say. Sarah had weighed the situation and decided to drive back to Boston sometime during the afternoon; it would be neither fair nor prudent to leave Charles alone at Tulip Street. She'd had to let Mr. Lomax, who'd been tending the Ireson's Landing property since before Sarah was born, know that his services as caretaker would be particularly needed this week. It wasn't a good idea for the seaside house and grounds to be left unwatched and she didn't know how long she might get stuck in Boston.

At least this ordeal of a meal could not go on much longer. Sarah managed to suppress a sigh of relief as the sullen young waiter took her plate away. She'd done all that could reasonably be expected of her. She'd made admiring noises about the polled Herefords, she'd struggled to find words of praise for the stiff, garish, ruthlessly clipped and weeded plantings about which even Cousin Anne, consummate gardener that she was, couldn't wax enthusiastic. Because Anne had said Cousin Sarah was an artist, she'd been herded into the painfully restored barn and forced to look at the ever so quaint, mildly pornographic, too devastatingly folk-arty mural that some vandal had painted on a long panel knocked together from beautiful pumpkin pine boards, each nearly two feet in width. Those boards must have weathered at least a century of legitimate use, only to be sacrificed to an idiot's whim. Sarah felt queasy again at the recollection, or perhaps it was the boeuf bourguignon.

Fortunately, dessert was nothing more deadly than melon sherbet dribbled with Amaretto, served in squatty green glass goblets and garnished with the sort of expensive cookies that get sold through mail-order catalogs geared to the affluent suburbanite. Elwyn Turbot gobbled his sherbet in two spoonfuls, heaved himself to his feet, and made a quick switch from genial country squire to masterful man of destiny.

"First off, Mrs. Bittersohn, would you kindly tell me why your husband failed to show up for this meeting? I thought I'd made it sufficiently plain to your cousin that I wanted Bittersohn present."

Sarah had sensed something like this in the wind, she was not a bit surprised. "I'm sorry you're disappointed, Mr. Turbot, but my husband's away on business. Percy, why on earth didn't you explain that to Anne before you badgered her into phoning me?"

It was a rotten thing to say, but Sarah was not a bit sorry she'd said it. This was the first time in her life that she'd ever got the chance to watch Percy Kelling squirm.

Percy was one of the rock-ribbed, horse-faced Kellings. For approximately half a second, his craggy features were suffused with the exact same shade of russet as the Turbots' Herefords; and his wife's with the identical look of bland satisfaction that Sarah had noticed on those gentle, white-jowled ruminants' faces. Still, the Kelling code was inflexible. Percy could not be left hanging. For once, it was Anne who got her oar in first.

"Oh, Percy doesn't have to explain things to me. We both knew Max was off on one of his hunting trips, but we didn't see that it mattered. Sarah and Max are equal partners, Elwyn. When one's too busy, the other takes over. Percy knew that Sarah could cope and that you're eager to get going on your new project, so there was no reason to keep you waiting. Isn't that right, Percy dear? Shall I tell Elwyn and Lala how Sarah rescued our sweet little girl with the parrot?"

Percy's aplomb was back in order. "Er—perhaps later, Anne. I believe Elwyn has some questions about the Wilkins Collection which I'm sure Sarah can answer to his complete satisfaction."

Turbot loomed over his empty dessert dish with his head lowered, like a bull getting ready to charge. "Then suppose you answer me this, Mrs. Bittersohn. Give me one good reason why, as chairman of the board for the Wilkins Museum, I shouldn't slap you and your equal partner with a lawsuit for breach of contract."

The only sound in the room was the nonstop jangling of Lala Turbot's bracelets. Her husband continued to loom and glower, Percy Kelling looked more than ever like a horse with a frog in its throat. Anne's face was a careful blank. Sarah fought down an impulse to giggle.

"I assume you're talking specifically about a contract with the Wilkins Museum, Mr. Turbot."

"Of course."

"Then the answer is simple. You have no grounds on which to sue because there is not now and never has been any contract between the Wilkins and the Bittersohn Detective Agency.''

Turbot wheeled on his accountant. ''What the hell is she talking about? God damn it, Kelling, why can't you follow instructions? I suppose, because you couldn't get hold of Bittersohn, you thought I'd fall for this dumb little cutie-pants and let her waste my afternoon.''

Lala yawned without bothering to cover her mouth. Her husband glared at her. Percy Kelling might have wanted to glare at his cousin, but that would have been unsubtle. He took a deep breath and pasted a grim smile to his lips.

''Perhaps, Sarah, you may be able to clarify the situation?''

''I'll be glad to, Percy, though I certainly don't want to waste any more of Mr. Turbot's valuable time. Could you tell me, please, Mr. Turbot, how long you've been chairing the board of trustees?''

This was pure devilment. There was no way that Sarah couldn't have known, considering how long she and Max had been involved with the Wilkins. If she shut her eyes she could still picture what had happened on her first visit: the screaming peacock, the sprawling body, Max Bittersohn dashing down the grand staircase, Brooks Kelling standing staunch to his trust between a bogus Gainsborough and a broken-down sedan chair with a bad case of woodworm. At that time Sarah hadn't seen Brooks for ages. After the tumult had died, she'd invited him back to the boardinghouse for supper. A staff member named Dolores Tawne had gone along with Brooks, and seen the handwriting on the wall when Theonia Sorpende helped him to a slice of something rich and delicious.

Thus had Madam Wilkins's palazzo become once more a part of the Kelling family saga, though there was one chapter that Sarah had never told anybody. After the old security guard's death, when Max Bittersohn was trying to sort out the pieces, he'd persuaded his then landlady to accompany him on a surveillance mission to the Madam's, both of them disguised as Hindus. With the help of a sedan chair and a safety pin, Sarah had managed to cope when her sari came unwrapped. The real sticker had come when they stopped at Max's office afterward to get rid of their disguises and Sarah got hopelessly stuck in her too-tight bodice.

There had been only one thing to do, and Max had risen to the occasion. That episode was one link in the long chain of circumstances that had brought her here now and forced Elwyn Fleesom Turbot to admit that he'd only held office since Thursday afternoon. She pressed her case.

"Is it correct to say that until now you'd never served on any art museum board?"

This question went down even worse than the first. Turbot was blustering like a north wind at the corner of Park and Boylston streets on a January day.

"It was high time for new blood! The place was going to hell in a handcart, they begged me to take the chair because I'm a man who gets things done. Half those old fogies are in their dotage and the rest not far behind. I'm going to straighten that bunch out in a hurry, and don't you think I won't."

"I'm sure you will," Sarah cooed with her fingers crossed. "My husband and I will be delighted to draw up a list of competent art experts if you'd like. Are you a serious collector yourself, Mr. Turbot?"

If he was, Sarah hadn't noticed any sign of it. So far, she had seen only that disgusting travesty in the barn and a slick portrait of Lala over the drawing room fireplace. It reminded her of covers she'd seen on the kind of lurid paperback novels that Cousin Mabel bought for a pittance at garage sales and burned in her fireplace to show her contempt for such trash, though not before Mabel had read them. Here in the dining room there were only matted and framed color photographs of polled Herefords, each with a blue-ribbon rosette from one cattle show or another attached to its frame.

Lala hadn't rated a blue ribbon, Sarah didn't see any reason why she should. When the surly waiter served the sherbet, he'd left the Amaretto bottle close to Mrs. Turbot's hand;

she'd been adding extra dribbles of the liqueur to her sherbet as the spirit moved her. Now she splashed in a sizable dollop, raised the heavy goblet in a swift but all-inclusive toast, drained it dry, ran her tongue around her lips, and took it upon herself to answer Sarah's question.

"You bet he's a collector, cutie-pants. But don't get any ideas. He only collects cows."

While Turbot was trying to pretend that he found his wife's vagaries amusing, Percy cleared his throat and took the floor. "We seem to be straying from the subject here. You were about to explain, Sarah, why no contract exists between the Wilkins Museum and the Bittersohn Agency."

"Thank you for reminding me, Percy."

Sarah was easily the youngest woman there and looked even younger than she was by contrast to her weather-beaten cousin the gardener and that well-preserved tribute to the cosmetologists and the haute couture. The sedate jacket dress and the Psyche knot into which she'd twisted her baby-fine light-brown hair suggested a sub-deb wearing her mother's clothes, as in fact Sarah had done more often than not during her less affluent years. Her eyes were an interesting mixture of brown and gray, one set a whisker higher than the other in a pale squarish face that could blush like the rose or set like a statue of Queen Boadicea as occasion demanded. At the moment, Sarah's demeanor was nobly bland enough to have made anybody who knew the signals tread warily. Turbot would learn soon enough.

"Since you're so obviously new to the art world, Mr. Turbot, I should explain that it's simply not possible for us to give our clients any guarantee as to when or whether a stolen work of art will ever be recovered. One problem with paintings is that they're so easy to disguise."

Turbot didn't like being lectured, he scowled. "Disguise how?"

"Lots of ways. Some thieves lay a fresh ground over the

surface and paint a different picture over it that can be wiped
off without harming the original."

"Huh. What kind of picture?"

"Anything, or nothing in particular. It's amazing what trash
can pass for art these days." Sarah was still bitter about those
vandalized barn boards. "Another way is to hide a valuable
canvas under a not-so-good one and fasten them both to the
same stretcher. That's an amateur's trick but it still gets tried
and sometimes works."

"I could make it work." Now that she'd been refueled, Lala
was showing real interest. "What else do they do? Suppose I
walked into the museum and stole a painting in broad day-
light."

"You'd be caught and sent to jail. That's why museums
have security guards."

"How about if I took along an accomplice? We could be
dressed just alike. One could keep the guard interested while
the other cut the painting out of the frame with a razor blade
or something and stuffed it under her clothes."

"That wouldn't be so easy as it sounds. In the first place,
two women dressed just alike would be noticed, and watched.
If one did manage to cut the painting out of the frame, she'd
have to be awfully quick and careful or the blade might slip
and do serious damage. If she stuffed the canvas inside her
clothes she'd most likely crack the paint surface and lower
the value of the painting. But again, it does happen. My
husband once caught a thief in the men's room of a place I'd
better not name. He'd cut a nice little Sargent beach scene
out of its frame and was taping it to a plaster body cast that
he was wearing."

"What did your husband do?"

"Flashed his private detective's license and yelled for a
guard to call the police. Luckily the painting wasn't badly
damaged, though of course it had been somewhat reduced in
size by the cutting."

"But still salable?" Lala insisted.

"I suppose so, if the buyer was gullible enough."

"How about that?" Lala's bangles were making such a racket that she had to quit waving her arms to make herself heard. "There we go, Elwyn. After your next board meeting, you just stick a few masterpieces under your coat and wear them home. We then paste photos of the cows on top, take them to Palm Springs, peel off the cows, and peddle the Rembrandts to the movie stars. How about you, Percy? Care to join the mob?"

Mr. Kelling was not amused. "Thank you, Lala, but I hardly think grand larceny is my métier. Just out of curiosity, Sarah, what if the painting one wanted to steal was too big to carry?"

"Like that big—ah—Titian, is it?" Elwyn Turbot had been silent too long to suit him. "The one with the—"

Anne Kelling shifted a bit in her chair and coughed behind her napkin. Percy threw his wife a glance of approval and took up the torch.

"Quite so, Elwyn. By all accounts, the Titian—the original Titian, I should say—was the gem of the Wilkins Collection."

"Which Bittersohn was supposedly going to get back," Turbot snarled.

Percy made a neat job of not noticing that he'd been interrupted. "Think of the thousands upon thousands of art lovers who have admired that work of genius, but how many have recognized its historical aspect? Even you, Sarah, may not be aware, though you certainly ought to be, that the woman in the painting was a noble Roman matron named Lucretia, or Lucrece. A paragon of beauty and a model of domestic virtue, she was depicted by Titian as being—ah—mishandled by one Tarquinius Sextus, a son of Tarquinius Superbus. Lucrece's husband was a first cousin of that brilliant statesman Lucius Junius Brutus, who wrested the reins of power away from Tarquinius the Elder, drove the Tarquins out of Rome, and established a republic."

"He and his cousin?" teased Lala.

"So what are relations for?" Sarah seemed to be the only

one who heard what the surly young waiter mumbled. He gathered up the dessert service, carried his laden tray to a swinging door that must lead to the kitchen, and kicked it open with quite unnecessary violence. Not batting an eyelid, Percy finished his history lesson.

"After having informed her husband and father of the outrage to which she had been subjected, and having exacted from them a solemn vow of vengeance upon the Tarquins, the noble lady, preferring death to dishonor, took her own life."

"How times have changed." Having resumed her lady-of-the-manor manner, Lala rose from the table. "What do you say, anybody? Would you care to go back to the pasture and pat the pretty moo-cows?"

# Chapter 3

There were no takers. Percy glanced at Anne, Anne glanced at Sarah. Sarah nodded. Anne did what was proper, as always.

"This has been delightful, Lala, but we really ought to be getting along. Percy has things to do." Which would consist of switching on the television to some sports program or other, settling into his armchair, and going to sleep in front of the tube. "And Sarah's expecting a long-distance call from her husband."

Turbot wasn't letting that pass without a parting shot. "Then will you kindly remind your husband for me, Mrs. Bittersohn, that even if he doesn't have a written contract with the Wilkins, there's still such a thing as a gentlemen's agreement. I haven't yet had time to go into the matter thoroughly, but so far it looks to me as if Bittersohn's been dragging his feet over that Titian for the past six years, and it's high time he showed some action. You might also mention that there are plenty of other operators in his line of work who'd be only too glad to take on the assignment without soaking us for another of those fat fees he's been so punctual about collecting."

Cousin Percy froze stiff as a fly in amber. Cousin Anne was regarding Turbot as though he were a jimsonweed that had suddenly popped up among her gypsophila. Sarah was the coolest of the three.

"You seem to have been misinformed, Mr. Turbot. My husband has not been dragging his feet, he hasn't asked for a penny that wasn't earned several times over, and he's tried very hard to interest other agencies in taking on some of the Wilkins work. The response has been mostly negative. The trails were too cold and the fees too small to be worth their time and risk. If you can locate any reputable agency willing to take on the job without demanding hefty retainers up front and no strings attached, I strongly suggest that you accept their offer."

"Hunh. So you're backing out too, is that it?"

"No, Mr. Turbot, that is not it. I'm merely trying to point out to you some of the realities you'd have done well to consider before you accepted the chairmanship. Right now, all I can tell you is that we still have not the faintest clue as to where the Titian might be."

Turbot must have practiced snorting with one of his bulls, he did it beautifully. "It's been taken out of the country, naturally. How stupid can you get?"

"Not stupid enough to fall for such a jejune solution, Mr. Turbot." Sarah expected another snort, but Turbot didn't appear to know what jejune meant, so she went on. "We have a widespread and reliable international network of informants, none of whom has come up with anything. The Titian is too large and far too precious to be smuggled any great distance without enormous risk. The logical assumption is that it's hidden somewhere not far away from where it was stolen. Since no ransom demand has been made, we assume it's being held for other reasons."

"Such as what?"

"Maybe the thieves think it's still too hot to offer for sale, or maybe some cuckoo just likes it to look at."

Sarah made a move toward the door, but Lala wasn't ready to let the party die.

"Percy, you're the one who knows all about high finance. How much would they want for a ransom? Do you mean that crooks actually kidnap paintings instead of people?"

Didn't the woman ever read a newspaper? "Oh yes, Lala." Percy must be reminding himself by now that the Turbots were lucrative clients. "It happens. Frequently an insurance company becomes involved."

Sarah was growing very tired of this conversation. "There isn't any insurance in this case. Madam Wilkins was too cocksure of her security arrangements to believe that anybody would dare to steal any of her treasures. And of course art robberies weren't such a big business then. Furthermore, the endowment that seemed so munificent at the time of Madam Wilkins's death is drastically reduced by now, partly because everything costs so much more and partly because, as you must have found out at the trustees' meeting, Mr. Turbot, there had been some milking of the funds during the previous chairman's tenure."

"Is that supposed to be a hint?" Turbot growled.

"Only if you choose to take it as one. I did leave my handbag in the foyer with yours, didn't I, Anne? Thank you for a most interesting visit, Mrs. Turbot."

It was a relief to get back in the car, even with Percy at the wheel. Knowing his views on women who chattered while he was trying to keep his mind on the road, Sarah and Anne had opted for the back seat. Anne took advantage of a sympathetic ear to explain in detail what the Turbots' landscaper should have done instead of what he did. Sarah made appropriate noises from time to time and continued to wonder why the board of trustees, some of whom were still at least partially compos mentis, had turned over the reins of office to a man so patently wrong for the job as Elwyn Fleesom Turbot.

Sarah rather wished she could be a fly on the wall the first time Turbot locked horns with Dolores Tawne. Mrs. Tawne was not even on the board, but she'd have made a far better chairman than the lot of them put together. For roughly three

decades, Dolores had been the Wilkins's chief prop and main-
stay, taking on all the odd jobs from mending the moth holes
in the tapestries to doctoring the peacocks and deadheading
any flower in the courtyard that dared to fade before the
gardeners' weekly visit. All in all, her dedication and skill
had been utilized so zealously that they'd led, among other
malefactions, to two murders and a near miss.

Because the trustees could not imagine how the museum
would be able to stay open without Dolores, particularly after
visitors had quit coming in hordes and the cash flow had
slowed from a torrent to a trickle, they had voted unanimously
that the catastrophe hadn't really been her fault. Having
already figured that out for herself, Dolores had thanked them
for their vote of confidence, risen above the ruins, and sol-
diered on as usual, dusting the bibelots and berating the security guards with unflagging zeal.

Dolores would be Turbot's greatest asset, Sarah was thinking, if only he'd have sense enough to give her the chance.
Not that Dolores would need much of a chance; she was
bullheaded enough not to take any lip from a blustering neo-
phyte and old enough to get away with telling him off. Sarah
had noticed often enough how those big, strong man-of-des-
tiny types tended to quail before women who reminded them
of their mothers. Turbot wouldn't have tried his bullying
stunt on Sarah Kelling Bittersohn, she decided with some
resentment, if she'd been twenty years older and fifty pounds
heavier.

Anne Kelling voiced something along the same lines, keeping her voice low so that Percy wouldn't overhear and tighten
his lips. Having covered the ground from unimaginative landscaping to Lala's bangles to that young waiter's lack of savoir
faire, she remarked, "Don't you think, Sarah, that it was out
of place for Elwyn to make such a fuss about Max's being
out of town? You handled him well, I must say."

Sarah shrugged. "So did you. I expect Mr. Turbot tried to
give me a hard time because he didn't think I'd bite back.

Cousin Dolph used to bluster like that sometimes before Mary Smith took him in hand, bless her heart. Dolph's quite human now."

"So I've noticed. I must drop Mary a note about those plants for the Senior Citizens' Recycling Center."

"You really are an angel, Anne. You know, I don't think I'd better stop at your house any longer than to pick up my car. I need to push on to Tulip Street and see what's happening there."

"Oh dear, I was hoping you'd stay for tea. How long will you be in Boston?"

"I wish I knew. With Mariposa gone, I'm not too keen on leaving Charles there by himself for any great length of time. He's so used to being directed when he's acting and being bossed around by Mariposa when he's butling that he keeps looking for a prompter to feed him his lines. When he does try to take the initiative, it tends to backfire."

"But Uncle Jem's right there on the Hill," Anne pointed out. "Can't he and that nice valet of his move in for a few days and keep Charles company?"

"That's a case of the cure being worse than the ailment," Sarah replied. "Egbert alone would be fine, but Uncle Jem's helpless without him so it has to be both or neither."

"I do wish there were some way I could help," Anne fretted. "Perhaps I could nip over tomorrow and put in a little work on your flower beds."

Anne would never have dreamed of offering to take Sarah's child for a day; Sarah's perennials were quite another matter. Sarah understood perfectly and gave Anne an A for Agriculture.

"Would you really, Anne? Mr. Lomax will be around, but his rheumatism has been acting up so that he can't do much bending or stooping. Please don't ask him how he feels, though, he likes to pretend he's as good as he ever was. I don't have a spare house key to give you, but Mr. Lomax will have one. He knows who you are, of course, just tell him

I said to let you in. And please feel free to use the kitchen. You'll be wanting a cup of tea and Max's mother sent over some lovely pastries with prune filling. Help yourself, they're in the fridge.''

"What fun! This will make a nice change for me."

Sarah couldn't quite see how weeding somebody else's perennial borders would be all that different from weeding one's own, but she wouldn't have said so for all the tea bags in Chinatown. Their talk turned to Sarah's landscaping needs; at least Anne talked and Sarah did her conscientious best to listen. With October's bright-blue weather approaching, Anne was all for blending massed chrysanthemum plants in shades from yellow to rust at the top of the drive for a splash of autumn color. It sounded lovely. Sarah took out her pen and checkbook on the spot, wrote a check made out to Anne's most-favored nursery, and told her cousin to do as she thought best. Anne accepted the check with awe and wonderment and vowed to be true to her trust, though not in those precise words.

Anne really was a dear in her own funny way, Sarah thought as she put her wallet back in her handbag. Max had his wife well-trained by this time; Sarah's house keys were locked in the glove compartment of the car that she'd left parked in Percy's driveway. Her charge cards, her checkbook, her driver's license, and her ready cash were in the slim wallet that she'd slipped into a pocket sewn inside her skirt before dropping her handbag with Anne's on the refectory table in the Turbots' front hall. Anybody who might have cared to investigate her comb, lipstick, and clean handkerchief would have been welcome to do so.

Always having to be on the qui vive was a boon to the reflexes but sometimes a pain in the neck. Sarah wondered how it might feel to be fixated on chrysanthemums instead of criminals for a change. Dull, probably. She did wish she could go back to Ireson's Landing, if only for an hour or so, but that would be silly. The whole purpose of driving her own car to Percy's had been to shorten the drive to Boston.

Brooks and Theonia had commandeered Max's elderly leviathan, which was ideal for driving on long trips now that Ira had fitted it with a less gas-hungry engine and every other environmentally acceptable safeguard he could think of. Basically, this was the same car in which the enigmatic Mr. Bittersohn had driven semi-hysterical Mrs. Alexander Kelling from Ireson's Landing to Beacon Hill only a few hours after she'd been told that she was a widow. The car had been almost new then. Since she'd become Mrs. Bittersohn, Sarah had driven it scads of times. She didn't begrudge the travelers their comfort today, she was content with the less opulent but easier to park mid-sized American model that she'd bought when it became obvious that a backup vehicle was essential to their growing family business.

Sarah had picked this car not only because she liked the way it behaved but because it was identical with many others of the same make and color. Sometimes, being just one more in a crowd could be an advantage. In a supermarket parking lot, trying to sort out her own vehicle from all the other look-alikes was more apt to be exasperating, so Sarah kept a shocking-pink ribbon at hand to tie around her aerial when she went grocery shopping. She also carried a blaze-orange pennant in case of emergencies but so far she'd never had to use it. As she said good-bye to the Percy Kellings and turned the ignition key in the lock, she was inwardly hoping to goodness that she wouldn't find yet another emergency waiting for her on Tulip Street.

Sarah could easily have run into one before she ever got there. Two idiots in a gray Toyota tried to give her a hard time. Little did they know that this dainty lady had been on familiar terms with every bump and jog in the road before she was out of her teens. She led them a merry chase until she caught the blue flash of a state police car, ditched the Toyota slick as a weasel, slowed down to a decorous forty-five, and caught a gratifying glimpse through her rearview mirror of the two silly fellows—she supposed they were fellows—getting hauled over to be dealt with as they deserved.

This seemed to be her day for handing out comeuppances. Sarah was feeling rather smug by the time she turned up Tulip Street. Evidently some of the neighbors weren't back from their Sunday drives, parking was less dire than usual. Charles must have been watching through the window, he was out on the sidewalk and opening the car door before she'd had time to switch off her motor and unfasten her seat belt.

"May I assist you to alight, moddom?"

Sarah tried to keep a straight face and failed. "Don't overdo it, Charles. Here, take these flowers."

The handsome bouquet had been a last-minute offering from Anne, who'd had the flowers conditioning in a bucket beside the greenhouse in case Cousin Sarah couldn't stay for tea on account of all the exotic and important things she had to do. Anne had made a professional job of overcoating her offering for the road in wet paper towels and plastic baggies while Percy was unlocking the door and disconnecting the burglar alarm that he'd talked himself into buying after a skinny thief had wriggled in through a small vent in the greenhouse roof. It was sweet of Anne to share her flowers, but just now Sarah's mind was on other matters.

"Has Max called yet?"

"The mahster checked in at precisely two twenty-three pip emma. Negotiations appear to be proceeding, though less rapidly than he'd hoped because everybody keeps wandering off and taking siestas on horseback. He left a number for you to call back, not that he holds out much hope of your getting through to him any time in the immediate future. He says nobody down there seems to know what immediate means, and they're none too clear on future, but you know the mahster's penchant for hyperbole. Would you wish me to leave the car where it is, or take it over to the garridge?"

"Good question. Let's think about it."

Sarah rushed into the house and made a beeline for the telephone. Charles refrained from offering to dial for her and went off to find a suitable vase, vahse, or vawse, as the mood might seize him. Having played so many butlers, valets, and even an occasional housemaid in his sporadic acting career, he'd had a fair amount of training at arranging flowers; he would do full justice to Anne's handsome offering. It was a pity, Sarah thought as she started to dial, that the family wouldn't be around to admire the result.

She picked her way through the intricacies of international dialing, waited in fidgets until somebody said something in Spanish, and made the mistake of asking for Mr. Bittersohn. If she'd said Señor Max, she'd have saved herself some grief. Eventually, however, she managed to sort out her husband's voice from a wild twanging noise that she took to be technical problems on the line.

"Max, is that you? We have a dreadfully noisy connection."

"Sorry, querida, it's the best I can do. For some unfathomable reason, every telephone in the area's gone on the fritz except this one, which is in the only bar for fifty miles or so. Ay, compadres, quieto! Shut up! My esposa's on the teléfono."

"Whom are you shouting at?" demanded the esposa.

"Twenty drunken guitar players who want to serenade you. They've played 'La Paloma' for two hours straight while I've been sitting here waiting for your call. What the hell kept you?"

"Idiocy. I made the mistake of letting Anne and Percy drag me off to luncheon with the new head of trustees at the Wilkins."

"Did you tell him about the Watteaus?"

"I never got the chance," Sarah confessed. "Max! Have you got them?"

"Sí, señora. At least I think I have. There are still certain formalities to be gone through, if you get my drift. What's the guy like? Note that I take it for granted he's a him. It comes of hanging out with all these macho vaqueros."

"Oh, then you and Mr. Turbot will have something in common. He raises polled Herefords."

"You mean cows that vote?"

"I don't suppose they do, but I shouldn't be surprised if they could. They're too pedigreed for words. Darling, is your leg giving you trouble? You're not trying to ride the llamas or anything silly, are you?"

"No, querida, I'm saving myself for you. What's happening back there? Where's Davy? Can you put him on?"

"No, I can't. He's at the lake with Miriam and Ira. We have a bit of a situation here."

"What kind of situation? Is Davy all right?"

"Yes, dear, he's fine. It's just that Brooks and Theonia have gone off in your car with Jesse as you knew they were planning to do. Which was fine too. But then Mrs. Blufert came down with some kind of bug, so she couldn't come. Friday night Mariposa got word that her great-aunt—the nice one with the twenty-seven goats—was either dying or already dead. So Mariposa had to fly down to Puerto Rico yesterday morning and I've no idea when she'll be back. But Charles is here and Anne's going to help Mr. Lomax plant chrysanthemums around the driveway at home, so we'll muddle through. But I do miss you, darling."

"You damned well better. Look, if I don't get things wrapped up here within the next couple of days, I'll just say the hell with it and come home to help out. Okay, kätzele?"

"Of course it's not okay. You can't back away so long as there's a chance of getting what you went for. Trust me, Max. I can cope."

# Chapter 4

Brave words, but Sarah didn't for one moment suppose that Max was any more thrilled to hear them than she'd been to utter them. While she was trying to think of a more appropriate good-bye, the line went into a frenzy of sputters and died. She put down the handpiece and stood there wondering until Charles came back with his floral offering.

"That's lovely, Charles. It didn't take you long."

"Piece of cake. Mrs. Percy had already stripped the stems so that the water wouldn't get fouled by dead leaves. All I had to do was pop the flahs in the vawse and fluff them out a wee bit. I'll set them in the bay window, shall I?"

"Why not on the coffee table?"

"Because Mrs. Tawne is coming to tea."

"Charles, you beast! Why didn't you tell me?"

"I was going to, but you didn't give me a chance."

"I don't suppose I did, now that you mention it. Did Dolores say what time she was coming?"

There wouldn't have been any point in telling Dolores Tawne not to come. It was typical of her to invite herself, set her own time, and arrive spang on the dot, expecting to find the tea tray set out and the kettle at the boil. Somehow or other, by telepathy or smoke signals, she must have got wind of Sarah's visit to the Turbots; she'd be itching to air her own views on the new chairman.

Sarah could understand that. She wouldn't have minded airing a few of her own views if she hadn't learned early on that great dustups from little tongue-slips grew. "Five o'clock, as usual, right? Do we have anything to feed her?"

"No fear. As soon as she'd called, I nipped down to the corner and bought a package of those squishy-wishy ooey-gooeys she likes. We also have cheese and crackers in good supply and I can whop together a plate of tuna-fish sandwiches to fill in the chinks. Crusts off, right?"

"Crusts definitely off. You'd better light a fire, Charles, so that the room will be warm when Mrs. Tawne gets here."

Not that it would matter to Dolores, she was about as close to a fire-breathing dragon as a human could get; but Sarah herself was feeling a nip in the air now that the sun had gone around. She remembered a cardigan that she'd left in the downstairs bedroom closet along with a few other garments, and was glad.

"I'm going across the hall and write some letters. Keep an eye on the clock for me."

"Your wish is my command. Shall I thump or just bellow?"

"Whichever you think the script calls for. I'll see you in a while, then."

Back in the boardinghouse days, Sarah had turned her drawing room into a downstairs bedroom for an elderly tenant. After Brooks and Theonia took over and the boardinghouse became again a private dwelling, there'd been talk of turning it back to its original state, but nothing had been done. Elderly visiting relatives liked not having to climb two or three flights of stairs to find a place to sleep. The room had been particularly useful after Max had suffered some cracked ribs and a badly smashed leg this past April, spent far too long in Massachusetts General Hospital, and been released in late May on condition that he stay in town and report for therapy on a regular basis.

Having to miss the whole summer at Ireson's Landing had

been a disappointment, but ferrying Max back and forth would have been far harder on both patient and family. He, Sarah, and Davy had all settled in with Brooks and Theonia; life on Tulip Street* had proved to be more interesting than they'd expected. Seeing Max progress from walker to crutches to cane and finally to his own two feet with no help needed would have been worth any sacrifice to Sarah.

During those early weeks when Max had needed to rest much of the time, Sarah had brought a small but sturdy table into the bedroom and appointed herself his secretary, writing letters and taking notes from his dictation. Being able to maintain an active role in his far-flung business even when he could barely wiggle his toes was probably the best therapy Max could have had. Knowing herself to be part of the healing process had helped Sarah to keep up her own spirits as well as her husband's.

Sitting here now, doing a few of the odd jobs that she'd promised to take care of in his absence, Sarah didn't feel so far away from Max. Concentrating on the work, she quite forgot until Charles thumped at the door to announce that Dolores Tawne would be arriving in exactly ten minutes. She flung off the cardigan, put the blue silk jacket back on, tidied her hair, freshened her lipstick, and sailed out to greet her guest.

Sarah needn't have rushed. Five o'clock came, Dolores did not. The time passed. By half past five, Sarah and Charles were staring at each other with a wild surmise.

"You're quite sure she said five o'clock, Charles?"

"Quite sure, moddom. I wrote down the time on the pad before I sent out to get the squdgy-wudgies. We Admirable Crichtons do not make mistakes."

"But Dolores is never late, not by a minute. You don't suppose . . ."

*The Resurrection Man

"I never suppose, it's unbecoming to my station in life. May I suggest a tuna-fish sandwich to calm your nerves?"

"Oh, Charles, quit acting. Is that the phone?"

Sarah beat Charles to it. "Hello. Dolores?"

"Oh, M-Mrs. K-K—have I the r-r-r-ight n-n-n—?"

"Mr. Melanson! I haven't spoken to you in ages."

"But you recogn-n—" overwhelmed by the incredible honor of hearing his voice remembered, the timid soul faltered into total incoherence.

"For Christ's sake, Milky! Give me that phone."

Sarah was good at voices; Vieuxchamp's combination of whine and bluster was as easy to spot as poor Joseph Melanson's stammer. Philip Vieuxchamp would not have been her choice to fill old Mr. Fitzroy's place as head of security. He had been Dolores Tawne's, however, because he made a good appearance in his dark-green uniform and was lazy enough not to resent her taking over and running the museum her way. He and Melanson held the longest tenure among the guards, Melanson was by far the more conscientious but he couldn't have said "boo" to a peacock, much less function in a position of authority.

There was nothing shy about Vieuxchamp, he was bellowing into the phone. "Where's Brooks?"

"I'm sorry," Sarah replied somewhat crisply, "he's not here."

"Then find him! I've got to talk to Brooks."

"I told you he's not here. We're expecting Dolores Tawne to tea, can't she—"

"No, she can't!" His bluster had become a shriek. "Jesus, isn't there anybody I can talk to?"

"Mr. Vieuxchamp, stop that screaming. I'm Sarah Kelling Bittersohn. You know me. What's keeping Dolores? Where is she?"

"She's sprawled out flat on her face in that big clump of green stuff next to the pink stuff in the courtyard. We can't wake her up."

"How long has she been lying there?"

"How the hell do I know? That new head of trustees was on my case Thursday about not letting the staff run up overtime, so I let them all go but Milky and me. We were locking up; Milky's the one who found her."

So it was all Milky's fault. Sarah was ready to do some screaming of her own. "Mr. Vieuxchamp, are you trying to tell me that Dolores is dead?"

"How do I know? I'm no doctor."

"Then get one. Dial nine-one-one immediately. Tell them you need a police ambulance at the Wilkins right away. Don't try to move her until it comes."

"I can't call the police!"

"You have to. It's the law."

"Then can't you call them?"

"No, I can't. Listen to me, Mr. Vieuxchamp. You're the one who's supposed to be taking Mr. Fitzroy's place. Can you imagine him trying to wiggle out of making a simple telephone call?"

"Aw, hell! Why do women always have to complicate everything?"

He slammed down the phone. Sarah picked up one of Charles's carefully decrusted tuna-fish sandwiches and bit into it, there was no sense in wasting them. It tasted good, she took another. She was about to suggest that Charles make them that pot of tea they still hadn't had when the telephone rang again. Again, it was Vieuxchamp.

"Okay, Miz Kelling, they're here. They say she's dead. A stroke or something, they don't know. What do I do now?"

"Call Mr. Turbot. Did you get his home telephone number while you were talking with him on Thursday?"

"Dolores did, I guess. She always takes care of stuff like that." His voice dropped, it must have hit him that Dolores might no longer be around to take care of stuff like that. "I don't suppose you'd be willing to—"

"I don't suppose so either, Mr. Vieuxchamp. All I know,

and you'd better write this down before you forget it, is that his full name is Elwyn Fleesom Turbot and he lives on a cattle farm in Cowley."

"Where's Cowley?"

"Somewhere near Foxford is the best I can tell you. Call Information, the operator should know. If that doesn't work, ask a policeman."

That was mean, but Vieuxchamp deserved it. Sarah drank her tea when it came, without a qualm, wondering what would happen to the Wilkins next. Dolores Tawne had been grudgingly respected, sometimes feared, by no means well-loved by the rest of the staff. As long as Mr. Fitzroy remained in charge, he had courteously but firmly kept Dolores in her place, or thought he had. Since his retirement almost a year ago, there had been much talk but no action with regard to a new director. During the interim, Dolores Tawne had maneuvered Vieuxchamp into Mr. Fitzroy's place, then proceeded to make that place considerably less than more, constantly undercutting his already tenuous hold. By the time of Turbot's appointment, she had been pretty much running the show to suit herself.

The truth of the matter was that Dolores had been a better man than the lot of them, though naturally none of the guards would have admitted it, except perhaps Melanson. That Dolores Agnew Tawne should die just as the new chairman of trustees was in the process of taking over did strike Sarah as being almost too much of a coincidence.

Now that Turbot had appeared on the scene, change would be inevitable. He clearly meant to take an active role in the running of the museum, he'd insist on knowing exactly where its funds came from and where the money went. Somebody might still have had sound reason to worry about what information Dolores might let fall into Mr. Turbot's ears.

Dolores had had her virtues and her limitations. She'd been a more than capable painter without a glimmer of creativity. She'd been a zealous, competent worker, ready to take on any job that came to hand, never once stopping to consider toward what end that job might be leading. Even a cataclysmic shock that she'd suffered seven years ago didn't appear to have sharpened her sense of awareness; she'd been just as pigheaded as usual when Sarah had last met with her a month or so ago. Was it so impossible that what had been done before might have been done again; that somebody else— most likely one of Dolores's co-workers, since she'd been so single-mindedly involved with the Wilkins—was taking advantage of her blind spot to cash in on her abilities?

Now here had come a new broom intent on a clean sweep. Somebody as big and bristly as Elwyn Turbot might have looked like vengeance to a man—it would have to be a man because Dolores was the only woman aside from Madam Wilkins herself who'd ever been allowed an active role in the palazzo's workings—who was running a little business on the side at the museum's expense.

After years of somnolence on the board of trustees, that visit of Turbot's on Thursday must have been a rude awakening. Sarah could envision him barging around from floor to floor and guard to guard, barking out orders right and left, letting everybody know who was going to be boss even if he couldn't distinguish a Rembrandt from a Rubens or a Manet from a Monet. Dolores Tawne, who had been an undisputed asset to the Wilkins on Thursday morning, could have become a dangerous liability by closing time that same day. Too dangerous, perhaps, to be let live until Mr. Turbot came again.

This was all conjecture, of course. Dolores could have fallen dead from a sudden heart attack, or choked to death on a cough drop. Sarah looked at the few tuna-fish sandwiches that were still on the tray and shrugged.

"Charles, do please take away those ghastly squoodgy-woodgies, or whatever you call them. Poor Dolores, one always got the impression that she'd go on forever. I hope somebody knows who her relatives are, assuming that she

had any left after her brother died. Brooks might know; I
wish we knew how to get hold of him."

Not that it made any difference, Sarah supposed. Some
long-lost nephew or cousin, or even the husband whom Dolores had never talked about and her co-workers thought must
be long dead was bound to show up and claim the body, along
with anything of value that was to be got from the studio in
which Dolores had lived and done her unlikely homework
for so many years. There'd be some money put by, not a great
deal but enough to pay for a decent burial.

In this respect, if in no other, Dolores would have looked
ahead; she was that sort of woman. With Jimmy gone, the
odds were that she'd leave whatever there was to the Wilkins,
along with a handsomely calligraphed epitaph extolling the
artistry of Dolores Agnew Tawne and the years of dedicated
service she'd given to the museum. She'd have left a note
with it giving precise instructions as to where on the courtyard
wall a bronze plaque was to be fastened; she might even have
had the plaque all engraved and ready to be hung once the
date of her passing had been inserted.

What a crazy thing to be thinking. No, it wasn't crazy at
all, it was what Dolores would have wanted and what she'd
have made sure she got if she hadn't died so abruptly. If such
a plaque either existed or was mentioned in her will, would
anybody care enough to put it up? Sarah would, Max would,
Brooks Kelling would if they were given the chance; but none
of them was officially a member of the Wilkins staff. Even
Jimmy Agnew would have carried more weight if he'd been
still above ground.

Jimmy had been around the museum almost as long as his
sister. He'd managed to hold his job ostensibly because Dolores had covered up his alcohol-inspired absences. In fact, as
it later transpired, Jimmy had been kept on the payroll as
messenger for a former bigwig who was now living in
restricted quarters at the public expense. Nobody had blamed
Jimmy for what he'd done, nobody had ever expected much

of him in the first place. His co-workers had tolerated him well enough, partly because he was a likable chap in his way, and partly because they'd pitied him for having a sister like Dolores.

When he'd got run over, the other guards had been mildly regretful to see him go. A few had voiced their puzzlement as to how the accident happened. The day had been fine, the pavement not a bit slippery, the traffic no heavier and Jimmy no drunker than usual. He'd used that same crossing day after day for years and years because his favorite pub was across from the museum's back entrance. But dead he'd been, and nothing to be done but attend the obsequies and then gather at the bar to hoist one for Jimmy.

Sarah and Brooks had attended the funeral out of courtesy to Dolores. She had not appeared to be overwhelmed with grief. Once Jimmy was safely tucked away, she'd accepted Sarah's invitation and come back to Tulip Street for tea and sympathy. With a glass of sherry under her belt, Dolores had as much as admitted that she was well rid of her brother. He'd been getting more cocky, harder to manage. Could that mean that Jimmy Agnew had taken on a second job running errands on the q.t. for some other member of the museum's staff?

More guesswork. Sarah poured out tea for Charles while he laid another log on the fire, and motioned for him to finish the sandwiches. When the tuna-fish was gone, they ate cheese and crackers with a couple of Early Transparent apples that Sarah had picked from one of the trees at Ireson's Landing. When the food was all gone and the teapot empty, Charles went into the dining room and came back with the brandy decanter and two glasses.

"To Dolores, moddom?"

"To Dolores, Charles."

Sarah took a ritual sip, wondering whether anybody else anywhere was sorry that Dolores Tawne was dead. Vieux-champ hadn't sounded at all bereft, his grief would be for himself and the extra work he'd have to do without Dolores around to do it for him. Turbot would be on Vieuxchamp's neck, no doubt, once he noticed that the museum was not being properly kept up, which it certainly wouldn't be unless somebody new was hired to take Dolores's place. The trustees would have their hands full trying to find a replacement who could function capably as a curator, housekeeper, assistant gardener, and peacock doctor, and was willing to work for a relative pittance.

And what about Max? Sarah wondered, down in Argentina at his own expense, exercising his training and diplomatic skills to get back another of the Wilkins's looted treasures with nobody left on the staff who cared enough to rejoice in its recovery or could distinguish the original from the copy.

Other museums had fund-raising societies formed for their benefit by interested patrons. There had never been a Friends of the Wilkins. Even if the trustees had sanctioned it, Dolores Tawne would have thrown a wet blanket over any such amateurish nonsense in her domain. Maybe Lala Turbot would get interested, at least it would be a change from looking at livestock. Whatever happened, Sarah was well aware that, after the way she'd spoken her mind to Elwyn Turbot, the Bittersohn Detective Agency would be finished with the Wilkins Museum once the Watteaus had been delivered and the new chairman of trustees had tried unsuccessfully to gyp Max out of his fee. It was the end of an era. She raised her glass again.

"Bottoms up, Charles. This one's to us."

# Chapter 5

Sarah went to bed early but didn't get much sleep. She kept waking up and trying to remember all the things that needed to be done now that the usual support group had—temporarily, she hoped—dwindled away to Charles and herself. Mostly what came to her mind, however, was Dolores Tawne as Sarah had known her, the living image of a teakettle coming up to the boil, clumping around in sensible thick-soled tan walking shoes, her sensible beige gabardine shirtwaist covered by a smock that had seen far too many wash days and been patched under the armpits at least once too often; radiating a sort of ferocious warmth when things were going her way, turning up the heat to full blast when anybody tried to cross her.

In her own way, Dolores had been a personage. It was hard to think of her as she must be now, lying stiff and still in a drawer at the morgue with a cardboard tag tied to her bare big toe. She'd have loathed being seen naked. Whoever was doing the autopsy had better watch his or her step; even from beyond the veil, Dolores might arise long enough to pick a bone or two. What a blessing it was, finding something to smile about, here alone in the dark. Sarah sent a wave of comradely farewell into the blackness, trusting that it would find its way to the right place, and dropped at last into a sound sleep.

At Ireson's Landing, the only night noises would be those of wind and water and occasional local fauna out on the hunt. Summer in the city, though, had re-immunized her even to police and fire sirens; Sarah didn't wake up until almost half past seven. By the time she'd showered and rummaged something halfway wearable out of the closet, she could hear Charles astir in the kitchen. She hoped to goodness he wasn't thinking of some essay into haute cuisine such as eggs Benedict; toast and coffee were about the limit of his culinary powers.

Fortunately, he'd only got so far as to be holding a box of pancake mix at arm's length, trying to read the directions on the box without his glasses on, when Sarah entered the kitchen.

"Don't go to all that bother for me, Charles. Is there any bread in the house, or did you use it up on the sandwiches yesterday?"

"Yes, I did, but there's one of Mrs. Brooks's coffee cakes in the fridge. She left two, but the other one sort of melted away."

"They do, don't they. Why don't you bring what's left and pour us some coffee?"

Not that Sarah couldn't have poured her own coffee, but Charles did burn to be useful and it was generally safer to draw the boundaries while yet there was time. Charles might be a little tired of coffee cake by now, but that was just too bad. She'd better check the larder and make sure there was enough for them to eat during the next few days. Charles could do what shopping was needed down on Charles Street, it always gave the self-appointed butler a proprietorial thrill of satisfaction, and the exercise would do him good. He'd pass the time of day with some of his numerous cronies, then spend the afternoon doing some of the chores that Mariposa would have nagged him about before she left.

Sarah's own plans were, first, to phone Miriam and find out whether Davy was homesick or enjoying the lake, then either go to pick him up or else stroll across Boston Common to the office, check the mail and the answering machine, and put in some work on the books while there was nobody around to interrupt her. She had appointed herself to the job shortly after she and Max were married. During the years with Alexander, she'd become quite capable at handling correspondence and keeping books for various charitable organizations in which her blind, deaf, keen-minded, and keener-tongued mother-in-law had been involved. After her remarriage, she'd turned her experience to advantage. Keeping the accurate records that Max hadn't had time to maintain had become a major contribution to the smooth operation—relatively smooth, anyway, some of the time—of the Bittersohn Detective Agency.

They'd talked of hiring a bookkeeper; instead, Cousin Brooks, who could do anything, had set up a computer system and taught Sarah to use it. He himself didn't mind putting in some time at the console when he had the chance, which wasn't often because Brooks could always find some new challenge to his ingenuity. Sarah did wish he and Theonia would get in touch, but they probably wouldn't. Charles had got the impression that they planned to remain incommunicado for much of their time away; they hadn't told him why and he didn't think it was a butler's place to ask.

That was all right. Brooks and Theonia must know what they were about and Jesse was proving to be almost too resourceful. They'd break their silence when they felt the urge or the advisability. It was unlikely, Sarah thought, that they'd be needing any help from the home front, but somebody ought to be at hand to take their call if it came. At least she could do that much.

She spent a little time with Charles over the shopping list, then phoned the Rivkins at the lake and heard just about what she'd expected. Davy was down by the lake with Ira. He'd eaten up every bite of his breakfast and taken a piece of bread out to feed the minnows. He was wearing Ira's old straw hat and one of Mike's T-shirts to keep from getting sunburned.

They were going to have a cookout on the beach at suppertime and surely Sarah wouldn't mind if they kept Davy with them till Max got back, so that she could get her work done.

What could a mother say? That she'd talked with Max, who'd sounded hale and hopeful but there'd been trouble with the telephone so she couldn't tell when he'd be back. That Mr. Lomax and Cousin Anne were minding the house at Ireson's Landing. That Anne could phone Mrs. Blufert and tell her to stay home and nurse her bug now that Davy was with Miriam and Ira. Yes, Charles would be here to make sure that Sarah didn't get kidnapped or burglarized. She wasted no breath on describing her visit to the Turbots' and said nothing about Dolores Tawne's sudden demise. She entreated Miriam to give Davy an extra kiss and hug from his mother. She began to feel too bereft, rang off and got down to business.

"Be sure to pick up a *Globe* while you're out, Charles. There might be something in the obituaries about Dolores."

"Yes, moddom."

Getting away from the house was always the hardest part. Sarah donned a light raincoat over the too-summery outfit that she'd elected to wear because the blue silk was too dressy for the office and there wasn't much else in the closet to choose from. Once on her way, she enjoyed her walk to the Windy Corner, which was no more than agreeably breezy this morning, pushed through the door into the lobby, and checked in at the reception desk. The receptionist knew her, of course.

"Well, Mrs. Bittersohn, we haven't seen you around here much lately."

"No, I've been staying at home, catching up on things. The office won't be open today. I'm just here to work on the books and don't want to be interrupted, so please don't send anybody up unless I scream for help."

They both found this notion mildly amusing. Sarah took the elevator up to her floor, unlocked the office door with Brooks's magic key which only worked if one recited the proper mantra, went in, and took off her raincoat. There was nothing impressive about the Bittersohn Detective Agency's headquarters except the gold-leaf lettering on the door. The old flat-topped oak desk and creaky swivel chair that Max had inherited from some previous tenant took up too much of the meager floor space. An impressive array of file cabinets along one wall and a couple of straight-backed, slimly padded chairs that didn't encourage droppers-in to stay and chat once their business was done were the only other furnishings, unless one counted a few shelves that held office supplies and some pegs that Brooks had screwed to the wall because there was not room enough for a coat rack. Sarah hung her raincoat on one of the pegs and got down to business.

A fair amount of mail had been poked through the slot since Brooks was last in the office. Sarah picked the envelopes up off the dingy green-linoleum-covered floor and dumped them on the desk before she checked the answering machine. There were only a few messages on the tape, none that sounded important or urgent, the usual one or two from persons who were either mentally deranged or trying to be funny. Sarah jotted down those names and numbers that might be worth following up and turned to the mail.

Once the junk had been weeded out, she found her task rewarding in every sense of the word. There were no fewer than five checks, two of them for large sums that were long overdue, two that were almost equally impressive, and one that verged on munificence. She'd drop them in at the bank when she went out for lunch. This would not be a late meal or a meager one; it was high time she got some real food into her for a change. She'd done too much snacking since Max left. Charles's tuna-fish sandwiches hadn't been particularly filling. As for that Sunday luncheon at the Turbots', the best she could say was that the food had been no worse than what she'd have got at Cousin Mabel's. She hadn't spoken to Mabel in ages. How nice.

The immediate tasks done, Sarah opened a ledger and got down to what she'd come for. This was work that many would call boring. So would she, perhaps, if she weren't doing it for Max and Davy and the rest of the crew. She gave her small pile of checks a satisfied nod and went on with the next piece of business. There was the job book to be brought up-to-date, summarizing how many hours had been spent on a specific assignment, how much the operatives' expenses had come to, all the picky details that the IRS could be so stuffy about if they weren't properly documented.

Sarah's particular care and pride were the oversized notebooks that described, often with carefully detailed sketches from her own pen, the wide variety of precious objects that Max and his cohorts had either recovered or were still looking for: their age, their provenance, their appraised values, their full descriptions; all valuable working data and possible reference for other investigations. Since these notebooks were Sarah's special province, and since there would have been no room for more than one or two at a time in the office or in any of the small rooms at Tulip Street, they were generally kept at Ireson's Landing as part of a reference library that occupied a good-sized room of its own and might require another if Sarah kept on as she was doing.

After having pored through shelves upon shelves of art books at the Boston Public Library and a great many more at the Museum of Fine Arts, she'd developed a sure sense of what would be useful and begun prowling the bookstores. Sarah's private library was proving to be of immense value to the agency, not to mention the insurance companies that were Max's steadiest clients. To her personally it meant being able to spend more time at home with her child and her beautiful house while still pulling her oar in the agency boat.

However, the computer, the job book, the mail, all the bits and pieces that needed to be dealt with on a daily basis, and too often were not, had to be kept at the office. Theonia could have been helpful here if figures were tea leaves and cabinets contained only tarot cards. As it was, her notions of office procedures were so esoteric that she had to be enjoined from taking on any task except making coffee and cooing into the telephone when a potential client who sounded like real money happened to call. When she began to coo like a *Zenaida asiatica*, or white-winged dove, even her husband was quite willing to step aside and let her do what she did best; invariably to the ultimate satisfaction of all concerned except any misguided miscreant who mistook her for a pushover.

By noontime Sarah felt she'd earned that ample luncheon. She put on her raincoat, tucked the checks and the deposit slip in her handbag, and made sure she had her keys. The door would lock behind her, but Brooks's magic key must still be turned to wind up the spell or it wouldn't work next time around. The women's washroom was less intricate to get at, one simply walked down the corridor and opened the door with the key supplied to tenants by the management.

Sarah had the washroom to herself, it looked as if there'd been nobody here except the cleaners. This was as it should have been. A large firm that needed more space had petitioned to have the entire floor put at its disposal. Other firms had agreed to take new space on other floors, all but the Bittersohn Detective Agency. Max had been offered various inducements, such as a snappy paint job and a more up-to-date entrance, but he'd turned them all down. He was quite content to be an anachronism; he'd been around so many Kellings by now that he was beginning to think like one; he'd stood his ground and won his point. Sarah was proud of Max for maintaining the family tradition, but she did find it a bit spooky being all alone on the floor. She was glad when the elevator came up empty and took her down alone; she went over to the bank and made her deposit, then headed for a restaurant where she and her co-workers were well-known.

"All by yourself today, Mrs. Bittersohn?" The head waiter in person was ushering her to the coziest table, presenting her menu with a bow and a red rose out of the splendiferous arrangement in the reception area. "Where's the rest of the crew?"

Sarah was not about to broadcast the fact that she was alone in the office. "Oh, they're galloping off in all directions as usual. Somebody may come in later on, but I'm hungry now. How are your scallops today?"

She called them scollops, as any true-born New Englander would have sense enough to do. On being assured that the succulent bivalves were A-One and thoroughly guaranteed, she ordered them simply broiled, with coleslaw on the side and a pot of tea. She didn't have to specify which kind of tea, the waiter already knew. He brought brown bread instead of white and offered neither milk nor lemon with the tea because Mrs. Bittersohn was not one for extraneous fripperies. He disappeared to consult with the chef, returned with her scallops done exactly as she liked them, and paused to watch with quasi-paternal pride as she sampled one and found it good.

Sarah could have done with less solicitude. Fortunately the restaurant was filling up and the waiter had to get on with distributing his smiles and his menus. She finished her excellent meal at a leisurely pace, signed the check, picked up her rose, and debated taking a short stroll before going back to work. Once outside, however, she changed her mind. The sky had turned sullen and the wind was picking up; it would make more sense to put in another hour or two at the books and walk back to Tulip Street before the storm broke. If she overstayed and got wet it wouldn't matter; she had a comfortable robe and slippers to change into.

Dinner wasn't going to be anything special, Charles was no chef and Sarah didn't feel like cooking. They'd broil the steak that she'd told Charles to buy, grill mushrooms and tomato halves along with it, and skip dessert. Afterward, Charles could slip downstairs to his own quarters, watch something or other on television, and wonder when Mariposa was coming back. Sarah was not a fan of the tube, she'd sit in the library and read or listen to a concert on one of Boston's excellent classical music stations.

She supposed it would be only civil to give Uncle Jem a ring and let him know that she was in town for an as yet undetermined but preferably short period of time. Jeremy Kelling and his sorely tried henchman, Egbert, lived just over on Pinckney Street; they might like to come to dinner tomorrow night unless Jem had something livelier on the docket. He probably hadn't. J. Lemuel Kelling was no longer the bon vivant he'd been during those halcyon years before a cruel bureaucracy tore down Scollay Square and rebuilt it as Government Center, though he still liked to think he was.

Before making any plans for herself, however, it occurred to Sarah that she ought to find out whether a funeral service for Dolores Tawne had been announced. Charles hadn't left a message on the answering machine, as he probably would have if he'd found anything in the paper while Sarah was out to lunch. She'd better pick up a later edition on her way home. If all else failed, she'd have to get hold of Vieuxchamp at the museum; surely he would know by then, if anybody did.

By the time she'd battled her way back down Boylston Street to the Little Building, Sarah was glad to get inside. She never minded being blown around on the cliffs overhanging the ocean at Ireson's Landing, but feeling somebody's discarded hamburger wrapper trying to wrap itself around one's ankle was a far different and wholly revolting situation. After checking her nether limbs to make sure she wasn't bringing other people's trash into the building, Sarah walked over to the reception desk.

"I'm back for a while. I don't suppose anybody's been asking for us?"

"You just missed him," the man in charge told her. "Or her, or it. Who can tell? Anyway, a messenger. This must be for you."

" 'Biterman Det. Agy.' Close enough, I suppose. Could be someone's idea of a joke. You didn't tip the messenger, I hope?"

"Are you kidding? They always add it to the tab anyway. You're not planning to stay on after five, by chance?"

"Oh, no," Sarah assured him. "I'll be well away before then, I don't like the look of that sky. Thank you for taking the package."

# Chapter 6

Brown manila envelopes delivered by anonymous messengers of indeterminate sex were no surprise at the Bittersohn Detective Agency. Neither were misspellings of Max's family name. This could be anything from an oddment that Brooks had been trying to track down through some unchancy source for some reason that only he could have thought of to a small stolen object that an anonymous somebody had found too hot to handle.

Thus far, nobody had sent the agency a letter bomb; but it was not outside the bounds of possibility that somebody, some day, might. Sarah was not one to panic but she did experience a moment's discomfiture. Should she open the envelope? Should she not? Should she take it to the rest room and dunk it in a basin of water? Should she just leave it on the desk with a note of gentle warning? Should she mention it to Max if by some miracle the line got repaired and he phoned again tonight? Should she drop the envelope quietly in the wastebasket and pretend it had never arrived? Should she just lay the thing on the windowsill out of the way and get on with what she'd come to do?

Slightly ashamed of her pussyfooting, Sarah pushed the envelope to the far corner of the desk, opened her job book, and picked up her pen. She was having a hard time to concen-

trate but plugged on anyway; she'd just about got her mind
nicely set on her task when the phone rang. It was Charles,
wanting her to know that he'd found nothing about Mrs.
Tawne in the morning paper and wondering if he ought to
squander the price of a later edition. Sarah told him not to
bother, she'd pick up one on her way home. She asked whether
Mariposa had called, learned that she hadn't, and suggested
that Charles polish the silver as a nice surprise for Mariposa
to find when she got back from Puerto Rico. This was almost
certainly not what Charles wanted to hear, but it was the best
Sarah could think of at the moment. She broke the connection
and picked up her pen again.

It wasn't working. The scallops might have been a mistake,
though Sarah couldn't think why they should have been. She
wasn't feeling sickish or sleepy or anything in particular, there
was just this odd creepiness up and down her spine. Maybe
it had something to do with the impending storm, more likely
it was just being up here all by herself. Unless it was the
ghost of Dolores Tawne trying to nag Sarah about something
that hadn't been done properly before she'd passed through
the veil. Too bad Theonia wasn't here to take the message,
revenant spirits were more in her department. Sarah locked
away the job book in a drawer that was labeled "Bird
Sightings," started to put on her raincoat, then hesitated.

Oh, all right! Why make something out of nothing? She
picked up the still unopened envelope and gave it a gingerly
prod. Whatever was inside weighed next to nothing, all she
could feel was something like a knitting needle with a bump on
the tip. She ripped open the envelope and burst out laughing.

Not long ago, an old friend of the family named Lydia
Ouspenska had shown up at a funeral wearing a circa 1900
walking ensemble with a hobble skirt, a redingote with lapels
down to her knees, and a huge cartwheel hat worn very much
to one side and skewered in place with a formidable hatpin.
Lydia had looked absolutely stunning. Sarah could never have
worn such an outfit but Theonia had lusted after it, most

particularly the hat. A talented and ingenious needlewoman like her was easily able to concoct one out of a child's hula hoop, a yard or two of black velvet, a few more yards of white satin, and some feathers from the Wilkins's white peacocks that Theonia had scrounged from Dolores Tawne in return for a two-pound box of homemade peanut brittle, to which Dolores had been much addicted. The hat was a smashing success, the only problem was how to keep it on.

Women before World War I had had hair, lots of hair. The beauty who could actually sit on the end of her mane was entitled to brag about it, and generally did. The one who could claim no such crowning glory might eke out her scanty tresses with pads made from her own combings and referred to for good and sufficient reason as rats. Others might sport a switch or postiche made from hair that was human but not their own. For women who couldn't afford to be stylish, a fine head of hair might become a salable commodity, as witness Jo March's great sacrifice in *Little Women* and the young wife in "The Gift of the Magi," who sold her beautiful hair to buy the chain for the gold watch that her husband had pawned to buy fancy combs for his wife's beautiful hair.

Logistically, hatpins meant to anchor so formidable a freight of frippery to coiffures of such luxuriance had to be up to the job, to be instruments of strength and endurance as well as of fashion. The end meant to show would be ornamental: a gilded butterfly, a Chinese intricacy carved out of red cinnabar, a multi-colored glass marble, a cone or sphere set all around with imitation sapphires or rubies, pretty trinkets of no great value lending their own small touch of charm to milady's toilette.

The business end of the hatpin, on the other hand, would have been six or eight inches of tempered steel wire, stiff as a ramrod and sharpened to a point that was able to penetrate whatever elaborate concoction a milliner might dream up. It could glide through stiff fabric, through switch and rat, through whatever came in its way, emerge on the opposite side without inflicting painful wounds on a lady's scalp, if she was careful, and send her out literally dressed to kill should the need arise. In an emergency, a few inches of needle-sharp steel vigorously applied could be an effective way to dash the hopes of a too-ardent male. Anxious mothers and saucy vaudeville performers alike were particular in reminding skittish young misses that girls who went strolling without their hatpins ran the risk of losing more than just their hats.

Theonia Kelling had a fine head of hair all her own and had never, so far as Sarah knew, been forced to resort to cold steel when it came to cooling down a man with a plan. All she needed a hatpin for was to keep her hat on. Naturally Theonia didn't want just any old toad-stabber after all the time and trouble she'd spent creating her antique hat. The previous week, she and Lydia Ouspenska had spent most of an afternoon scouring Boston's many antique shops and come away empty-handed.

There had been hatpins, but none that would suit Theonia's purpose. Most of the big ones had been cut down; neither husbands nor policemen liked the idea of a dangerous weapon kicking around the boudoir. The few hatpins that were long enough had failed to come up to specifications otherwise. Once-jeweled ornaments had lost their stones, gilt gewgaws that had twinkled like stars a century ago were by now dull and unsightly, not worth restoring.

Evidently Lydia had found a hatpin that she thought would do, and had got somebody or other to drop it off as a surprise for when Theonia returned. That would account for the bungled address; Lydia could barely speak English, much less spell it. Sarah slid the pin out of the envelope to get a better look at the head.

Theonia was going to be disappointed. The head had been nothing special to begin with, just a small knob covered with tiny black beads, perhaps intended to anchor a widow's long mourning veil. Too many of the beads were gone, the steel retained its sharp point but showed some rust and discoloration along the shank. Sarah got the impression that it might have been used to unclog a bottle of ketchup.

Whatever had Lydia been thinking of? There must be other hatpins less ugly than this and in no worse shape. Perhaps she'd seen this one lying somewhere and taken it as a good omen. "Find a pin and pick it up and all the day you'll have good luck" was a charm in which many people still believed; a pin this size ought to convey a whole week's worth of good fortune.

But Sarah didn't think it would. Lydia took superstition seriously, she must know that luck wasn't transferable. Furthermore, luck or no luck, Lydia would hardly have sent this ugly thing along without at least scouring the wire with a steel-wool pad and doing something about the head, if only to dip it in gold paint and pretend it was a nugget. Why hadn't she bothered?

Because, obviously, it was not Lydia Ouspenska who'd sent the hatpin. Sarah tried to think who else might have heard about the hatpin hunt and either tried to help Theonia out or tried to be funny. There must have been some of Great-Aunt Matilda's hatpins among the welter of stuff that Cousin Dolph had inherited from Great-Uncle Frederick, but everything that wasn't nailed down had been auctioned off some time ago on behalf of the Senior Citizens' Recycling Center.

Aunt Appollonia in Cambridge was a likelier prospect. Her house was almost as big as Dolph's and even more cluttered. She'd have been only too delighted to hunt out a hatpin for dear Cousin Theonia; it was unthinkable that she wouldn't have one somewhere. It was even more unthinkable, however, that Appie would remember what she was supposed to be looking for, much less send it all the way here by special messenger at ruinous expense while the ghost of Uncle Samuel growled in her ear, "Waste not, want not."

Three of Appie's grandchildren, Jesse's dreadful brothers Woodson, James, and sweet little Frank, would no doubt love to stage a hatpin hunt for reasons of their own. At this time, however, they were safely penned up in an expensive boarding school that combined the better features of an institution of learning with those of a high-class reformatory. They wouldn't be let out until Thanksgiving, the thanks, no doubt, being given by their beleaguered teachers. With sincere regret, Sarah crossed the boys off and racked her brain for likelier suspects.

It was a waste of time. She wasn't getting anywhere, the sky was even more ominous, the wind beginning to howl around the windows. Or was that the wind? No, it wasn't. The noise was coming not from outside but from the supposedly empty office next door. Some workman must be in there using an electric drill.

But why? Brooks had told Sarah before he went away that renovations were not scheduled to begin for another month. Even if the schedule had been moved up, three o'clock in the afternoon seemed an odd time to begin work. Almost of its own accord, her hand reached out to the telephone and punched the number for the reception desk.

"Hello, this is Sarah Bittersohn. I'm sorry to bother you, but it was my understanding that there wouldn't be any work going on next door. It's been quiet all day, but now there's somebody in there using an electric drill. It almost sounds as if they're trying to drill through to our office."

The receptionist was interested. "How long have you been hearing this noise, Mrs. Bittersohn?"

"Just these past few minutes. I thought at first it was the wind, but it's the wrong kind of noise. Do you suppose some workman may have got in there by mistake?"

"I don't see how, he'd have to be pretty dumb. Nobody told me about any work on your floor. I'd better check with maintenance. In the meantime, stay where you are and lock your own door."

"It's already locked, thank goodness. I hope I'm not making something out of nothing."

"Don't you worry about that, Mrs. Bittersohn. Just sit tight, we'll send somebody to check it out."

The receptionist rang off, there was nothing for Sarah to do but wait and hope she wouldn't have occasion to use that hatpin. She wasn't really worried; anybody trying to bore a way through the connecting wall would run into a bigger job than he'd bargained for. The agency's steel filing cabinets were stacked five feet high the whole length of the wall and every drawer was padded at the back with old telephone directories.

The phone books had been Brooks's idea. He'd learned sometime or other that outdated directories had been used to line railroad cars in certain potentially explosive countries, as insulation against guerrilla attacks. Brooks had never exactly envisioned a shootout from next door but, being a Kelling, he'd thought it wouldn't hurt to get some practical use out of bulky tomes that, at the time, not even trash collectors had wanted to lug away.

It was impossible to concentrate on anything but the noise next door. The drilling went on, where was that security guard? Startled as she'd been by the sudden noise, she felt even jumpier when it stopped. After a brief silence, she heard a knock on the door and a male voice calling, not loudly, "Anybody in here?"

Sarah didn't recognize the voice, she hesitated a moment, then reached for the phone and called reception again, speaking as softly as she could.

"Hello, Sarah Bittersohn again. The noise just stopped and there's somebody at the door asking if anybody's here. I haven't answered and I don't think I'm going to until I'm positive it's somebody I know."

"I can't say I blame you, Mrs. Bittersohn. The trouble is, I can't leave the desk. I did check with maintenance and they say nobody's supposed to be working on your floor until the plans for renovation have been finalized, which won't be for another couple of weeks. They said they'd send one of the crew up in a while, but—"

"All right, I understand. What I'm going to do is not answer the door until I've sent for our man Charles to escort me home. You know him, he's been in and out of the building at various times. He's fairly tall, dresses well, and has curly blond hair. Just to make sure of his identity, he'll be carrying a group photograph in which he appears along with myself, my husband, Mr. and Mrs. Brooks, and our new trainee, Jesse Kelling. He'll show you the photograph and ask to be accompanied upstairs by some member of the building's staff. I shan't open the door until the two of them arrive together. I'm not an hysterical woman, if that's what you're thinking, but I'm not taking any unnecessary chances."

"How long do you suppose it'll take your man to get here?"

"Ten or fifteen minutes, if he's at home now. He'd only have to cross the Common from Tulip Street. I'll call him as soon as you and I hang up."

"What if he isn't there?"

"Then I'll call the police."

She wouldn't have to. Charles was on the qui vive and only too eager to dash to the rescue. He'd bring not only the photograph but also the Kelling umbrella, a relic of another era with a formidable steel shaft and a heavy blackthorn handle. Sarah's father had carried it, and his father before him, and his father's father. After Walter Kelling's death, the ancestral bumbershoot had come down to his favorite cousin, Alexander, who'd also inherited Walter's unfinished history of the Kelling family, his collection of pressed mushrooms, and a pair of ornate gold cuff links inherited from the great-uncle for whom Walter had been named, which he'd never worn because they were too pretentious. Alexander had never worn them either, for the same reason. Sarah still had the cuff links but didn't suppose Davy would ever want to break with precedent. More or less as an afterthought, Walter had also bequeathed to Alexander the guardianship of his young daughter, Sarah; but that was hardly germane to the issue at hand.

There had been times in its long history when the Kelling umbrella had proven its worth as a weapon. Charles was right to bring it now, it might serve again in a pinch, although that hideous old hatpin would be handier and perhaps even more effective.

Sarah wished she could forget the hatpin, she was developing what Jesse would call an attitude about the thing. It must mean something to somebody, though; she shouldn't have ripped the envelope so carelessly. Not that it mattered, the fingerprints would be hers and some anonymous messenger's. Maybe scads of unknowns'. How could she know where the ugly thing had come from and how many hands it had gone through before it wound up here?

Nevertheless, Sarah tucked the pin back into the torn envelope, closed the envelope inside one of the zip-top plastic bags that Brooks kept in various sizes for sometimes unfathomable reasons, and stuffed the *tout ensemble* into a tote bag that Theonia had left hanging on one of the pegs. Perhaps it was foolish, but she didn't like the idea of having such a potential weapon in her handbag.

Now there was nothing to do except poke through some of the likelier file drawers, trying to see whether the drill had got through the wall. Sarah didn't make much headway, there were too many drawers at various levels and the phone books had been jammed in too tightly. She was unutterably relieved when she heard two sets of footsteps marching up the hall, heard the right kind of knock at the door, and the right voice calling out, "Are you there, moddom?"

# Chapter 7

"I'm so glad you're here." Sarah was already putting on the raincoat that Charles was holding for her, while addressing the woman in overalls who'd come with him. "Are you security or maintenance?"

"Maintenance." The worker wasn't wasting any time on amenities. She nipped into the office that was supposed to be empty, took one quick look and came back. "Mind stepping in here for a second, Mrs. Bittersohn? Is this where you heard the drilling?"

"I think so." Sarah examined the small hole in the plasterboard, then knelt to study a whitish heap not much bigger than an anthill on the floor. "Yes, this is it."

"You sure? Looks to me like dust from the plasterboard."

"I don't think it's that simple. Charles, would you bring that big magnifying glass off Brooks's desk?"

"Toot sweet."

Charles was off and back with the speed of light. Heedless of her nylons, Sarah knelt beside the evidence, took the glass, and satisfied herself that she was in fact seeing what she'd expected to find.

"Take a look."

The maintenance worker shrugged and obliged. "Just plaster dust. Oops! Metal shavings. And—what the heck? Looks like ground-up newspaper."

"Right on all counts. The metal shavings are from the back of a filing cabinet that was lined with an old telephone book. I expect the ground-up paper fouled the bit. Yes, here it is on the floor."

Charles whipped out one of Brooks's small plastic bags. "You'll be wanting this, I assume?"

"Thanks." Sarah picked up the short, spiral-grooved metal bit very carefully by the clogged-up end and slipped it into the bag. "Get me another bag, Charles, and a piece of stiff paper to scoop with."

"Allow me."

While Charles swept the telltale debris into a clean bag, Sarah chatted a moment with the maintenance worker. "So you see I wasn't imagining things, in case your boss wants to know. If I type up a quick note about what we've found, would you mind signing it as a witness?"

"Not a bit, I'll be glad to. You're a real detective, huh? Are you going to call the cops?"

"No, I think we'll just drop off what we've found at the station. There's nothing much to be done here now that the phantom driller's gone," Sarah answered as they walked back to the Bittersohn office. "Have you any idea how whoever was here managed to get through security? I thought your people were pretty tight about letting anyone upstairs without proper identification."

"They are, but you know how it is. There's ways. For instance, if you showed up wearing jeans and carrying a tool box, claiming you're here to install some piece of equipment for one of the tenants, the receptionist would call up to the tenant. Somebody would say to go ahead and send you up, they were expecting you. Only what the front desk doesn't know is that it's your girlfriend on the switchboard giving the okay. So you get a pass and go up. Once you're inside the building, you're in, if you get what I mean. Like I say, there's ways. You just have to remember to turn in your pass when you leave, and to use a false ID when you sign in. Of course that's kind of a production, you'd have to be darned sure of your connections or you'd be out on your ear."

"I see. Thanks for the information." Sarah had been typing as she listened. "Would you sign your name, your job title, the date, and the time? Also your home phone number, if you don't mind."

"Sure, glad to."

The worker, whose name turned out to be Pansy Pottle, signed with a flourish and went back to work. By this time, the anticipated storm had broken. Sarah called police headquarters, explained what had happened, and said not to bother sending anybody over. She and Charles would drop off their evidence on the way home; they were ready to leave and Charles had brought an umbrella.

That was fine with Boston's Finest. Sarah and Charles performed Brooks's mantric ritual of the office-door locks without a hitch, went down in the elevator thinking up implausible ways to fox the security guards, and signed out in the most law-abiding way possible after giving the man at the desk a quick rundown on what had happened upstairs and special thanks for having come to Sarah's rescue. Then Charles raised the Kelling umbrella and they stepped forth into what was already beginning to look like a real soaker.

The umbrella accommodated them both without crowding, they could have taken in one or two more. The police station was not far away. Sarah only wished she'd put on more suitable footwear, preferably a pair of Wellingtons. Except for her feet and thanks to Charles's deft manipulation of the family heirloom, she was still respectably dry when they entered the red brick building with the blue lights in front.

The sergeant at the desk was an old acquaintance; Sarah had expected to be greeted affably, but not with cries of joy. "Mrs. Bittersohn! Am I glad to see you! Lieutenant Harris has had us burning the wires. Wait a second, I'll tell him you're here."

The words were barely out of the sergeant's mouth when a tall, tired-looking man in civilian clothes came out to greet her. "Well, Mrs. Bittersohn, that was quick. We just put a call on your office machine. You must have been—uh—down the hall or something. Come back here, will you? We need to talk."

He ushered her and Charles into a small, shabby room with nothing much in it except a battered wooden table and a few straight chairs. Charles stood at attention until Sarah had introduced him, then pulled out a chair for Sarah and stood behind her with the umbrella furled but ready, Sarah couldn't imagine what for.

"Do sit down, Charles, I hate to be loomed over. Lieutenant, I don't understand why you were looking for me. Didn't the sergeant tell you I'd already phoned to say we were coming? All I want is to deliver some evidence."

"What evidence?"

"A mixture of plaster dust, steel shavings, and shredded paper from an old telephone directory that we swept up in the office next to Max's after somebody tried to drill a hole through the wall. It didn't work because your friend Brooks had lined up our filing cabinets along that wall and stuffed the backs of the drawers with outdated telephone directories. I explained all that over the phone."

Harris shook his head. "I guess we've got our wires crossed here. Would you mind telling me why it's such a big deal that somebody drilled a hole through the wrong wall? Couldn't it be an electrician trying to run a wire or something? Did you go in and speak to him?"

"I did not," Sarah answered. "I stayed in our office with the door locked and telephoned down to the receptionist, who told me no work was scheduled to be done on our floor until next month. So I sent for Charles here, who's our butler and general factotum at Tulip Street, and told reception to send up somebody with him because I was not about to leave the office until they came. When Charles and a woman from maintenance showed up, we all went into the empty office and found the hole, the dust under it, and the bit from the drill lying on the floor, clogged with paper from the phone book. Charles, would you show Lieutenant Harris the evidence?"

The lieutenant turned the plastic bag over in his hands. "Huh. Good thing you kept your head. How come you were alone, Mrs. Bittersohn?"

"The office is closed this week because everybody's somewhere else," she told him. "I thought this would be a good time to catch up on some bookwork but now I'm not so sure. What was it you wanted to see me about?"

"It's about Mrs. Dolores Agnew Tawne, Jim Agnew's sister from the Wilkins Museum. You knew she'd died there Sunday afternoon, I expect."

"Yes, but that's all I do know. Charles has been trying to find out about the funeral, assuming there's going to be one."

Harris shrugged. "I guess that will be for you to say, Mrs. Bittersohn. Weren't you aware that Mrs. Tawne had named you her executrix?"

"What?" Sarah was thunderstruck. "Surely you can't mean that. Why me?"

"Who knows? Maybe she didn't have anybody else, with Jim gone."

That was all too probable. Sarah didn't know what to say. Lieutenant Harris hadn't time for poignant pauses.

"One of the museum guards turned over her handbag to us. According to the address book we found inside, she lived at the Fenway Studio Building. Is that right?"

"Yes," Sarah answered, not wanting to talk but knowing she must. "She'd been there for ages. But how did you find out about her will? Don't tell me Dolores carried it around in her handbag."

"No, but her lawyer's name and phone number were in

the book. We called his office a while ago and the secretary or whatever she is referred us to you. Redfern and Redfern on Milk Street. Would you know anything about them?''

''I ought to. Redferns have been handling legal business for various Kellings since long before I was born. There's only one Redfern left now. Come to think of it, I was the one who recommended him to Dolores Tawne. This was after the big blowup at the museum, before her brother died. I gave her Mr. Redfern's name because he was the only lawyer I knew. Funny, I'd forgotten all about that.''

''Seems to me it's pretty strange that she'd go ahead and put you down as executrix without bothering to ask you first,'' said Harris.

''It seems strange to me also,'' Sarah replied with asperity. ''But that's typical of Dolores. She never could see any point of view but her own. It was quite in character for her to take it for granted that I'd do whatever she wanted done and no questions asked. As I will, I suppose, but I do wish she'd landed somebody else with the job.''

''So you didn't like her.''

''No, Lieutenant, that's not true. I did like her. But there are different ways and degrees of liking, you know. It might be nearer the mark to say that I respected her. Dolores was not a comfortable person to know; she was too bristly, too bossy, too quick to take umbrage if one ventured to express an opinion that ran contrary to her own. On the other hand, she was loyal, useful, even kind in a gruff sort of way, and so thoroughly honest, as you well know, that she was an easy target for a plausible crook.''

''I still can't get over it,'' Harris confessed. ''That one woman copying all those paintings so perfectly that even the experts didn't catch on, and that other one pirating the originals as fast as she knocked out the fakes. Twenty years of it. God! And she never got a cent of the money?''

''She wouldn't have taken it. She honestly believed she was performing a grand and noble work for the museum.

When the bottom fell out, she could have got herself plastered all over the newspapers and television screens. She was all set to mount the stage and receive the accolades when she was faced with the reality of the situation. Two people were dead, and a third close to it. She was an art forger. If her name had been made public, she'd have had to choose between going to jail as an accomplice to theft and murder or being branded a gullible old fool, which would have been even worse. So she kept mum and went on dusting the majolica and doctoring the peacocks, never once uttering even the hint of a complaint about how unmercifully she'd been deceived and exploited.''

By this time, Sarah was pretty well choked up. Heaven only knew how many tears must have been shed across this banged up old table; Harris passed an open box of tissues and waited while she blew her nose and repaired her lipstick.

''Thank you, Lieutenant. So what I'm supposed to do now is claim the body and arrange the funeral. Is that right?''

Harris made a noise in his throat. ''Er—there's more to it than that. The medical examiner's not ready to release the body because he's still not sure how she died. She was found in the courtyard, but there's some evidence that she might have spent some time in one of those sedan chairs on the first balcony. Know what I mean?''

''Oh yes.'' Sarah was making her voice sound brisk and businesslike to keep the tears from coming back. ''I fell asleep in one when I was supposed to be lookout the night Max and Cousin Brooks caught two overage hippies trying to steal the big Titian, not realizing it wasn't a Titian but a Tawne. Poor Dolores always considered that painting her chef d'oeuvre, and well she might. It really is a remarkable piece of work.''

''You never got back the original, though.''

''We never say 'never.' The Titian was almost the last to be lifted, as Dolores used to put it. After the bomb went off, so to speak, she became a real help in providing information as to when certain paintings were taken from the museum, which has been a great help in tracking them down. I simply can't think of her as being dead. Doesn't the medical examiner have any idea at all as to what killed her?"

"He did say something about possible brain damage, but that's as far as—"

"Brain damage?" Sarah felt an ugly prickling of her own scalp. "Did he happen to notice a tiny wound, not much bigger than a pinhole, at the base of her skull?"

"Wait a minute! What are you getting at?"

"This." Sarah reached into Theonia's tote bag and pulled out the plastic bag that contained the hatpin and its envelope. "It was left at the reception desk while I was out to lunch. As you see, the envelope's sketchily addressed, but we're used to getting odd communications." She shook the hatpin out of the torn envelope. "What do you think?"

Harris was unimpressed. "All I'm seeing is a piece of wire."

"Look again, but don't touch the point." Sarah gave Harris a brief rundown on Theonia Kelling's quest for the perfect hatpin. He remained unstirred.

"So she wanted one, now she's got it. Offhand, I'd say one of Mrs. Kelling's friends was trying to do her a favor."

After the day she'd put in, Sarah was not to be talked down. "I do not believe this pin was sent as a goodwill gesture, Lieutenant. To begin with, it's unattractive and in poor condition. Second, what's left of those tiny black beads suggests that the hatpin was meant for a widow in mourning, which isn't something to joke about. Third, that stuff smeared on the shank of the pin looks to me like—I thought at first it might be ketchup or something, but—ugh!"

Harris knew an "ugh!" when he heard one, he got out of the way in a hurry. "To your right and around the corner."

Sarah made it to the washroom, but not by much. She emerged seven or eight minutes later, trembly and still a trifle green around the mouth. Charles was ready and waiting, a paper cup in one hand and an opened can of cola in the other.

"You'd better sit down, moddom. I know you hate this stuff, but it does help to settle the stomach."

Sarah eyed the cupful he'd poured out for her, shuddered, and turned her head away. Charles persisted. She finally steeled herself to take a sip, then another. The men watched, anxious as two father hens; she managed to keep the cola down and drank a little more.

"Thank you, Charles, I'm all right now. The thing of it is, I've been reading the published diaries of Amelia Peabody Emerson, a truly remarkable woman archaeologist of the late-Victorian and Edwardian periods. She led an amazingly venturesome life and was known as the *Sitt Hakim*, or woman doctor, although she'd had no formal training in medicine. At one point in her narrative she mentioned quite offhandedly that it was easy to get away with murder, simply by driving a hatpin, which would have been as essential to a woman's wardrobe then as her buttonhook or her glove stretcher, into the base of the skull. The victim's hair would cover the tiny wound, and thrusting the pin directly into the spinal cord would instantly—"

Sarah had to pause and drink more cola. "You see, few people nowadays would even think of a strong hatpin like this, much less own one. You might want to mention this to the medical examiner and have the wire tested for—"

Harris made a quick grab for the cola can. "Steady, Mrs. Bittersohn! Want some more?"

"No, thank you." Sarah heaved a sigh that came all the way from her wet feet. "All I want is just to go home and lie down."

# Chapter 8

"You're sure you feel well enough to go out?"

Harris was overdoing the solicitude, and Sarah knew why. "Don't worry, Lieutenant, I'll get hold of Mr. Redfern first thing tomorrow morning. As soon as he fills me in on what an executrix is supposed to do, I'll start things moving. No doubt the building manager will be anxious to have Mrs. Tawne's studio cleaned out, there's probably a waiting list already."

"Fenway Studio Building, right? Do you know where it is?"

"Oh yes, I've been there a few times. Did you find the keys in her handbag?"

"There's a big bunch of them, I'll get somebody to sort them out. Just let me know when you're squared away with the lawyer."

"If it's too much bother, I expect the building manager would let me in, provided the studio isn't sealed and I have written authorization from you and Mr. Redfern. We can see about that tomorrow. You have our office number; I probably won't be there but Charles will be able to pick up your message at the house. Are we ready to go, Charles?"

"Ready and waiting. This way out, right?"

Sarah was relieved to get out in the air, even though the

ozone level must be bad enough to kill a canary. Rush hour
had begun, the streets were jammed with cars trying to fight
their way to Storrow Drive or the turnpike. The rain was
making a bad situation worse, as it always did. Home-going
office workers were scuttling toward the subway entrances,
choking the sidewalks, jaywalking through the crawling traffic
without regard to others just as wet, tired, hungry, and ruthless
as themselves.

Trying to hail a taxi would have been an exercise in futility.
Sarah and Charles joined the scuttlers and headed back toward
the Common, Charles still managing somehow to keep the
umbrella over himself and the lady he served without poking
out somebody else's eye in the process. Some hopeful souls
were standing in doorways, waiting for the rain to let up,
which it obviously was not about to do. This was going to
be an all-nighter. Sarah could have told them that, she'd grown
to be weather-wise living so close to the sea. There was not
a blessed thing anybody could do in the circumstances except
grin and bear it or else scowl and utter the sort of imprecation
that would impel Aunt Appollonia Kelling, were she here, to
address the cussers with gentle suggestions that there were
many beautiful words in the English language and it would
be a far, far better thing were they to learn some.

The result of Appie's ministry was that Appie had got to
learn some new words herself, which she didn't know the
meanings of but feared they were not quite nice. Nevertheless,
her determination to brighten whichever corner she happened
to be in never flagged. Sarah felt some small relief in the fact
that her aunt wasn't there now; she herself was in no mood
to brighten anybody's corner. Particularly that idiot's who
came flying out of a doorway just as she was passing and
jostled her so hard that she bumped into Charles, almost
making him lose both his aplomb and his grip on the Kelling
umbrella.

"Sorry, Charles, that man shoved me on purpose. You don't
suppose he was a bag-snatcher?"

It was perhaps not the thing for a butler to smile, but Charles smiled anyway. The handbag Sarah carried was one that Max had had custom-made for her; a modern version of the sturdy old Boston bag, with a formidable brass catch, leather straps that wrapped around and fastened with brass buckles, and handles strong enough to hold a rearing mustang.

"I should venture to say, moddom, that anybody who tried to snatch that suitcase you're carrying would need either an acetylene torch or a chain saw. He didn't hurt you?"

"No, but he startled me. Charles, I think we ought to get on the subway."

"But it's only one stop from Boylston to Park. And we'd still have to walk down Beacon to Tulip."

"I know that. Humor me, can't you? Have you any tokens for the turnstile?"

"Oodles. Would it be presumptuous of me to ask where we're going?"

"I don't care where, I just think we ought to go. We'll take whichever train comes along first."

Sarah was not at all sure why she was behaving so eccentrically, but that hand-delivered hatpin and the hole drilled through the office wall into one of Brooks's telephone books so soon after Dolores Tawne's unexplained death were quite enough for one day. She was not about to take a chance that the person who'd just lurched into her was planning to follow her and Charles home.

Getting hold of the Bittersohn Detective Agency's business address was no problem. Anybody could pick up a Boston phone book and open it to the right page. Anybody could read the company name on the directory in the lobby. Anybody could have been standing around the front desk when she got back from lunch, seen her picking up the envelope with the hatpin inside, and heard the receptionist address her by name. She and Charles could have been trailed to the police station. That alleged messenger could very likely be tailing them right now, in the hope of finding out where they lived.

On the other hand, maybe he—or she—wasn't. What was the sense of putting herself and Charles through this smoke-and-mirrors routine? They were just two more raincoats in the crowd. The last thing Sarah wanted to do was cram herself into a packed train among a human logjam and fight her way out when the train stopped someplace where she didn't want to be. Just getting down those iron steps was a test of endurance, being shoved through the turnstile by the weight of others behind her almost landed her on the tracks.

By some miracle, however, a Riverside car pulled up at precisely the right spot and spilled out enough bodies so that Charles was able to practice some deft swordplay with the furled umbrella, maneuver Sarah into one of the few empty seats, and anchor himself like a limpet to the handgrip behind her. She gave up trying to think and let the waves of fatigue wash over her. She didn't snap out of it until the woman in the window seat crammed her Danielle Steele paperback into an already brimming tote bag and tried to worm her way past.

"Excuse me, I'm getting out here."

"Oh, sorry." Sarah stood up to let the woman by, noting as she did so that they were out of the tunnel and coming to a stop at Brookline Village. She'd meant to change cars at Kenmore to muddy the trail further. So much for trying to be clever.

At least she knew where they were; it was as good a place as any. Max and she had come here one night back when all those things were happening at Madam Wilkins's palace. They'd ridden in a taxi following another that held Lydia Ouspenska and a drunken piano player named Bernie. That had been the first time in her life she'd ever been kissed passionately in a taxicab.

Or anywhere else, for that matter. Her elderly first husband's caresses, on the rare occasions when he'd bestowed them, had been so chaste that she might as well have been a novice in a nunnery rather than a lawfully wedded wife. Poor Alexander, what a time to be thinking of him. She took the arm that her butler offered, not for auld lang syne but because it was a long step down and she still felt unsteady on her feet.

Once he'd assisted her safely off the train, Charles asked quite reasonably, "Now what shall we do?" He'd forgotten to add "moddom," he must have wearied of playing the faithful servitor. Sarah didn't blame him a bit.

"You know the Village, Charles. Where can we get a drink and some decent food? Preferably quiet, not too adventurously ethnic, and close by."

"Gotcha. This way to the peaceful."

On the relatively few occasions when she'd been there, Brookline Village had struck Sarah as an agreeable place to be. Charles knew exactly what she was hoping for. A few minutes later they were shedding their raincoats in a cheerful bistro where Charles appeared to be on amicable terms with all three waitresses and most of the patrons. The question of drinks came up. Sarah was not much in the habit of drinking anything stronger than white wine or a little of the sherry that used to be a dinnertime ritual at the boardinghouse back when Charles would buy it in gallon jugs at bedrock prices and decant it into Waterford crystal in order to improve the aura, since not much could be done about the taste. Sarah still kept sherry in the house, but not in gallon jugs and not at bedrock prices. Tonight, however, she ordered Scotch and water.

"For medicinal purposes," she explained, kicking her wet shoes off under the table and hoping she'd be able to squeeze them back on when it came time to leave. "I'm still not sure why I dragged us both into this, Charles. There was just something about that man—I'm sure it was a man, don't ask me why—darting at me the way he did. He reminded me of somebody, I can't think who. I wish I'd got a look at that messenger who left the hatpin."

"It's probably a good thing you didn't."

Their drinks came, the waitress hovered. Charles ordered the special, whatever that might be, without bothering to look at the menu. Sarah decided that plain broiled scrod would be safest after her recent upset, and took a careful sip of her watered-down Scotch.

"I suppose I'm reacting to—oh, the whole situation. Dolores Tawne dying the way she did. Myself being named her executrix. By the way, please remind me to phone Mr. Redfern at ten tomorrow morning; that's when he gets in. I do wish I hadn't made that dreadful scene in front of poor Lieutenant Harris. Perhaps I let my nerves run away with my head, but I just didn't dare go straight back to the house."

Sarah and Charles had both been keeping their voices low. As their waitress approached with salads and hot rolls, they changed the subject and turned up the volume to normal pitch.

"Have you heard from Mariposa yet, Charles?"

"Yes, she called around noontime. It's different there, of course, I think they're ahead of us. Anyway, the aunt's died and left her something, I couldn't make out whether it's a goat or a coat or what. You know Mariposa when she gets excited and starts mixing her languages, I caught about one word in six. I understand 'hasta la vista' well enough, though, and I sure hope she meant it. By the way, she wants you to phone her."

"Did she say when?"

"Mañana, which could mean either tonight or tomorrow or sometime when you happen to be in the mood. She gave me the number, I'll copy it out for you when we get back to the house."

A lone diner at the next table was exhibiting signs of interest; Charles winked at Sarah and began to improvise.

"Do you still want to fly over to Bimini tonight, or should we try the puppet theater?"

"Let's think about it," Sarah replied. "Did you know George Junior is planning a huge birthday party for Anora? He'll be tapping you about the catering, I expect."

"Sounds like fun. When's it going to happen?"

"When George gets around to it, I suppose. You know him,

he takes after his father. Don't look now, Charles, but that luscious blond over there is trying to catch your eye."

"Oh, her. She's been trying for quite a while." Charles shook his own blond curls and bestowed a sickeningly sweet smile at his admirer. "I'll tell her you're my rich aunt from Brazil, where the nuts come from."

"Tell her anything you please. Just don't expect me to pick up the pieces when Mariposa finds out what you've been up to."

They kept up their inconsequential banter, dropping a false clue now and then just in case one of the other diners was Sarah's nemesis in disguise. It got to be plain silly, the Scotch was helping, but Sarah decided she'd better not have another. Perfectly broiled scrod with rice and buttered squash was the best medicine for a diner who'd lost her lunch. The restaurant was as satisfactory as the food; quaint but not cute, clean and cozy, with real flowers in the vases and real candles dripping real wax into the saucers under the candlesticks. They took their time and enjoyed their meal.

As a smashing grand finale, Charles ordered a whopping dessert, something fudgy topped with whipped cream, nuts, cherries, and various other bedizenments that Sarah tried not to look at while she toyed with a modest scoop of lime sherbet. Charles took coffee, Sarah took tea. Charles put on a dapper blond mustache and a dapper Vandyke beard to match. Sarah put on her still-damp but not quite so squidgy shoes. They held an amiable squabble over the bill for the benefit of Charles's audience; in fact the meal would go on the office-expense sheet no matter which of them paid. They flipped a coin and Charles magnanimously let Sarah do the honors.

At fairly long last, they put their raincoats back on and ventured forth again into the teeming night, wondering at the tops of their voices whether to take a taxi to George's or ride the T out to Chestnut Hill and pay Mary a surprise visit so that she could admire Charles's beautiful new beard. By this time Sarah was past caring what they did. She let Charles assist her into the Red Cab that the cashier had kindly ordered for them and tell the cabbie where to go.

Charles's choice was a delicatessen over in Allston, where he stocked up on enough pastrami, salami, corned beef, chopped liver, rye bread, and kosher pickles to keep body and soul together for the rest of the week. Then it was back to Brookline, where they paid off their driver and ducked into a bakery for croissants and cheese Danish. The driver had seemed not to notice or perhaps not to care that Charles had switched in the cab from his smart Vandyke to a bushy black beard and donned an exotic black rain hat with a peak in front and a little curtain at the back reminiscent of those worn in the Foreign Legion.

Charles had also produced from his raincoat pocket a gaudy print head scarf of Mariposa's. Sarah had tied it on and pulled it as far down over her forehead as was feasible. Her distinctive handbag was out of sight inside the plastic carrier that also held the Danish and the croissants. They stood by the car tracks under the umbrella, a train marked "North Station" came along three-quarters empty. They climbed aboard and sat down several seats apart on opposite sides of the aisle, not only for purposes of dissembling but because the smell of salami at close quarters in the cab had turned out to be more than Sarah's stomach had bargained for.

Park Street Station felt like Mecca. They climbed the stairs, crossed Beacon, slipped behind the State House and through the back alleys until they'd worked their way to a sturdy green-painted wooden door that opened on Cousin Brooks's tiny garden and led to the basement entrance of the Kelling brownstone. All in all, this had turned out to be quite a day.

# Chapter 9

To her surprise, Sarah slept late and woke refreshed. Charles had coffee made and croissants warming by the time she entered the kitchen decently mantled from head to toe in a floor-length robe woven in many shades of red and pink with a hood attached and soft red leather bootees to match, which Max had picked out for her in a Moroccan bazaar. She allowed Charles to serve her with coffee, a croissant, butter, and apricot jam, then told him for goodness' sake to sit down and eat.

"Yes, moddom. I was going to iron the morning paper for you, but I got sidetracked reading the funnies."

"That's quite all right, it's yesterday's paper and I haven't time to read it anyway. I need to call Miriam and make sure Davy isn't homesick, then get dressed and go over to see Mr. Redfern. I suppose there are papers one has to sign, I've never been an executor before. Poor Dolores! I wish I could stop saying that."

"Have a Danish," Charles suggested.

"I'll think about it. Have you checked the answering tape this morning?"

"I have. Do we wish to purchase top-quality aluminum siding at reduced rates for a limited time only?"

"Not today, thank you. Is there more coffee?"

"Sí, señora. May I take your request as a tribute to my culinary efforts?"

"You may take it or leave it, just pour me about half a cup and drink the rest yourself. And for goodness' sake, go to Fuzzleys' sometime when you have nothing more pressing to do and have them make you a new beard. That ratty old bush you put on last night looks as if you'd been hatching sparrows in it."

"You wound me. You might at least have said budgerigars, there's some class to budgerigars. Then you want me to go to Fuzzleys' this morning?"

"Of course not, I want you here to straighten up the kitchen and answer the telephone. Lieutenant Harris might call while I'm out and you'll have to talk with him. I don't know what the protocol is about getting Dolores's stuff out of the studio, or whether they've managed to locate any heirs. I may need you to chauffeur later on."

Sarah sliced a small piece off one of the Danish pastries and slid the rest over to Charles. "Here, you finish it. I really must find out what's happening at the lake."

Miriam had been waiting for Sarah's call, or said she had. All was roses. Davy was developing into quite a fisherman, he'd succeeded in scooping a live minnow into his net, shown it to everybody, then carefully put it back in the water and waved bye-bye as it swam away. He told his mother that he was going to catch the minnow again today because it was nice and it liked him.

Sarah reminded her son that there were lots of nice minnows in the lake and perhaps a different one might like a turn at being caught today. Then Ira took Davy off to check out sites for possible sand castles and Sarah told Miriam about having been landed with the job of executing Dolores Tawne's will and she wished to heaven Max would come home. She said not a word about the mysterious hatpin or the hole that some-body had drilled in the office wall while she was up there by herself. Why get them all upset when they were having such a lovely time?

Having allowed herself the luxury of an extra few minutes' chat, Sarah told Miriam that she'd better get dressed and go see what Mr. Redfern had to say, not that it would be anything she'd want to hear. She promised further bulletins when there was anything to report, called Miriam an angel, which was not so far from the truth, and went to do what must be done.

The blue silk jacket that she'd worn to the Turbots' would not be inappropriate for a visit to a lawyer who still wore starched collars and a pearl stickpin in his tie and kept a filled inkwell on his desk. Even though she'd gained control of the trust fund her father had left her and was married to a man who would have been only too willing to give her the moon if they'd had any place to put it, Sarah could still take pleasure in the fact that she would never again have to face persnickety old Mr. Redfern wearing one of her late mother's hand-me-downs. She added her late mother's modest but genuine string of antique India pearls, borrowed a mohair stole of Theonia's, for last night's rainstorm had brought a fallish nip to the air today, and left Charles to carry on as best he might.

The lawyer's office was over in the financial district, just a pleasant morning walk for a healthy young woman who'd grown up threading her way among the winding streets that were supposed to have been laid out by early settlers' cows meandering down to enjoy a communal graze. Punctuality being the courtesy of kings and Kellings—some of them, anyway—Sarah got to her appointment right on the dot of half-past ten. Nothing in the Redfern offices had changed since her last visit some time ago. Nothing had ever changed; Sarah got the feeling that nothing here ever would change. Miss Tremblay, who had greeted at least three generations of Kellings at various times, rose from the straight-backed swivel chair behind her unpretentious desk and gave Sarah her ritual greeting: a token nod, a fleeting smile, and a reasonably cordial "Good morning, Mrs. Bittersohn."

This being Tuesday, Miss Tremblay was wearing a dark-brown dress. Had it been Monday, her dress would have been plum-colored. Wednesday's color was navy blue, Thursday's hunter green, and Friday's slate gray. All the dresses were cut by Miss Tremblay herself from the same simple pattern; none of them ever showed a wrinkle, much less a spot. Each had its special hand-crocheted lace collar: mauve for Monday, beige for Tuesday, sky-blue for Wednesday, leaf-green for Thursday, and silver-gray for Friday. What she wore on the weekends none of the Kellings had ever discovered.

Invariably, the collar would be fastened by a really good antique gold bar pin set with seed pearls and three sapphires of small size but fine quality that must be a family heirloom. Her salt-and-pepper hair was worn in a bun at the back of her neck, held in place by four tortoiseshell hairpins and a next-to-invisible hairnet. She smelled, only faintly, of violet talcum powder. Her shoes were laced-up black oxfords with one-inch heels. Her stockings were a darkish taupe that was neither sheer nor opaque. They gave the impression that she must have bought a job lot of them sometime in the dim past and was still trying to use them up, as why should she not? Miss Tremblay had achieved a style that was right for her and saw no reason to change it. Sarah found her wholly admirable.

The office protocol was familiar. Sarah smiled, not too broadly, and refrained from offering a handshake. "Good morning, Miss Tremblay. It's nice to see the sun after that downpour last night."

"Yes, that was quite something. But at least the rain washed some of the dirt and trash off the sidewalks. I believe Mr. Redfern is ready for you, Mrs. Bittersohn. Just let me make sure he's not on the phone."

This was part of the ritual. As always, Miss Tremblay stepped noiselessly across the dark-green heavy-duty indoor-outdoor carpeting and opened the inner office door exactly eight inches. "Mrs. Bittersohn is here, Mr. Redfern."

"Ah, good, right on time. Thank you, Miss Tremblay. Please show her in."

As always, Miss Tremblay opened the door wider and stepped back. As always, Sarah found Mr. Redfern making a fussy gesture with a sheaf of papers; she'd often wondered whether he kept that same sheaf handy as yet another part of the ritual. As always, he laid them down with exaggerated care on his immaculate green desk blotter and half-rose to shake hands across his desk rather than waste his valuable time walking around it.

Not that she cared a fiddle or a fig, but it did occur to Sarah that Mr. Redfern would have walked around if his visitor had been Cousin Dolph or Uncle Jem. And this notwithstanding Jeremy Kelling's having committed the fiscal sin of dipping into his capital and Adolphus Kelling's squandering the better part of his late uncle Frederick Kelling's enormous fortune remodeling an old factory on prime waterfront land into a far too lavishly appointed communal residence for indigent senior citizens.

However egregious their follies, Mr. Redfern would continue to hold the family in high esteem. A Kelling was, after all, a Kelling; and most of them, even scatty Appollonia, still had sense enough to keep their legal affairs in his capable, conservative hands. The truly horrific way in which the late Caroline Kelling had mishandled her dead husband's estate had caused Mr. Redfern extreme perturbation, as well it might; but his darkest day of all had dawned when young Sarah Kelling Kelling married out of the family and out of her caste and turned over the major portion of her legal business to her second husband's uncle, Attorney Jacob Bittersohn.

Sarah had, however, left the Tulip Street property in Redfern's hands, so he could hardly be too cavalier in his greeting. As always, he ran through a litany of inquiries as to the well-being of various Kelling connections—but not a word about the Bittersohns—before he clasped his hands, as always, over his gold tie clip in the shape of Justitia's scales and got down to business.

"Now then, Sarah."

Mr. Redfern had been calling the late Walter Kelling's only child by her first name ever since she'd first appeared at his office in white knee socks and black patent Mary Janes. Sarah would no more have expected him to drop the habit at this late date than she would have ventured to call him James. He cleared his throat, as always, and switched smoothly from old family friend to trusted member of the Massachusetts Bar.

"We seem to have a somewhat distressing circumstance on our hands, Sarah. As you may recall, about six years ago, if memory serves me, you recommended me to Mrs. Dolores Tawne, a member of the staff at the Wilkins Museum, who wanted a will drawn up. This was a small matter. I drew up the will in accordance with her wishes and, quite frankly, gave neither the client nor the will any further thought until about six o'clock yesterday evening, when I received a telephone call from the Boston Police Department."

Mr. Redfern rather went in for dramatic pauses, but Sarah was in no mood for histrionics. "Yes, I know," she said. "Two of the museum guards called me at half past five. She'd been found dead in the garden and they didn't know what to do. I told them to call the police and the head of trustees; evidently they did."

"Er—yes. Her body had, I was told, been taken to the city morgue in accordance with usual procedure. Her handbag had been opened at the scene of her demise by the officer in charge, in order to discover her place of residence and inform her family, if any. They had thus far been unable to locate a next of kin and were looking for an executor. Fortunately I was able to give them your name and your Tulip Street address."

"But why me?"

The lawyer went so far as to raise an eyebrow. "Because you are the executrix, of course. Sarah, is it possible that Mrs.

Tawne failed to get your permission before she so named you in her will?"

"Oh yes, quite possible. Dolores was like that. I don't know why she didn't pick on Cousin Brooks, she'd known him longer than she did me." But that was before he'd married the beauteous Theonia. Oh, well. Sarah had been getting stuck with odd jobs ever since she was twelve years old, why make a fuss over this one? Somebody had to do it and really, who else was there?

"All right, Mr. Redfern," she said. "What am I supposed to do?"

"Ar-hunh." True to form, Mr. Redfern, having cleared his throat, would now take out his handkerchief and use it to polish the lenses of his eyeglasses. As always, he didn't speak again until the glasses were safely and spotlessly perched again on his sharp little beak of a nose, the handkerchief refolded and tucked just so into his breast pocket, and the fingers of both hands tented together over the tiny effigy of Justice on his tie clip.

"In principle, Sarah, what the executor—or, as in your case, the executrix—must first do is to procure a signed court order making him or her—in this case, you—responsible for the deceased's estate and everything pertaining to it."

Oh dear. "And how do I get the court order?"

"In point of fact, you already have it, thanks to the—ah—diligence of some early-rising underling from the offices of Mr. Elwyn Fleesom Turbot, who brought it here to me immediately after having procured it from the court officer. If you'll just sign this receipt for the record . . ."

In for a penny, in for a headache. Sarah took out the elegant gold pen with a small ruby on the tip that Max had given her to add a touch of glamour to her ledger-keeping and appended her signature. Mr. Redfern nodded his approval.

"That's it, Sarah. You are now officially in full charge of the Tawne estate, for whatever it may be worth. There will be certain formalities, such as advertising for possible heirs, which I am quite ready to perform as lawyer for the estate, under your direction and with your consent. Do I have your permission to do so?"

"Yes, please." Sarah hoped there'd be money enough to pay for Redfern's services but the odds were that she herself would wind up footing the bill. Well, as Max's mother was given to saying, what could you do? "Just tell me where to start."

"Ah, yes. Your most immediate duty should be to make a judgment with regard to the—er—remains and to arrange the funeral, should you deem it appropriate to hold one. Any costs incurred in cremation or interment may be billed to the estate, unless you decide to pay them yourself and claim reimbursement after the will has been duly proved and whatever funds there are made available for distribution. I might just mention that there is no need to tie up your own money; funeral directors are quite accustomed to extending credit."

"For how long?"

Redfern shrugged. "For as long as it takes, is the best answer I can give you. Usually about a year. This brings us to your next most immediate duty, which is to secure the original will. Since Mrs. Tawne elected to keep it in her own hands, leaving only a copy in our files, I assume the original will turn up either among her papers or in her savings deposit box, if she has one. Once you've located the will, all you need to do is bring it to me and I'll initiate the process of probate. We may assume that the judge of the probate court will declare the will to be legal and reasonable, since I can think of no reason why it should not be so found. This takes about a month, usually, after which the process of probate can begin. Probate entails settling all outstanding debts and liens against the estate, such as income tax and so forth. I did not get the impression that Mrs. Tawne's estate would be either large or complicated, but one never knows."

"That's true enough," said Sarah. "Now I suppose the next thing is for me to go to the police station and collect Dolores's keys. May I use your phone to call and see if they're available?"

"They are." Mr. Redfern shuffled a few more papers in a haphazard way. "Lieutenant Harris left a message on our machine to the effect that the keys to Mrs. Tawne's—er—studio would be made available to you at the station on presentation of your court order. In fact, there's no way he could keep you out," the lawyer added a bit spitefully. "He added that Mrs. Tawne's handbag and her set of keys to the museum are being kept as evidence, though he didn't say to what. He also left her address. It's—"

"In the Fenway Studio Building on Ipswich Street," Sarah finished for him. "I've been there a few times. I'd better get over to the station, then."

"Now, Sarah, there's no need for you to rush off. Perhaps you might care for a cup of coffee, I'm sure Miss Tremblay would be glad to—"

Sarah didn't think Miss Tremblay would be at all pleased to have her morning's routine disturbed by a cup of coffee; she wondered whether the lawyer's offer had been prompted by solicitude for her delicate sensibilities or by plain, old-fashioned snoopiness. "Mr. Redfern," she said, "you're not by any chance trying to spare my fragile feminine feelings? I was the first to suspect that Dolores Tawne was murdered by having an old-fashioned hatpin shoved into her spinal cord. In fact, I'm the one who turned over the hatpin to Lieutenant Harris and suggested having the medical examiner look for a pinhole wound at the nape of her neck."

"Really, Sarah!" The old lawyer's neck was as red as a turkey cock's wattle. "I must say I—God in heaven, what would your father have thought?"

"I can't imagine what my father would have thought, Mr. Redfern, but you may rest assured that he wouldn't have been thinking about me. Now is there anything else I ought to know before I leave? What about money to pay the light bill and so forth? May I draw on Dolores's bank account?"

Redfern took a few deep breaths and got back on familiar ground. "You would be best advised to have the bank transfer any checking or savings accounts to your own name as trustee for the estate of Dolores Tawne. Do you know where Mrs. Tawne did her banking?"

"I think it's the High Street Bank, but I'm not sure," Sarah answered. "Dolores was more what might be called a business acquaintance than a close friend. Brooks knew her best. He used to work with her off and on at the museum. They socialized to some extent, but were never on intimate terms as far as I know. Dolores never seemed to me to be the sort of person who needed close relationships, she was too self-sufficient."

"Too full of herself" would have been a more accurate description but Sarah could never have said so, at least not to stuffy old Mr. Redfern. "I'd better be getting along. Thank you for letting me take up so much of your time."

"Not at all, that's what I'm here for."

Redfern was all set for a long, fatherly chat, but Sarah was not about to oblige him. She skated over the bare facts as fast as she decently could, then picked up her gloves, handbag, and borrowed stole. "I'll bring you the will when I find it. Thanks for your help."

Once outside the building, she could see the wind puffing up dust and debris from the pavement; she hugged Theonia's stole around her and decided it wouldn't be a bad idea to take time out for some shopping. Her silk suit was too light, this deep-crimson stole too eye-catching. What she needed was a seasonable outfit as different as possible from what she had on without being freakish. In fact, the duller might be the better.

# Chapter 10

Taking time out for a change of wardrobe before Sarah picked up the keys from Harris and pushed on to Ipswich Street would make no difference to the dead woman now. If there was anything to certain theories held by some of Theonia's former colleagues in the transcendental line, Dolores must be busy dusting off the astral plane by now and having the time of her transmigrated life. Since nobody had ever been able to tell Sarah for sure what would happen to the liberated spirit once the bar had been crossed, she was content to hope for the best and turn her attention to more mundane affairs.

A mannequin in a window on Newbury Street caught her eye; it displayed a warm-looking green jacket and a kilt that was mostly green and blue with a thin red stripe. Sarah hadn't bought anything green in ages, she stepped inside and started browsing through the racks. She decided against the green; the businesslike young woman who left the shop half an hour later was soberly but tastefully clad in a darkish-gray flannel jacket and skirt and a lighter-gray silk shirt. Her light-brown hair was mostly hidden beneath a gray felt fedora with a black grosgrain band such as Kelling ladies had been wearing since the days of the Gibson girl, whether anybody else was wearing them or not. Her pearl earrings were small but genuine. She wore black kid gloves and low-heeled black pumps, she carried a black handbag that could have been her grandmother's and a paper shopping bag that bore the name of the fairly exclusive boutique she had just patronized.

Anybody looking inside the bag might have glimpsed a fuzzy mass of crimson mohair and possibly a flash of blue silk, but nobody did because pink tissue in multiple layers had been so neatly tucked in on top. The bearer might have been executive secretary to somebody important, or a rising young member of the bar. A more discerning eye would have spied a dedicated young matron of the so-called leisured class on her way to organize something respectable and meritorious.

Sarah Kelling Bittersohn had affairs of her own to organize, she'd better get cracking now that she'd taken on the appropriate protective coloration. There were still Dolores's keys to be picked up, and the original will to be found. She hadn't even thought about a funeral, except in passing; she hoped to goodness Dolores had left instructions as to what sort of send-off she wanted.

It would have made sense, Sarah thought, to ask Mr. Redfern to show her his copy of the will while she was in his office; but he always made such a pother over everything. He'd have insisted on reading the whole document aloud to her with a running commentary in tedious legalese at every whereas and whyfor; she'd have been ready to fly into fits before he got to the parts that mattered.

Her shopping bag was bulky but not heavy. Rather than take a taxi and get caught up in traffic, she cut across Boylston and legged it for police headquarters. Nobody paid any attention to a small woman in dull, sensible clothes, dull, sensible shoes, and a face-hiding hat. She ducked pedestrians, dodged traffic, and made good time to the station. Lieutenant Harris was not in but he had left an envelope at the desk for her. He'd also instructed a uniformed policeman to drive Mrs. Bittersohn to the Fenway Studio Building and stay with her while she made her search of the late Mrs. Tawne's apartment.

That was good news to Sarah; she hadn't relished the

thought of having to ransack a murdered woman's premises all by herself. Officer Drummond, as he turned out to be, stowed her shopping bag in the back seat of the police car and suggested that she sit up front with him because he'd had to rush an injured dog to the Angell Memorial after a car smash and hadn't had time yet to brush the hairs off the back-seat upholstery. That said, he left her alone and concentrated on his driving while she delved into the lieutenant's envelope.

As she'd expected, Dolores Tawne's keys were inside, identified as hers by a cardboard tag on a string. A note written on lined yellow paper with a ballpoint told Sarah what she'd already surmised. According to the medical examiner's report, the hatpin which Mrs. Bittersohn had brought in was indeed the murder weapon. Whose hand had wielded it was not known and perhaps never would be; a beaded hatpin in a bad state was not the optimum object on which to hunt for fingerprints. As for Mrs. Tawne's effects, Harris had made a preliminary examination without finding anything that looked to him like a clue. There was a will, but he hadn't found any bankbooks in her handbag or in the apartment. He hoped Mrs. Bittersohn would have better luck.

Sarah hoped so too. It was considerate of the lieutenant to have provided her with an escort; although she couldn't help thinking he'd have been remiss not to, considering what had happened yesterday at the office. Maybe she and Officer Drummond ought to stop at the Little Building after they got through at the studio and check the office for further signs of unauthorized entry or potentially lethal souvenirs. Then again, maybe they oughtn't. She'd have to think it over. But first things first, and here they were turning into Ipswich Street. She tried not to wish they weren't.

As a young member of an old family, Sarah had on more than one occasion been stuck with the task of sorting over the effects of a dead relative for proper disposal. There'd been her mother, who'd died early and slowly of cancer; her father, who'd died before he'd known what ailed him; her gentle, handsome, self-sacrificing first husband and his blind, deaf, imperious mother, who'd died together in the wreck of a 1920 Milburn electric runabout. Those had been the hard ones. There had been other deaths, but always people she'd known well. How was she going to feel when she got upstairs about rummaging through a studio in which she'd set foot only three other times, and those before she'd married Max?

The first time around, Sarah had more or less invited herself to tea. A man she'd known and detested had shown up and Lydia Ouspenska had walked off with Dolores's tea cakes wrapped up in one of Dolores's napkins. The other visits had taken place unannounced, two nights in a row. Both nights, Dolores had answered the door in a plissé kimono, a headful of old-fashioned metal crimpers, and a raging temper.

Each time, the studio had been in next-to-perfect order. What would it look like now, with policemen's footprints in the dust on the floor and nobody bothering to wipe them up? Sarah remembered a line from *The Mayor of Casterbridge:* "And all her shining keys will be took from her, and her cupboards opened, and things a' didn't wish seen, anybody will see; and her little wishes and ways will be all as nothing."

Dolores had had her wishes and ways, she'd voiced them often enough. How could nursing the peacocks and dusting Madam Wilkins's bibelots have led to a hatpin through the neck in the flower-filled courtyard of the museum that had been her great and perhaps her only love?

The will that Harris had turned up and not stopped to read might possibly give some kind of clue. Harris's note had said only that he'd found one in Mrs. Tawne's top dresser drawer, glanced through it, and left it for the executrix to deal with. As was right and proper, but Sarah wondered why Dolores had left so important a document—important to herself, at any rate—in so easily accessible a place. It wasn't as if she'd lived like a hermit when she was not at the museum. She'd entertained a member of the board of directors to tea on a number of occasions that Sarah knew about; her brother would no doubt have been a frequent visitor, and so had Lydia Ouspenska during the years when she'd occupied the studio underneath Dolores's and scraped out a precarious living by painting antique Byzantine icons.

Lydia would not have been above snooping, nor would she have refrained from broadcasting anything that caught her interest to anybody who'd stop to listen. Max's friend Bill Jones, for instance; Bill always liked to know things. Sarah had no idea where Bill was sleeping these days, but he'd often shared Lydia's bed before she'd deserted la vie bohème in favor of steady employment, a comfortable home with congenial people, and three square meals a day. Not that Bill would have passed on any gossip about either Lydia or Dolores except possibly to Max Bittersohn or Brooks Kelling, but there it was.

If only Max would come home! Or Brooks or Theonia, or even Jesse. The city had taken her summer away; Sarah had been back here only since Sunday afternoon and she was sick of it already. Why couldn't she simply dump this job on somebody else, stop at the Rivkins' hired cottage to watch Davy commune with his friend the minnow, drive home to Ireson's Landing and let Anne teach her how to bed out chrysanthemums? Sarah wanted her husband. She wanted her child, she wanted her house, she wanted her own life. But she must not take what she wanted until she'd earned it; because that was how she'd been reared. And it served her right for not having the intestinal fortitude to squirm free of the Puritan ethic.

Having sublimated her snit, Sarah took Dolores's keys out of Harris's envelope and braced herself to enter the studio. She must forget that the murdered woman had eaten at her table on several occasions. But how could she not remember that last nighttime meeting when they'd rousted Dolores out of bed and Max had accidentally thrown the artist into ecstasy by mentioning what superb copies she'd made of the Wilkins's greatest treasures; how she'd rushed in her nightgown and curlers to put on the teakettle and rushed back with a trayful of chocolate marshmallow coconut fluffs; and how Max had recoiled in horror when she'd urged him to eat one?

Dolores had been lifted to the heights and dashed to the nethermost pit. She'd climbed out and dusted herself off and picked up the pieces and got on with her job. She had, in her way, been an admirable person.

Like Miss Tremblay, Sarah thought. Admirable people did not always get the best seats in the house or the biggest slice of the loaf. Perhaps, in a way, it was not so bad that Dolores Agnew Tawne had been spared further humiliation. Sarah could not for the life of her see how Dolores could ever have worked in anything like harmony with the Wilkins's new head of trustees.

Elwyn Fleesom Turbot had already made it plain that his was going to be the hand that cracked the whip. Dolores Agnew Tawne had appointed herself chief bullier ages ago. She'd known everything there was to know about the Wilkins. It had been her knowledge, her experience, her skill that had kept the museum going so well for so long, especially through the dark years that by now had shown signs of brightening. Turbot hadn't a clue about running a museum, yet he had the power to call the shots. He'd have driven Dolores until she balked, then fired her for insubordination and incompetence.

The giving or withholding of pensions was, according to the museum's charter, at the discretion of the board of trustees. Mr. Fitzroy had got one, and deserved it. An elderly, unattractive woman who'd threatened Turbot's supremacy, as Dolores certainly would have, could have been turned out to beg on the streets and not one of the bemused old trustees would have ventured to question the big man's judgment. But this was no time to sit and fume about what might have been. Officer Drummond was double-parking at the front door since there was no empty space at the curb.

"Why don't you get out and wait for me inside, Mrs. Bittersohn? I'll find a place to put the car."

"I could go on up to the studio," Sarah told him. "I know where it is."

"I'd rather you waited for me in the lobby, if you don't mind. My orders were to stick with you as much as possible. Here's your shopping bag."

Sarah couldn't see why he hadn't just locked it in the cruiser for the short time, she hoped, that they'd be here; but no doubt Officer Drummond knew best. She took the bag, hit the right key on the second try, and let herself into the lobby. About two minutes later, Drummond rapped on the door and called, "Mrs. Bittersohn?"

"That was quick," she remarked.

The policeman shrugged. "Can't arrest a cop on duty for a necessary parking violation. Where do we go?"

"Upstairs and to the right, as I recall."

There was an elevator in the foyer, but Sarah didn't bother with it. Her feet seemed to know the way well enough, they stopped at the door that displayed Dolores Agnew Tawne's card in a tarnished brass holder. She sorted out the right key and let herself and Drummond in, half expecting to hear the thump of sensible shoes climbing the short flight of stairs from the studio up to the small balcony where they'd entered. Dolores would have invited them in and galloped back down to put on the kettle and get out the chocolate marshmallow coconut puffs, unless the policeman's uniform put her off. If she'd been here.

Sarah knew that an arrangement had been worked out with the interim board of trustees that each of Dolores's meticulous copies would be returned to her as soon as its original was back in the museum. There was no reason why Dolores shouldn't have displayed her own paintings in her own studio, Sarah was surprised that the artist hadn't hung more of them. By now she must have amassed an impressive collection.

Sarah was both amused and touched to see that Dolores had given pride of place to a full-figure portrait of one Ernestina Kelling, whose husband had been an attaché at the Court of

St. James while John Adams was Minister Plenipotentiary, trying to form fresh diplomatic links between their former mother country and the by-then extant United States of America.

Why Ernestina, middle-aged, lantern-jawed, and tough as a minuteman's boot, had elected to have herself portrayed by the fashionable Mr. Romney as Venus, complete with doves and roses, was anybody's guess. Why Dolores Tawne had never caught on that the supposedly original portrait Madam Wilkins had bought for her palazzo had been even then no more than a pretty good copy of Romney's less than first-rate work was a question to which not even Max Bittersohn had found an answer.

The actual simon-pure, incontrovertible Romney that Romney himself had painted was in Kelling hands, as it had been ever since Ernestina had got into a hairtangle with Abigail Adams and been sent home with her doves and roses and a piece of Abigail's mind. For two centuries the genuine portrait had hung over one Kelling mantelpiece or another, most lately in Sarah's Aunt Emma's spacious drawing room. The alleged Romney that was neither a Romney nor a Tawne had easily been reclaimed by the museum once a too-gullible art collector had been made to realize that this particular Ernestina was both stolen and bogus. The painting was back at the Wilkins now, and few visitors knew or cared that she was just one in a series of Ernestinas.

Regardless of its debatable provenance, Dolores had given the Tawne Romney her best shot, skimping neither the scrubbiest feather on the skinniest dove, the most wanly blushing petal on the sickliest rose, nor the calculating glint in Ernestina's eye. She had worked hard on her subject, probably harder than Romney had done; a painter who'd preferred pretty young women as models and had managed to squeeze in nine thousand sittings in twenty years would hardly have taken time to dawdle over a subject so little to his taste as a middle-aged termagant from Boston, Massachusetts.

Dolores had produced a thoroughly professional duplicate, using the right pigments for the period on an old canvas of the right size that must have taken her ages to locate. Once the painting was done and dry, she'd imparted by dark and devious methods exactly the right patina of antiquity, dirty enough but not too dirty. She'd considered Ernestina one of her all-time greats, she'd been entitled to get some enjoyment out of having her work to herself at last. Poor soul, she'd paid for it dearly enough.

Dolores Agnew Tawne had really been a superb copyist, far too good to have been let run loose in a small museum where she'd had things pretty much under her own control. It was a marvel that someone so uniquely talented and so insurmountably gullible had been allowed to stay alive as long as she had. Why wasn't Dolores murdered sooner?

What a shocking notion to be entertaining, here in this studio that had been Dolores's home for so many years. But one did have to wonder how she'd survived that fantastic debacle seven years ago, had managed by sheer gall to keep her foothold at the Wilkins and promote herself, for all practical purposes, to being its curator.

One thing that Dolores had never done at the Wilkins, so far as Sarah knew, was to paint. Every stroke in that prodigious body of fakery had been laid on here in this studio, much of it done at night under special lamps, getting touched up in the morning's light, and overlaid with enough tobacco-spit brown varnish to conceal any slight deviations from the original. But what had she done lately? The air here now wasn't heavy with odors of oil and turpentine, the way it used to be. Even that half-finished canvas of a dead pheasant on a silver platter that Dolores had kept as a prop to hide what she was really up to from the few acquaintances who happened to wander in was missing. Had she given up painting entirely?

The tools of her trade were still here: the big easel, the battered wooden table beside it that held tubes of paint in orderly rows, a scraped-down palette, a jug of brushes. But there was no canvas on the easel, no preliminary sketches, not even a stick of charcoal. This wasn't a working arrangement but a still life, a dead thing. The whole setup ought to be taken away and burned. Sarah turned her back on the easel and considered the rest of the studio.

Over by the staircase, Dolores had arranged a sort of living-room area with one comfortable easy chair and a rickety wrought-iron floor lamp beside it, a couple of wooden chairs with thinly padded seats that must once have belonged to somebody's dining set, and a nondescript coffee table about which nothing much could be said except that it looked sturdy enough to hold a tea tray laden with plenty of chocolate marshmallow coconut puffs.

Sarah had a memory for detail. These chairs had been shabby the day she'd first visited the studio; another seven years of city grime had not improved them any. Nor had the glare from the oversized windows that had been such a boon to so many artists over the years, even though they were heavily coated with dust from the constant flow of traffic going on and off the turnpike. There was no way to keep them clean, neither the windows themselves nor the thin curtains that were used in studios to soften the light or let in more according to the artist's need. Sarah remembered Dolores's curtains as having been a queasy yellowish gray in contrast to the immaculate room. The curtains she was seeing now were almost chalk-white.

That was mildly interesting. These curtains couldn't have been hung very long ago or they'd have been filthy from the smog. The fact that Dolores had gone to the bother and expense of putting them up suggested that she'd had no plans to move even though the rent must be fairly impressive by now.

Dolores had been a frugal woman; she'd have had to be on what the Wilkins paid her. She'd known it was hopeless to keep curtains clean here, she couldn't need them as light-breakers if she wasn't painting. As long as they weren't actually falling apart, she'd have been more inclined to leave them alone. Did the fact that she'd so recently invested in a new set suggest that she'd been intending to get back to her easel? Had she already taken Elwyn Fleesom Turbot's measure and realized that she wouldn't be able to run him the way she'd run the interim board? Could she have borne to fall back into being just another employee now that she'd had her taste of power? Had it actually penetrated her stubborn head that she might soon be out of a job, and had she been preparing to meet the crisis with her paintbrush at the ready?

# Chapter 11

Years ago, before she'd been recruited to the Wilkins by a far-seeing crook who'd been astute enough to recognize an almost unique talent going to waste, Dolores Agnew Tawne had been in some demand as a painter of meticulously rendered, deadly dull portraits of company executives and deceased relations, all done from photographs. Had it been in Dolores's mind to work up a new clientele in that same field? Surely she wouldn't have dared go back to copying old masters.

"Anything you want me for, Mrs. Bittersohn?"

"Oh." Sarah had almost forgotten that Officer Drummond was with her, it was hardly fair to keep the man standing around with nothing to do. "I'm sorry. I've been trying to get my bearings, it's so long since I've been here. Why don't you sit down in that armchair and take a rest while I poke around? It shouldn't take long."

She found pretty much what she'd expected. Partitioned off from the big studio was a slit of a bedroom with space for no more than a single bed, a tallish but not very wide chest of drawers, and a narrow standing cupboard of enameled steel that held Dolores's few beige or tan dresses and skirts, her sturdy tan working shoes and a slightly less utilitarian pair for dress-up, a robe, a nightgown, a pair of house slippers, and a couple of felt hats, one beige, one tan.

Off the bedroom was an even tinier kitchenette, barely more than a cubbyhole with a midget porcelain sink, a hot plate, a toaster oven, and a half-sized electric refrigerator doing extra duty as a food safe and a work surface. Some shelves above the sink held cups, saucers, plates, stainless-steel knives, forks, and spoons for four, a few cooking utensils, and a modest stock of groceries, including an unopened package of chocolate marshmallow coconut puffs. Sarah felt an insane impulse to have them buried with the woman who'd never gotten to eat them.

The studio had no bathroom facilities. Dolores had joked to Sarah once about having to go upstairs and across the hall in bathrobe and slippers with her soap and towel and hope that none of the neighbors would catch her in the altogether, taking a sponge bath and shampoo in a long black sink that had been installed for more art-related purposes. She'd lived that way for so long that she'd come to take such makeshifts as a matter of course.

Sarah wished she hadn't thought about Dolores having to squat in the sink, she was not liking this invasion of a dead woman's domain. Even though she had not only a right but a duty to be here, even though nobody was left to intrude upon, she still felt like an intruder. The mere thought of having to open that top dresser drawer was repugnant; she knew she was only staving off the moment of truth when she decided first to look for all those other paintings of Dolores's that Max had returned after he'd retrieved the originals.

What had Dolores done with them? Not under the bed; all Sarah could see was a film of dust that had already begun to collect. Not in the studio, certainly not in that pocket-handkerchief of a kitchenette. They must be in the storage closet, there was nowhere else. Officer Drummond was by now comfortably asleep in the easy chair, she slipped past him and climbed the stairs on tiptoe.

There they were, all shapes and sizes, not in the elaborate frames that were by now back on the original paintings, but still on their wooden stretchers, stacked with their faces against the closet walls. She turned one around. It was blank. So was the next, and so were the rest, every single one of them. These were obviously old canvases, the sort Dolores had prowled the junk shops for at her wicked patron's behest. Each had been sanded down to a smooth surface and primed with a fresh white ground. Dolores must have done this herself, but why?

One explanation might be that Dolores had gone back to picking up old canvases because she was not about to waste money on new ones, assuming she had in fact meant to resume painting. A pretty scene copied off a postcard might sell better if it was dressed up to look like an antique; an elderly artist who could be on the verge of losing her job had to think of these things. Dolores had always looked upon her work for the Wilkins as a sacred trust, even though it must have taken a good deal of denial to persuade herself that she wasn't involved in anything fishy.

As to these canvases, Sarah was only guessing about what Dolores might have planned to do with them; but it was impossible to believe that they were copies that Max had returned to her. Dolores had been proud of her work, as well she deserved to be, considering how many years it had hoodwinked the art-seeking public. She'd never have scraped the canvases down and painted over them just to save a few dollars. Then where were her copies?

Aside from these enigmatic blanks, there was little of interest in the closet: a brown winter storm coat worn threadbare at the cuffs, a pair of old-fashioned stadium boots with a rip in the back of the left one, a tan raincoat that had also seen its best days, a faded brown umbrella that bulged on one side from a bent rib, a couple of paint-encrusted smocks, an ironing board and a heavy old electric iron, a collapsible wire shopping cart, a mop, a broom, a long-handled feather duster, a few cleaning supplies, some canned goods that there wouldn't have been room for on the kitchenette's crowded shelves, all the odds and ends that couldn't be fitted in anywhere else. But not one finished painting.

Perhaps Dolores's will would shed some light. Much as she still didn't want to, Sarah went back downstairs. Officer Drummond was having a lovely snooze for himself; she slipped around behind him into the bedroom and eased open the top dresser drawer.

Yes, there was the will, lying on top of a carefully pressed and folded beige polyester blouse. Sarah sat down on the neatly made-up bed and began to read. Mr. Redfern's prose style was all too evident, she plowed doggedly through the wherefores and hereupons until, to her horror, calamity struck.

"Oh, my God!"

Officer Drummond could not have been that deeply asleep, he came flying. "What's the matter, Mrs. Bittersohn?"

"This ghastly will. It says here that Mrs. Tawne wanted to be cremated and have her ashes scattered among the flowers in the Wilkins Museum's courtyard garden."

"So?"

"Well, think of the consequences," Sarah sputtered. "Can't you imagine visitors strolling down the garden paths and suddenly coming upon bits and pieces of poor old Dolores poking up among the nasturtiums? I don't know whether you've ever seen what comes back from the crematorium, Officer Drummond, but it's not what you might think. My cousin Mabel has her father's and mother's ashes mixed together in a hideous china urn that she keeps on her dining-room mantelpiece. She insisted on showing them to me once and they were all gritty lumps and oddments of arm and leg bones. You could tell what they'd been. Some of them, anyway."

"And she keeps that thing in her dining room?"

Sarah couldn't blame Drummond for grinning. "Oh, yes, Cousin Mabel keeps everything. Goodness knows what will

become of that urn when she dies. If she ever does. I only
hope she doesn't will it to me, she's never liked me. But this
last request of Dolores Tawne's—I can understand why she
put it in, though. The Wilkins had been pretty much her whole
life for years and years, especially after her brother died. He
seems to have been her only relative; I see she's left everything
to the Wilkins."

"Including her bones."

Drummond had had his laugh, Sarah didn't think he was
entitled to a second. "Yes, unfortunately," she replied. "I'm
already in trouble with the new chairman of trustees, the
undertaker's waiting to be told what to do with the body, and
whoever owns this building will no doubt be after me to clear
out the studio so that a new tenant can move in. I don't
suppose the trustees will want to be bothered about Mrs.
Tawne's effects. The furniture's hardly worth carting away and
there's not much else except her clothes and a few groceries."

Plus the paintings on the studio walls and that lot of primed
canvases. Sarah was reminded of the brief lecture on art
thievery that she'd delivered over the Turbots' table and Lala's
less than amusing suggestion that her husband lift a few of
the returned originals from the museum to be faked up and
resold. She wished she'd kept her mouth shut. Maybe Dolores
hadn't been quite so noble as she'd presented herself to be,
and maybe those fresh white grounds would come off without
much coaxing if somebody needed a perfect secondhand copy
in a hurry.

Sarah herself was more an illustrator than a painter. Even
so, she had a fairly clear idea as to how an overpainting could
be removed without hurting the original painting underneath.
She wouldn't mind trying the process on one of those freshly
grounded canvases, but was she entitled to do so? For whatever it might or might not be worth, everything in this studio
was now the property of the Wilkins Museum. Even though
the executrix appeared to be stuck with the actual labor of
removing what the museum didn't want, it would be the board

of trustees who must first make the decisions about what to keep and what to throw away.

The thought that she, as the sole executrix, and Turbot, as the trustee best placed to give her the hardest time possible, might be obliged to work together was enough to make the blood run cold. Mr. Redfern had said he'd be willing to handle the details; she could ask when she took him the original will whether there wasn't some way that everything could be funneled through him. As far as Sarah could see, it was much ado about nothing anyway; the sooner they got on with the probate, the better for her.

Not much better, most likely. She put the will in her handbag, heaved a sigh, and began going through the dresser drawers to make sure she hadn't missed anything that might be of value, then putting everything back so that Mr. Turbot couldn't accuse her of malfeasance. She didn't relish the thought of having to take up the question of Dolores's tired old nightgowns and undies with the head of trustees. Maybe Turbot would consider the subject beneath him and stay home to commune with his polled Herefords. One could always hope.

It was easy to see that Dolores had been a member of the "use it up, wear it out, make it do or do without" school. Most of her things were well-worn, some of them patched or darned, but nothing was actually in tatters. Sarah assumed the hopeless cases had been used up as paint rags or for housecleaning. She saw nothing unusual in that, she'd had plenty of wearing out and making do during the lean years.

She kept on lifting and stacking, finding small oddments such as a black lace-and-satin sachet, what was left of a half-pint of brandy, which wasn't much; a stash of arty brass and copper jewelry that had been carefully tucked away inside a pair of bright-pink bed socks. Why Dolores would have worried about any burglar's coveting such stuff was beyond Sarah's comprehension, but beauty was ever in the eye of the beholder and at least the brass and copper handicraft hadn't clashed and clanked any louder than Lala Turbot's bangles.

A brittle cardboard gift box covered with Santa Clauses must have been sitting in this same drawer for a good many years. It held a cheap brown plastic handbag, never used. Sarah thought cynically that the bag must have been a present from Dolores's late brother at some bygone yuletide when Jimmy Agnew hadn't quite managed to drink up all his money. She opened the bag on general principles, pulled out the wad of crumpled paper that Dolores had never bothered to discard, and found a tiny brown envelope that contained a safe-deposit key.

"Well," she crowed, "this is interesting."

Officer Drummond had been standing in the doorway gazing past her at the unopened package of chocolate marshmallow coconut puffs. Now he focused on the open dresser drawer. "Found something, have you?"

"Yes, a safe deposit key." Sarah showed it to him. "Is there a branch of the High Street Bank around here anywhere? I remember Dolores mentioning once when I happened to have my checkbook out that she and I used the same bank, though not the same branch. Where is hers?"

"Right in Kenmore Square. She wouldn't have had much more than a ten-minute walk from here unless her corns were bothering her."

Sarah couldn't tell whether or not Drummond was trying to be funny but she smiled anyway. Not much to be done now, there was only the bottom drawer to check. Apparently this was where Dolores had kept the stuff that would have gone into her desk, if she'd had one. There wasn't much in it except a shoe box full of receipted bills, a scrapbook almost too big for the drawer, and a number of clippings out of old Boston newspapers.

Sarah recognized the scrapbook. Dolores had shown it to her that first afternoon when she'd come here to tea and been strong-armed into eating her first and so far her only chocolate marshmallow coconut puff. Here were all the presidents of Amalgamated Industries, over a hundred years of them, from the founder to the great-grandson who'd been in office when Dolores had finished the set. In the front of the scrapbook was a glossy eight-by-ten-inch black-and-white photograph of the artist having her hand shaken by a large man who bore a regrettably perfect likeness to the portrait that she had apparently just completed. Dolores herself wore the smug and self-satisfied expression that Sarah and Max had often seen on those occasions when she hadn't been raging at poor Melanson or Vieuxchamp or one of those other museum guards whom she'd contrived to make her serfs.

The photographs and cuttings which related to the Amalgamated Industries dynasty were all pasted in the scrapbook, along with some that testified to Dolores's work for various other clients. The clippings that had been left loose in the drawer all dealt with one group of seven who called themselves the Wicked Widows. Presumably they were female, though one never knew. The photographs that went with the text showed them wearing black fishtail evening gowns that hugged their rumps but fanned out into great poufs of black tulle from mid-thigh down to the floor. Each widow sported a huge black cartwheel hat perched almost vertically on one side of the head, as Lydia Ouspenska wore hers.

Either the Wicked Widows had grown their hair long and dressed it high with combs and hairpins or else they'd worn wigs. Hats of such dimensions would have needed firm foundations to pin into and long hatpins to keep them sitting pretty. Long black widows' veils were draped over their hats and faces but flung back over their shoulders to display as much cleavage as was feasible without letting it all hang out. Whether they'd sung, danced, or just stood around looking voluptuous and inscrutable was not made clear, at least not in the captions under the murky photographs. Glancing at her watch and feeling an emptiness in her stomach, Sarah decided it wasn't fair to keep Officer Drummond away from his lunch.

She could read this mass of yellowed newsprint later, and probably should; Dolores must have had some reason to save it.

The papers were dated from the mid-sixties. That Dolores could have been one of the Wicked Widows seemed preposterous. The Amalgamated Industries photographs of that same period showed the artist as a stocky, thick-legged matron with shoulders like a footballer's and a face that wouldn't rate a second look. *La vie bohème* would have been totally out of character for the Dolores Agnew Tawne whom Sarah had known, or thought she had. But did anybody ever really know anybody?

Bizarre things had gone on during the sixties and early seventies, at least some of Sarah's relatives said they had. She herself had been too young and too cloistered to know much of anything about the dawning of the Age of Aquarius, and her parents would have been the last people on earth to tell her. The only memory of the period that stuck in her mind was of being taken by her father's distant cousin and closest friend Alexander to a street fair over in the Back Bay where there was supposed to be a Happening.

They'd hung around for a while watching the crowd and wondering what was going to happen, but all they'd seen were people in overalls carrying garbage cans around, so Alexander had walked her back to the Public Gardens and treated her to a ride on the swanboats and a bag of popcorn to feed the ducks.

Before she was out of her teens, both her parents were dead and she'd been married to Alexander. The wedding hadn't been much of a happening either, nor had the marriage. Sarah had truly loved Alexander and duly mourned him. When she thought of him nowadays, though, it was never as the careworn elderly husband who had tried too hard to be a buffer between her and his domineering mother, but always the young Apollo in gray flannels who'd taken his lonesome little cousin to ride on the swanboats.

Alexander had never written Sarah a letter; he'd never had occasion to do so because they'd never been apart long enough to justify the expense of a postage stamp. Still, she'd have liked to get one. Maybe Dolores would have liked to get mail also. If she had got mail, she hadn't kept any. At least there were no letters in her bottom drawer, not even an empty envelope with her name and address written on it.

Unless Dolores had kept her personal correspondence in that safe deposit box. But why would she have bothered lugging it to the bank when there'd be nobody of her own to read the stuff once she was gone? Of course the poor soul hadn't known she was going to die when she did. Sarah shuffled quickly through the clippings; not until the drawer was empty did she notice the bump.

It wasn't much of a bump. Sometime or other, Dolores had lined her dresser drawers with brown wrapping paper, neatly and painstakingly, as she did everything, gluing the paper securely to the wood. Thus, when she'd wanted to poke a small, flat object under the lining, she'd had to cut a neat little slit to get it in. Typically of Dolores's act-first-and-think-afterward approach, the small object bumped up and showed through the slit, so she'd tried to mend matters by pasting a neat patch over the bump. By now the patch had curled up and become more noticeable than the slit alone would have been; Sarah picked it off with her thumbnail and fished out the thing that had caused the bump. It was a safe deposit key, but not a match for the key that had already been found.

"Officer Drummond, look at this. Why in the world do you suppose Mrs. Tawne was paying rent on two separate safe deposit boxes in the same bank?"

"Beats me."

Drummond's stomach chose that opportune moment to emit a growl too loud to be ignored. Sarah dumped the clippings, the scrapbook, and the boxful of receipted bills back in the drawer and jumped to her feet.

"I'm so sorry. We'd better get on over to Kenmore Square

and have something to eat. I'll keep these keys with me. I have to transfer whatever money she has in the bank to my own account as executrix, so we might as well open the boxes while we're there."

# Chapter 12

"Watch it!"

Miracles still happened. Half an inch closer, and Sarah Kelling Bittersohn would have been only a mass of pulp in the gutter. Officer Drummond's hand was biting into her arm, he was dragging her up over the curb, scraping her knee on the concrete. She could feel him shaking, she must be shaking too. Thank God she still had a knee to bruise.

Once she was safe on the sidewalk, he helped her to stand and relaxed his grip a little. "That son of a bitch! He deliberately tried to run you down. And I didn't even get his whole number. Seven-five something."

"Seven-five-three-two KG." Sarah had no idea how she knew that. She began to laugh, fighting hysteria. Her left leg was a mess, her nylon stocking one great run, her knee scraped raw, blood running down her shin. She opened the handbag that some kind passer-by had paused to salvage for her and rummaged out a handful of tissues. "What a nuisance, I'll have to buy some panty hose. Don't mind me, Officer Drummond, I'm babbling. Thank you. That sounds awfully feeble, doesn't it."

She must still be wobbly, Drummond was keeping a firm hold on her arm. "The car's a gray Toyota, I got that much. There can't be more than a thousand of them bombing through here every day. Seven-five-three-two KG, you said? I'd better call it in."

He let go of her just long enough to snatch out notebook and pencil and jot down the figures. "Seven-five-three-two KG, right? Come on, Mrs. Bittersohn, let's go in here and get you some coffee. You can sit down and pull yourself together while I'm phoning the station."

"Thank you." That sounded relatively sane, Sarah said it again. She let the policeman steady her into the coffee shop, he nabbed a waiter who had been peering out from behind the potted plants in the window.

"Take care of this lady, will you? She just missed getting creamed by a hit-and-run driver. You saw what happened, didn't you? I've got to make a report. Where's the phone?"

"Right over there beside the bar. Sure, I saw it, a gray Toyota. The guy did it on purpose."

"Are you sure it was a guy?"

"Well, yeah, I guess so. It might have been two guys, I didn't get a good look. But the car was a gray Toyota, I know that, I've got one myself. You okay, miss? Can I get you something to drink?"

"Coffee, please. Black," Sarah was amazed that she could get the words out, she felt as if she'd been stuffed and mounted like a hunter's trophy.

"Coming right up. Sugar's on the table."

Sarah had a vague notion that she ought to put sugar in the coffee that the waiter was going to bring. She hated sugar in anything, but it was supposed to be good for something. Shock, that was it. She didn't care, she didn't feel up to the bother of stirring. She just sat there regardless of the pain that she was feeling in her knee now that she had time to realize she'd been hurt. It would be better to let the numbness take over.

The young waiter came back with a mug and set it in front of her, where she could smell the steam. She stared at the mug, not even trying to pick it up. It seemed outside the bounds of possibility that somebody in a gray Toyota had made a deliberate, calculated attempt to run her down. Yet it had happened. Officer Drummond had said so, the waiter had said so, surely they wouldn't lie.

She tried flexing her fingers to see whether they still worked. Her hand made contact with the mug handle. She wondered what she should do next. There was something Officer Drummond ought to know about, it wasn't until he'd finished putting in his report and come to sit at the table with her that she remembered what it was.

"I was just thinking, Officer Drummond. There might be something more to this ... happening. I was driving into Boston from the north shore Sunday afternoon when two fellows in a gray Toyota started harassing me. You know, practically climbing my rear bumper, then cutting out and pulling around right in front of me when I tried to get away from them. That sort of nonsense."

"Ought to be locked up in a zoo," growled the policeman. "With the tiger, for preference. Here, drink your coffee while it's hot. So what did you do?"

Sarah managed to get a swallow or two into her, it helped a little. "Luckily for me, I've made that run so many times that I've picked up a few dodges myself. I strung the fellows along until I came to a spot I had in mind, then ditched them rather neatly, if I do say so. The thing of it is, when I rattled off that number just now, I can't honestly say whether I was remembering the one that I'd got several close looks at on Sunday or if it was actually the same number plate both times."

"You didn't write it down the first time, by any chance?"

"No. I was more concerned with not getting hit and watching my chance to shake them off." She tried a little more of the coffee and began to feel almost halfway human. "Don't you think it's time we ordered? You must be starving. I'm going to stick with something bland and simple, like a plain omelet, but you order whatever you like. Mrs. Tawne's lawyer says the executors are allowed to charge off expenses to her estate, assuming there is one.''

Drummond emitted a noise that might have become a laugh if he hadn't nipped it off short. ''You're a gutsy lady, Mrs. Bittersohn, if you don't mind me saying so. Now, where's that waiter?''

He glanced around in an authoritarian way and the young fellow reappeared. ''I guess we're ready to order. The lady wants a plain omelet and I'll try the roast beef sandwich. Tell 'em not to stint on the gravy.''

While they waited for their food, it was impossible to stay away from the topic that was uppermost in both their minds. ''Did you get a look at the driver?'' Sarah asked. ''Was there anyone else in the car?''

''Could have been. All I really remember is that crazy driver.''

''Male or female?''

Drummond shrugged. ''Who can tell, the way people dress nowadays? But I'm pretty sure it was a guy. Cops develop kind of a feeling. I don't suppose you got a look inside?''

''Oh no. I was wondering what Dolores did with her bankbooks. I wasn't even aware of the car until all of a sudden there it was, almost on top of me. Are you quite sure that swerve was deliberate? You know how flustered some drivers get if they're not used to our notorious Boston traffic.''

''I sure do,'' Drummond snarled, ''but I've had enough experience on traffic duty to tell who's just a stupid klutz and who to book for a charge of driving to endanger. That bas— er—driver was out for blood. And I'm going to get him. I don't know how, but he's mine. You want some more coffee?''

''I want my omelet.'' Sarah glanced at her watch. ''And I can see why, I hadn't realized it's almost half past one. I'm so sorry.''

''Ah, that's all right. I'm used to eating at odd times.''

The lunchtime rush was over by now, their food was not long in coming. Sarah's plain omelet was daintily garnished with four green grapes, a slice of orange, and a ruffle of kale; Drummond's roast beef sandwich was a great slab of half-raw meat swimming in gravy. Each of them tried to avoid looking at what the other was eating. Both relished the hot food, neither could let go of the bizarre incident that had shaken them so horribly.

"You know, Mrs. Bittersohn, it almost seems to me as if that driver might have been hanging around the square, waiting his chance. He and whoever was with him could have been double-parked over by the T station as if they were waiting for somebody, and speeded up when he caught sight of you in the crosswalk."

"But you were with me," Sarah argued.

"I was on the other side of you, watching out in case some cowboy made a quick left turn. The guy driving the Toyota might not have realized that we were together."

"How could he have known that I'd be here at all?"

"Not to alarm you, Mrs. Bittersohn, but let's assume he's the messenger who left the hatpin at the desk in the Little Building. He could have hung around watching until you picked up the envelope and been tailing you ever since."

Sarah shook her head. "Actually I think it's more likely that he lost me after my houseman Charles and I left the hatpin with Lieutenant Harris late yesterday afternoon, and picked me up again this morning when I stopped in at the station to get Mrs. Tawne's keys. I don't know whether Lieutenant Harris mentioned to you that somebody had tried to drill a hole through the wall into the office where I'd been working. That was why I'd phoned Charles to come and escort me home. Then I realized it wouldn't be a good idea to lead somebody with an electric drill directly to my house on Tulip Street, so Charles and I spent the evening in the rain confusing our trail. I bought this outfit as a disguise after I'd been to the lawyer's office this morning but it was probably a waste of money. All my stalker would have had to do was phone the station early and ask whether Mrs. Bittersohn had stopped by to collect Mrs. Tawne's keys, then wait in ambush until a woman about the right size went in and came straight back out. He must have got a jolt when he saw you helping me into a police car."

"Didn't stop him, though, did I?" Drummond replied somewhat bitterly. "He must have followed us to the studio building and made a lucky guess about Kenmore Square when he saw us leaving the building on foot."

"Yes, but your being with me would have forced him to change his plan of attack. If he was really out to murder me, it would have been easier and less risky to catch me alone in the studio and knife me or choke me or chuck me out the window onto the turnpike in front of a truck. Did you want some dessert?"

That was too much for Officer Drummond. "My God! Is that what they teach girls in those fancy finishing schools?"

"I wouldn't know," said Sarah. "My father didn't believe in schools for girls. If you'll excuse me, I'd like to wash up as best I can, I've used up all the paper napkins mopping the blood off my knee. Perhaps you wouldn't mind making a quick trip to the drugstore, if there is one, and bringing me back some gauze pads and adhesive tape, and a pair of knee-high nylons?"

"Sorry, nothing doing. My orders are to stick with you." Drummond made a halfhearted gesture toward the check that their waiter laid on the table but Sarah scooped it away.

"I'll take care of this. But please, may I be let off the leash for just a few minutes?"

"Okay, Mrs. Bittersohn, but I'll be right outside the door. Holler if you need me."

Sarah put money on the table, including a generous tip for the helpful young waiter, and let Drummond escort her as far as the women's-room door, which he insisted on her holding open long enough for him to make sure nobody was lurking behind the toilet bowl.

There was nothing she could do about her lacerations and

abrasions except sponge off the dried blood and the few trickles that were still running down her shin. Fortunately the gray flannel skirt was a bit loose around the waist; she pulled it as far down over her hips as it would go without falling off, trying to hide the extent of her injuries as best she could. Clean hands, combed hair, and fresh lipstick, a little of which she smudged on her cheeks so that she wouldn't look quite so much like the corpse she had almost become, lifted Sarah's morale a trifle; anyway, it was the best she could do. She opened the door just in time to catch her allegedly vigilant watchdog emerging from the men's room.

"There you are," she said. "Now the drugstore, if you don't mind. I can't go into the bank looking as though I'd lost a fight with wildcat."

She was limping badly, she couldn't help it. Fortunately Kenmore Square abounds in amenities. Officer Drummond explained to a kind pharmacist that the lady he was assisting had fallen and hurt herself. The kind pharmacist, a youngish woman, took Sarah behind the counter, helped her shed the remnants of her panty hose and wash out the sidewalk grit with peroxide, offered soothing antibiotic salve and heavenly feeling gauze pads, told Sarah to put ice on her bruises when she got home, and sent a clerk over to the hosiery rack for some dark-taupe knee-highs. She even knew where the High Street Bank's branch was situated, just a short hobble from where they were. Since it was not the Kelling way to hug strange pharmacists, Sarah voiced her gratitude in warm tones, paid her modest bill, and limped as nimbly as she could manage out of the drugstore and into the bank.

They didn't have much time, the bank closed at three. Sarah went directly to the reception desk and spoke to the middle-aged man in charge.

"My name is Sarah Kelling Bittersohn. I'm a depositor at your bank and executrix for another of your depositors, Dolores Agnew Tawne, who died Sunday afternoon. I'm supposed to transfer whatever money she had in your bank to my own trustee account. I haven't found any bankbooks yet, so I assume they're in one of her safe deposit boxes. Is there someone I can talk to?"

"Just a moment, please." The man flipped a switch and spoke into his headset. "Mrs. Fortune, there's an executrix here for the estate of a Mrs. Agnes Torn. She wants to talk to you, she's brought a policeman with her. Shall I ask them to wait?"

He listened, then nodded. "Mrs. Fortune will see you. Turn right past the counter, third door on the left."

Mrs. Fortune, a harried-looking woman of fifty or so in a gray suit much like Sarah's, emerged from some inner fastness. "What was the name again? Are you a relative of the deceased?"

"No, I'm executrix for the late Dolores Agnew Tawne. My name is Sarah Kelling Bittersohn and this is Officer Drummond, who's helping me. We found her safe deposit keys and her original will in her studio a while ago, but we haven't turned up any bankbooks; so I'd like to have her boxes opened in order to transfer any funds she may have left to my trustee's account."

Mrs. Fortune had brightened her businesslike suit with a pair of green-framed eyeglasses hanging from a string of pink and green beads. She put them on and peered suspiciously through the lenses. "You said boxes. Are you saying that this Mrs. Tawne had more than one?"

"She had more than one key, at any rate, and they're not mates."

Sarah took the two midget keys from her handbag and laid them side by side on Mrs. Fortune's desk. "I found this one in her top dresser drawer, with her will. The other had been hidden under the paper lining in the bottom drawer. Here are the envelopes, you see they're both marked 'High Street Bank' and have different numbers. It's possible, of course, that one of the keys might be to a box that she'd had some time ago and quit paying rent on; she was always careful about money. Anyway, I thought I should bring them both.''

Mrs. Fortune pecked at her computer, then shook her head. ''There's only one box listed under Mrs. Tawne's name.''

''Then I wonder if the second box could have been her brother's.'' Though whether the late Jimmy Agnew would ever have owned anything worth keeping at the bank was, Sarah thought, highly improbable. ''Or somebody else's,'' she modified. ''I expect you have ways of tracing a key number back to a name.''

''Yes, we can do that, if we have to. But not till you show me some identification.''

''Of course. Here's my court order, and my driver's license with my photo on it, and Mrs. Tawne's will with myself named as executrix. I'll be dropping off the will at her lawyer's office, he can vouch for me if you want to call him. His name is Redfern, his address is on the will. Is that enough for you?''

''Plenty.'' Mrs. Fortune even managed a grim smile. The top-drawer key was immediately matched to the name of Dolores Agnew Tawne. The other one put up a fight; it was not until an assistant brought Mrs. Fortune a typed card from an old wooden file in a back room that the computer was able to dredge up the relevant information. The box had been rented on December 3, 1967. Never once since that date had anybody requested access to it. This explained why the card had got shunted onto an inactive list despite the fact that rent was still being paid for it every year on the dot.

The name in the old file card matched the name on the computer; it was LaVonne LaVerne. Who she might be or might have been was probably going to take some finding now that Dolores was gone. Nobody of that name was listed in the Boston phone book or in any of the suburban directories that were the only reference sources Mrs. Fortune had ready to hand. No matter. There were places enough to look: the voting lists, the census, the Boston Public Library's unstumpable reference department. Personal ads could even be run in the Boston papers if all else failed, which seemed very unlikely.

Mrs. Fortune was not up for in-depth research, that was clear. She wanted LaVonne LaVerne to show herself or quit haunting that long-unopened safe deposit box. She seemed almost to suspect Sarah of deliberately withholding information.

"And you're absolutely sure, Mrs. Bittersohn, that Mrs. Tawne never once mentioned this LaVerne woman to you?"

"No, never," Sarah insisted. "As I've been explaining ever since Sunday, Mrs. Tawne was less a personal friend than a professional acquaintance. She could be sociable enough when she felt like it, but her conversation was generally related to the Wilkins Museum, where she worked. Her job seemed to be her major interest."

"The Wilkins Museum? Oh yes, I remember her now. Big woman with a loud voice. So she's dead. Well, we all have to come to it sooner or later. We'd better get to those boxes, we haven't much time."

# Chapter 13

Sarah hoped her knee wasn't going to start bleeding again. Luckily she hadn't far to walk before Mrs. Fortune ushered her and her bodyguard into a windowless room lined with safe deposit boxes, each to its own steel-lined cubbyhole and its own set of locks. Taking the two keys that Sarah handed her, she checked the number on the first box against the number on the key and the number on her list, and unlocked the little door.

"This is the Tawne box." Mrs. Fortune slid the long, narrow green box out of its niche. "Now, Mrs. Bittersohn, do you want to check the contents of this one and put it back before we take out the LaVerne box, or would you rather open them both together?"

"Together, please." Sarah's chief concern by now was to get through with what had to be done here and go home and put her leg up.

"This way, then. Here, you hold the first box while I take out the other one, that's so I'll have no chance to pull a switch on you. You may be wondering why I'm not getting written permission to open the LaVerne box, but since it's never been opened once in all this time and the key was presumably in Mrs. Tawne's possession, and since you're now the executrix, it's for you to say. It's quite possible, you know, that there never was a LaVonne LaVerne in the first place. We get some weird things happening here; people dying intestate and leaving boxes full of false teeth, glass eyes, stock certificates issued by companies that went bust half a century ago. We never know."

Mrs. Fortune had been getting the second box out as she spoke. She motioned for Sarah to follow her to a row of cubicles along the fourth wall, opened the door to one of them, and switched on an overhead light. "Please don't take too much time, we close on the dot of three. Be sure to hook the door from the inside."

She placed the LaVerne box on the shelf that served for a desk, backed out of the cubicle, and left Sarah to herself. It was like being shut up in a piano crate, there was barely room for a single wooden chair drawn up to the shelf. Sarah dutifully secured the outdated hook-and-eye fastening and opened the box that had been rented to Dolores Tawne.

Good, here were the bankbooks, two of them. One showed a total of just under fifteen thousand dollars, the other only a few hundred. Judging from the many small deposits and withdrawals, the latter must have been Dolores's method of handling her weekly expenses; the former, then, must be her life's savings. There had been withdrawals from the larger account also, though none recently. That biggest and latest one must have been her payment for Jimmy's funeral. Even in death he'd sponged on his sister. In life, how many of her hard-earned dollars had been poured unthinkingly down her brother's always-ready throat?

At least there was enough here to settle Dolores's small estate. Sarah put the two bankbooks in her handbag and lifted off a tan-colored silk scarf with a blue paint stain in one corner that had been laid over whatever else was in the box. She might have known Dolores would leave everything in perfect order, but why had Dolores gone to the bother of wrapping all her bits and pieces in Christmas paper, and tying them up with narrow red satin ribbon?

There were a fair number of these little packages, roughly five to six inches long, not more than two or three inches wide. Curious, Sarah slipped the wrapping off one of the packets. What she found was a purple velvet-covered jeweler's case, somewhat rubbed but still in excellent condition; she opened it and gasped.

The era of the beaux and belles, the macaroni, the nonpareil, and latterly the railroad tycoon was over. No man these days wore a great, flamboyant gem in his cravat or on the bosom of his boiled dress shirt; but somebody didn't seem to care. Sarah opened another of the elegant little cases, and another, wishing she had time to see them all. Some of the stickpins were relatively modest, if diamonds of only two or three carats in elaborate gold settings could be considered so; others were splendid enough to make a rajah sigh with envy.

Sarah knew what she was seeing, and it scared her stiff. There was no way Dolores Tawne could have come by this collection honestly. How in heaven's name had that handmaid to molting peacocks and housemaid to Madam Wilkins's hideous majolica managed to pull off a crime of this magnitude? And what was the position of the executrix with a court order that gave her full responsibility for the estate of Dolores Agnew Tawne?

If only Max were here! But he wasn't, and Mrs. Fortune must be having kitten fits outside the cubicle and the LaVerne box hadn't even been opened. Halfway excited, halfway dreading what she might find, Sarah raised the lid that had lain shut for thirty years.

What Sarah found was hardly anything at all, just a yellowed letter-size envelope stuffed with handwritten pages that she mustn't take time to scan, a half dozen or so black-and-white eight-by-ten photographs that had been rolled up for so long that they'd have to be wrestled apart and flattened under a heavy weight before one could get a proper look at them, and, of all things neither bright nor beautiful, six long, sharp, businesslike steel hatpins.

Each of them was much like the others, each had for an ornament a round knob the size of a glass marble, covered with tiny jet beads. All their steel shanks were darkened by time, or by something. All the pins were in better repair than the one that Sarah had turned over to Lieutenant Harris, but none was anything special to look at. Thirty years' worth of box rent for this? Paid by Dolores Tawne of her own free will? Preposterous! Paid by someone else? By whom?

Dolores had let herself be gulled once, but that was for what she'd been led to believe was a grand and noble purpose; not to mention the side benefits to her personally: the wide scope she'd been given in exercising her phenomenal skills as a copyist and the gratification to her never-sated ego of hearing thousands of visitors over the years swoon over what they took to be a genuine Duccio, a Botticelli, a Rembrandt, a Manet, even a Sargent; but was in fact a genuine Dolores Tawne every time.

The more Sarah thought about those fabulous stickpins, the less she could picture Dolores stealing them. Was it possible that the woman had been feather-headed enough to fall for another fairy tale? Had she let herself be manipulated into guarding stolen goods for that unconscionable rogue who was no doubt even now trying again to wangle a release from jail on the theory that money talked even louder than lawyers?

Dolores, never one to look before she leaped, could easily have failed to realize until it was too late that once more she'd let herself in for something too hot to handle. She'd have been afraid to keep what wasn't hers, but even more afraid that she'd be laying herself open to another charge of complicity if she tried to turn the stickpins over to the police. Just leaving them in her safe deposit box would have seemed the only sane and sensible thing to do. Notwithstanding all evidence to the contrary, Dolores had always prided herself on being sane and sensible.

As to this LaVerne box, Sarah didn't know what to think. Dolores had had so little for herself, why would she have gone on paying rent on it year after year? Unless she'd made some kind of promise that she'd felt bound to keep; Dolores had always perceived herself as essentially a noble soul. She'd nobly nagged her poor soak of a brother until he'd put an end to her eternal badgering by walking in front of a Huntington Avenue streetcar. She'd nobly kept silent during all those years when she'd been painting her guts out—her own words, spoken in bitterness on the night of revelation—for an occasional pat on the head and a bottle of cheap champagne. Perhaps she'd kept guard over that enigmatic little key in the name of nobility, but what was there to be noble about in this pitiful handful of shabby relics?

After a brief struggle, Sarah managed to separate one of the curled-up photographs from the roll and hold it down on the shelf. It showed what she supposed to be a line of chorus girls, seven of them, all wearing low-cut black evening gowns with flaring fishtail flounces of stiffened tulle, black cartwheel hats anchored almost vertically to one side of the head, and black mourning veils that obscured their features but were thrown nonchalantly back over their shoulders to reveal most but not quite all of their frontal elevations.

Sarah recognized the chorines at once. She'd seen newspaper clippings of these same photos this morning in Dolores's bottom drawer. She was wishing she'd brought the clippings along to read after dinner when Mrs. Fortune played a sharp tattoo on the cubicle door.

"Finished, Mrs. Bittersohn? It's two minutes to closing time."

"I'm coming."

Once Sarah let go of the photograph, it coiled itself back into a tight roll. She thrust it and the envelope that she hadn't got to open into her handbag, locked the two boxes, and unhooked the door. The stickpins left her a bit qualmish, but they'd be as safe here as anywhere until she could get hold of Max and find out what to do about them.

"Here you are, Mrs. Fortune. I've locked them both. I'll have to come back when there's more time."

Mrs. Fortune seemed less than enthralled by the prospect, she made quick work of tucking the two boxes away in their respective niches. "You'd better hurry. Go straight ahead as far as you can, then take a right. There'll be a security guard on duty."

Officer Drummond, who hadn't said a word since they'd entered the vault, offered a supporting arm; Sarah took it gladly and walked as fast as she could. By the time they got past the guard and out the door, her scraped knee was bleeding again.

Drummond noticed. "You okay, Mrs. Bittersohn? I'd be glad to bring the cruiser around, but I sure don't want to leave you standing here by yourself. Maybe the security guard—"

Sarah Kelling had not been brought up to expect pampering. What if the blood of her forefathers did flow a little too freely just now? The plastic-covered patch was seeping again but she could deal with it when they got to the cruiser; she'd swiped a few tissues from Mrs. Fortune's desk before they'd gone into the vault. And she didn't feel a bit guilty. There had, after all, been more than a touch of the freebooter in some of those early Kellings. Also in some of the later Kellings, but they'd called their privateering by a less pejorative name.

By the time she and Drummond got to where he'd parked the police car, she was thoroughly fagged and a trifle woozy, but that didn't matter. She'd be back at Tulip Street soon, God and the traffic willing. She climbed ungracefully into the passenger seat and examined the damage as best she could without shocking Officer Drummond's sensibilities. It wasn't so bad, actually. Her new skirt would have to be cleaned before she could wear it again, but the bloodstains around the hem didn't show up so badly on this dark-gray flannel as they would have on her good blue silk. She mustn't forget to take her shopping bag, she hoped nobody had had the gall to pinch

Theonia's mohair stole. She made a pad of Mrs. Fortune's tissues and held it against her oozing knee; by the time they got to Tulip Street, the bleeding had pretty much stopped.

"You stay put, Mrs. Bittersohn, till I get out."

Officer Drummond came around to her side, opened the door, and gallantly assisted her to the sidewalk. She couldn't let him go without once more expressing her gratitude. "I don't know how to thank you, Officer Drummond, as you surely must realize by now. I'm going to phone Lieutenant Harris as soon as I get inside and let him know how you risked your life to save mine. That maniac could have killed us both, you know."

"The thought did cross my mind," Drummond admitted, "but that was just part of my job. Want me to walk you up the stairs?"

"No, I'll be fine, thank you. There's my butler coming, he'll help me in. I do hope we meet again under less hair-raising circumstances."

"Don't forget your shopping bag."

He handed it over, there was no time for further demonstrations of gratitude. Like most of Beacon Hill, Tulip Street was inconveniently narrow for the volume of traffic that crawled up it each day. A single car double-parked for the minute or two that it took to let out a passenger could evoke a cacophony of honks and curses all the way back to Charles Street.

Even police cars were not immune, as several drivers were letting Officer Drummond know. He got back into his vehicle and broke the bottleneck by driving off with his siren howling. Charles bounded down the steps, relieved Sarah of her bags, and assisted her into the house as a good butler should, behaving as nothing more than an auxiliary mechanism constructed for the convenience of ladies in bloodstained skirts who were having trouble with their knees.

Sarah most gratefully allowed him to lower her into the nearest chair. "Thank you, Charles. I'm going to change as soon as I can get my legs back under me. Have we anything other than salami sandwiches for dinner?''

''Anticipating your query, I went down and bought us a barbecued chicken plus some veggies for a salad. There's plenty of that good bread left. Would you care for an aperitif before you change? You look, if I may say so, as if you could use a wee dram of the mahster's whiskey.''

''That's very perceptive of you, Charles. I'm going to take a quick shower first, though. Give me fifteen minutes or so.''

Getting out of her clothes and washing the blood off her leg, not to mention the dust from Dolores's studio and the general feeling of griminess, was an immense relief. The warm shower felt like a gift from the heavens. Sarah indulged herself in it for an extra few minutes regardless of the water bill, rubbed her fine, light-brown hair more or less dry, ran a comb through it, and poked at the natural waves that saved her so much in fuss, bother, and hairdressing fees. A clean night-gown, her all-concealing floor-length robe, a fresh gauze pad over the wounded knee and slippers on her feet were quite enough to cover the conventions as well as the wearer. Charles had been in too many backstage dressing rooms to go into a tizzy of disapproval over a housecoat at a potluck supper in her own house.

Sarah noted that Charles had put her whiskey and water on a small table beside one of the library armchairs. She collapsed into the chair and picked up her glass. This was just what the doctor would have ordered if one had been called upon for a professional opinion, she decided. And think of the fee she'd saved.

Sitting there easing her knee on a hassock and drinking her mild whiskey and water, Sarah felt as if this day had gone on forever. According to the clock on the mantelpiece it was a few minutes short of four in the afternoon. There was still time for a report to Lieutenant Harris; he ought to know what she and the invaluable Officer Drummond had been doing.

When Charles came in to ask whether she'd like her drink refreshed, she shook her head.

"I'm still working on this one, thanks. What I want you to do is bring me Max's portable phone and Lieutenant Harris's extension number at police headquarters. It's on the Rolodex. I don't want to get up because my knee still hurts, as you must have noticed."

"Would an ice pack help?"

"I don't know. Do we have one?"

"There's a package of frozen peas in the fridge that will work just as well and cost less. And you can eat them afterward."

"I'll think about it. How are you at getting bloodstains out of wool, by the way? I hate to send my new skirt to the cleaner when I've only worn it once."

"No problem. I've played enough valets in my time to know the drill. Sponging with cold water, plus judicious use of a pressing cloth and a warm iron should do the trick easily enough. Where did you leave the skirt?"

"Over the foot of our bed." The "our," of course, referred to Sarah's absent spouse. "Since I really don't have anything else that's right for this weather, I'd be grateful if you could have it ready for me to wear tomorrow."

"Your wish is my command. I'd better call the cops first. No, by Jove, I'll get you the mahster's telephone first."

Having made sure that the hassock under Sarah's afflicted limb was in the optimum position and Max's cordless phone ready to her hand, Charles went to fetch the bloodstained skirt. Sarah managed all by herself to dial Lieutenant Harris's number, only to find that he was even then on his way to deal with some malefaction heinous enough to warrant his personal attention. Having a phone in the car and an assistant to do the driving, however, he was quite ready to hear what Mrs. Bittersohn had to say. Her report was impressive enough to warrant his full attention.

"I'll make sure the incident goes on Drummond's record,

he's about due for a promotion. But you're okay, Mrs. Bittersohn?"

"Thanks to Officer Drummond, yes, barring a banged-up knee and a certain amount of shock. I cannot for the life of me understand how Mrs. Tawne had become possessed of those stickpins, unless she'd inherited them from a rich uncle or was keeping them for somebody else, which would have been more like her."

"Any idea who the somebody might be?"

"Only the one whom you put in jail, and that's rather unlikely considering what the judge said at the sentencing. You may be interested to know that Officer Drummond and I found a second safe deposit key in Mrs. Tawne's bottom dresser drawer, which turned out to fit a box that had been rented under a different name and paid for but never opened since 1967. What fascinates me is that there were six of those old-fashioned jet-trimmed hatpins in the box, and not much else. Would you by any chance happen to remember a showgirl from the sixties named LaVonne LaVerne?"

"Not me, lady. I've only been on the force for nineteen years and I never ran around with showgirls. First my mother wouldn't let me and now my wife won't. What I could do is have a search made in the police records in case—" Whatever he said next was drowned out by what sounded to Sarah like a burst of machine-gun fire, "Oops, I've got to go. 'Bye, Mrs. Bittersohn."

Sarah laid Max's cordless phone on the table beside her empty whiskey glass and shut her eyes.

# Chapter 14

Sarah could have sworn she hadn't been dozing for more than a few minutes, but it was three and a half minutes after five when the telephone woke her. She knew by instinct who was on the other end; she could picture Cousin Anne doing a countdown until five o'clock had struck and the cheap rate was on. Anne would have given herself an extra couple of minutes' waiting time just in case her own clock happened to be running a trifle fast. Not that it ever had, but one never knew when it might, and an ounce of prevention was greatly to be recommended. Sarah picked up the phone and braced herself for a half hour of horticulture.

"Hello, Anne."

"Sarah, how clever of you to know it was me. I hope this isn't a bad time to call, but Percy isn't home yet and I thought you'd like to know that Mr. Lomax and I have the terraced beds for the chrysanthemums dug up and he's going to bring a load of fish tummies from the packing plant tomorrow morning."

Anne allowed herself the frivolity of a giggle. "That's not what Mr. Lomax calls them. He really is funny, isn't he. Anyway, we're going to fork them in along with the peat moss while we're fresh and rested, then have a bite of lunch and drive over to the nursery in his truck. I've alerted Mr.

Greengage to set aside plenty of the right colors but of course it will take time to check them over one by one to be sure they're in top condition and just the right blending of shades. I know he hates to see me come because I'm such a pest about insisting on the best, but it does save fuss and money in the long run."

"I'm sure Mr. Greengage wishes he had more customers like you," Sarah lied politely, trying not to yawn as she spoke. "You're a dear to go to all this trouble."

"And you're a sweetheart to let me," Anne bubbled. "I haven't had so much fun in ages. I can't wait to get at all that lovely free fertilizer. I never in my wildest dreams thought I'd ever have a whole virgin hillside to landscape. Perhaps 'virgin' isn't quite the proper word, because there's not much virginity around these days, but you know what I mean."

Anne was in a merry mood, all right. "Honestly, Sarah, I can feel myself just spreading my petals and opening out like a night-blooming cereus. A gardener does need a new challenge every so often, but you know Percy. Every time I suggest making a truly meaningful alteration at home, he gives me his old soft-soap routine about how proud he is of what we've created together. Which is a lot of fish tummies because Percy never lifts a finger if he can help it. I'm learning a lot from Mr. Lomax, I can tell you that."

This was pretty wild talk from Anne Kelling; it prompted Sarah to bring up a topic that was even more organic. "Anne, there's something I'm longing to ask your advice about, though I'm not sure how to put it." She paused to swallow the watery lees of her whiskey. "The thing of it is, Dolores Tawne's death has put me in a most peculiar dilemma. I learned only this morning that Dolores had stipulated in her will that she wanted to be cremated and have her ashes scattered over the courtyard garden at the Wilkins Museum."

"I see nothing difficult about that, Sarah. Bone meal not only aids in improving soil quality, it also can be used to repel ants and keep them from spreading aphids, which I should think would be highly desirable in a public place like that. Furthermore, bone meal keeps leaf rollers away from strawberry plants, though I don't suppose leaf rollers are much of a factor at the Wilkins."

"But I'm not talking about the kind of bone meal one buys in bags from the garden shop," Sarah protested. "Hasn't Cousin Mabel ever shown you that urn on her mantelpiece that she keeps her parents' ashes in? It's all gritty little bits and pieces with chunks of bone big enough to be recognized as such. The Wilkins's garden is the one place visitors always want most to see; what would they think if they were strolling among the flowers and all of a sudden up came the remains of a leg bone or an eye socket?"

For some reason, Anne thought Sarah was being funny. "Sounds to me as though Mabel had patronized a cut-rate crematorium, which I wouldn't put past her for one minute. Anyway, I don't see the problem. All you need to do is run the ashes through your blender till they're all ground down into tiny bits, put them in a box or something until it's time for the gardeners to take up the fall flowers and prepare the beds for spring, and just dig in the ashes when nobody's looking. It's not as if you'll get any great heaps of bone meal, you know. What I'd do would be just to pick a favorite spot of hers in one of the beds and scatter her there. I'd be willing to help if you'd like me to."

Sarah could feel the wooziness coming back. Anne saw the blender as a sensible, practical solution with no qualms attached. Dolores herself would no doubt have been willing to grind up any number of calcined bones without turning a hair if she'd thought the museum's garden needed a pick-me-up. Whether the board of trustees could be induced to go along with such a plan was quite another matter.

Then why tell them? Those who had shared with Dolores Tawne the actual day-to-day work of the museum would have to know, of course. And what was wrong with that? Couldn't they organize a simple, private ceremony on a Monday when no visitors were admitted, and get the interment over in a seemly but expeditious way?

Dolores would have liked a tasteful bronze plaque commemorating her many years of dedicated service to the museum. Perhaps the trustees might be amenable if they didn't know that Dolores's pulverized remains were resting underneath it, and more particularly if by some miracle the fortune in stickpins that she'd left lurking in the strongbox should turn out to have been legitimately hers and therefore, by the terms of the original will that Sarah must deliver to Mr. Redfern tomorrow morning, a welcome addition to the Wilkins Museum's depleted coffers. Sarah wished she could believe in so happy an ending.

Never mind. Whatever final mess Dolores Tawne's unbounded zeal and lack of forethought had got her into, she had earned the right to rest whatever might be left of her bones in the spot where she'd wanted to lie. Perhaps the undertaker would attend to pulverizing the ashes, Sarah thought. They must get odder requests. Anyway, something had to be done about Dolores's remains; she couldn't be left lying in a refrigerator. And right now, Sarah Kelling Bittersohn was the only person authorized to order the body cremated. She'd call up Wasserman's in the morning; she could do it right now, if only Anne would get off the line.

But Anne was by no means ready to quit. Percy was out to an accountants' society dinner meeting and she had the bit between her teeth. She held forth nonstop for another forty minutes, by which time Sarah was too exhausted to think of doing anything at all except to eat whatever Charles set in front of her and totter off to bed.

The barbecued chicken was edible if not palatable. Charles's salad was excellent. The good bread, the salad, and a nibble or two of this and that from the supply of delicatessen they'd brought home last night made up for what the chicken lacked in flavor and succulence. Sarah and Charles lingered over their picnic supper, not saying much, each of them hoping that somebody—anybody who was amiably disposed toward either one of them—would break the spell of silence. Oddly enough, it was Jeremy Kelling who came through. Charles handed the phone over to Sarah.

The Anatomy of Melancholy was not the anatomy of Jeremy Kelling, but few could beat him at the Choleric. Jem was already in full hullabaloo when Sarah took the phone.

"A fine niece you turned out to be! Why was I not informed that you're in town?"

"Obviously you were or you wouldn't be chewing the carpet now," Sarah riposted. "How did you find out my guilty secret?"

"One of Egbert's spies saw you riding with a policeman. What did they pinch you for?"

"Consorting with elderly uncles of ill repute. My friend from the force will be around to collect you sooner or later, I expect. Seriously, Uncle Jem, I haven't been in touch with you because I quite literally haven't had the time. I've only been here since late Sunday afternoon, which was when Dolores Tawne, whom you surely remember because you never forget a female face, was murdered with an old-fashioned hatpin. It turns out that I'm her executrix."

"Humph. I suppose that's as good an excuse as any for not coming to the aid of an afflicted relative."

"What are you afflicted with? Don't tell me you've run out of gin."

"Nothing quite so dire. What I'm chiefly afflicted with is boredom. Egbert's off for the night with that female Gargantua who used to be Ed Ashbroom's gardener."

"Ashbroom? That's a familiar name. Wasn't he one of your Codfish friends?"

"Edward Ashbroom was and remains a member in bad standing of the Comrades of the Convivial Codfish. Ashbrooms have been Codfish since the days of the primordial slime; they haven't changed much. There's nothing I can do about Ed except remind myself from time to time that such things are sent to test us, and give way to occasional cries of pain and woe. I'm better at the woe, I think. Would you care to hear me in full lament?"

"No, I would not. I've heard too many lamentations already."

It was then that Sarah had her epiphany. "Uncle Jem, I've just had a beautiful thought. How would you like to toddle over here and let me show you a photograph that might interest you? I'm sure Charles wouldn't mind nipping over up to Pinckney Street and walking back here with you if you feel the urge for a companion. I think the photograph might have something to do with the estate which I'm supposed to be settling, but I don't know what."

"Sounds like the start of a glorious evening. What makes you think I'd be interested in an old photograph?"

"My feminine intuition, plus the fact that the photograph shows what looks to me like a line of chorus girls."

"Oh. Well." Chorus lines were right up Jeremy Kelling's alley. "Why didn't you say so in the first place? Charles can see me home later if he cares to. I daresay I can find my own way to Tulip Street since I happen to be lamentably sober at the moment. How soon do you want me?"

"As soon as you can get here. I'll have Charles light a candle in the window to guide your faltering footsteps."

"Don't be flip, young woman. You might have brought the photograph to me, you know."

Sarah showed no mercy. "The walk will do you good. I can't go to you because I have a banged-up knee as a result of somebody's trying to run over me in a 1989 Toyota."

"Great Scott! Couldn't you have waited for a Cadillac or a Mercedes? We do have the family position to consider, as your Aunt Bodie would be only too pleased to remind you if she happened to be in the vicinity of Tulip Street. Sarah, you have not, by any chance, been ingesting hallucinogenic substances?"

"Neither by chance nor by intention. You come over here and I'll show you my knee."

"Must you keep harping on your knee? Are you telling me the unvarnished truth?"

"I always tell the truth, except when it wouldn't be kind. Which is more than can be said for you, but that's beside the point. Please come quickly, Uncle Jem. I've had an exhausting day and I do want to be able to stay awake until you get here."

"All right, you nagging female. I'm on my way."

To everybody's surprise, notably his own, Jem made the distance from Pinckney Street to Tulip in fourteen minutes and thirty-two seconds. Charles could have done it in six, but he fussed over tubby little Jeremy Kelling as if the old goat had been Paavo Nurmi.

"You've made remarkable time, sir, if I may venture to say so. Can I offer you some refreshment?"

"You can, indeed. No barbarities this time around, I trust?"

Back when they were newly acquainted, Sarah's new butler had committed the faux pas of putting a pickled onion in Jeremy Kelling's martini, and Jem had never let him forget it. Tonight Charles was making no mistake.

"Oh, no, sir. No olive, no onion, no twist, no ice. Just the well-chilled gin in the well-chilled glass and the cork from the vermouth bottle waved slowly three times over the top, if memory serves me correctly."

"Bang on target, Charles. You've come a long way under my tutelage. Now then, Sarah, what's this business you want to show me?"

"I'm not just sure. There's a letter along with the photograph. I meant to read it before dinner, but I fell asleep. It might be a good idea to give you some background on what's been happening, if you can spare the time to listen."

Ensconced in one of the comfortable brown leather library armchairs that Alexander Kelling's grandfather had bought cheap at a house sale, his martini glass traveling happily from hand to mouth and back again, Jeremy Kelling was quite willing to let Sarah catch him up on the incidents that had taken place since Dolores Agnew Tawne had been found dead among the peacocks.

"So, Sarah, am I to understand that at approximately the time when somebody was murdering Mrs. Tawne with a hatpin, you were playing tag along the road to Boston with a carful of hoodlums?"

"Not a carful, Uncle Jem, only two. At the time, I took them for a couple of young imbeciles merely out for what they perceived as a bit of fun. As to just when Dolores's body showed up in the palazzo's courtyard, I don't know. It was half past five or thereabouts when Vieuxchamp called here looking for Brooks. The museum closes at five, so I suppose they'd have found her shortly after closing time. My own feeling is that she may have been killed earlier than that and her body hidden until the crowd and most of the guards had gone and the coast was clear except for Vieuxchamp and Melanson, who'd stayed to lock up."

"Only two of them, in that big place?"

"That's right. The museum has a new head of trustees who's cracking down on what he sees as unnecessary overtime pay among the staff. I don't even know if they still have a night watchman, come to think of it. Though they'd be pretty crazy not to, wouldn't they?"

"No crazier than the rest of what I'm hearing. And the hatpin was found in Mrs. Tawne's neck?"

"No, quite the opposite. The medical examiner hadn't been able to determine what she'd died from until Monday, when a messenger dropped off an envelope with that hideous old hatpin inside. As it turned out, there was still blood on the pin that matched Dolores's."

"Coffee, moddom?"

Now that they had a caller, Charles couldn't resist laying on a touch of pomp and circumstance. To humor him, Sarah took one of the tiny, translucent demitasse cups and sipped at the odd-tasting concoction that was in it, trying not to wince.

"But what I want to show you, Uncle Jem, is a photograph I took from another box that Dolores had a key to, which had been rented under the name LaVonne LaVerne back in 1967. I'd found the key in Dolores's bottom dresser drawer, along with some clippings that seemed to have a connection with the photograph. There was nothing in the LaVerne box except a few more photographs of the same kind, a handwritten letter that I brought with me from the bank but haven't read yet, and six more hatpins like the one that killed Dolores. What's particularly interesting is that, while the box rent was paid faithfully on the dot all these years, the box itself had never once been opened from the time it was shut until I unlocked it this afternoon. Charles, would you bring me my handbag?"

"*Con placer*, señora." Charles darted from the room and came back with the bag, self-satisfied as a spaniel retrieving a stick. "Anything else?"

"Yes, give Uncle Jem a hand with that photograph. It's been curled up so long that it snaps back. What do you think, Uncle Jem?"

"Don't rush me. Is there a magnifying glass available, Charles?"

"Coming right up, sir."

Jeremy Kelling had always possessed almost eerily keen eyesight, but presbyopia was finally beginning to catch up with him. While Charles wrestled with the stiff, glossy paper, Jem hauled a pair of Ben Franklin–style spectacles out of his waistcoat pocket, gave them a wrathful glare, stuck them on his nose, and picked up the magnifying glass in a properly Sherlockian grip. Charles, having managed to subdue the photograph, held it out for him to see. Jem threw down the

magnifying glass, whipped off the Franklin specs, and
snatched the photograph from Charles's hands.

"Great balls of fire, it's the Wicked Widows! How in the
name of Lucifer did your Mrs. Tawne get hold of this?"

"Don't ask me, but there it is," said Sarah. "She might
simply have been taking care of the safe deposit key for
somebody else."

"Then she'd been sitting on a keg of dynamite for the past
quarter of a century and more, whether she knew it or not."

"What do you mean? How could she?"

"Good question. I don't suppose you've ever heard of a
Happening. That's with a capital *H*."

"I know, oddly enough. Alexander took me to one when
I was still wearing white knee socks and Mary Janes. There
was some kind of street fair in the Back Bay and they'd
advertised a Happening. I don't remember much about it
except that we hung around awhile waiting for the Happening
to happen but all that happened was some people wandering
around in pink overalls dragging ladders and trash cans. So
Alexander bought me some popcorn and we went to ride on
the swanboats, which was much nicer."

"I'm sure it was. I must say I'm surprised at Alexander's
having taken the risk, though he probably hadn't realized
there might be any. Dear fellow, of course, but hardly safe
out without a keeper, thanks to that poisonous mother of his.
Anyway, there were seven of them, always dressed as you
see them here in this photo, which I'm surprised ever got
taken. The Widows didn't care for having their pictures
snapped while they were performing, if such it can be called."

"What did they do?"

"They appeared. Whether they did it for pay or just for
kicks nobody ever seemed to know. They showed up at one
of the Esplanade concerts in the Hatch Shell one peaceful
summer evening and set off a riot. They slithered onstage at

the Wilbur during a presentation of *Macbeth* and took the curtain calls themselves. And brought down the house, to the actors' chagrin. There was a terrible scene right onstage that spread out into the audience. People got hurt, the police had to be called, and when the dust had settled, the Wicked Widows were nowhere to be found, as was ever the case."

Jem was enjoying himself. "I mentioned Happenings because those were where the Wicked Widows really shone. There was quite a fad for such non-events during the hippie years. If the shindig Alexander took you to had caught the Widows' fancy, that dull little business with the trash cans would have turned into something resembling a saturnalian orgy."

Jem picked up the magnifying glass again and studied the photograph inch by inch. "Those veils they wore played the very devil; nobody could tell which of them was anyone. And that includes your friends on the force, who had in fact to be called out in force on a number of occasions I personally can recall and no doubt on even more that I missed. One never knew when, where, or whether the Widows might appear, or how they managed to get away with what they did. And they never got caught. Nobody ever laid a hand on them. Not once. It was almost as if they were evil spirits instead of ordinary flesh and blood. Gad, I must be drunk. Is there any more coffee, Charles?"

"Certainly, sir. *Uno momento.*"

Charles took away the empty martini glass with Jem gazing wistfully after it and spent a few minutes in the kitchen warming up the coffee while Jem rambled on about the Widows and Sarah studied each face as best she could through the hindering veils.

"Uncle Jem!"

"Hunh?"

"Were you asleep? I'm sorry. But look at those faces again."

"What for? They all look alike to me. These stupid glasses—"

"It's not your glasses, this is what I want you to see. The reason those Widows look the same is that they are the same. And they're all exactly like the Mona Lisa."

# Chapter 15

"Hand me that glass again, Charles."

Having fiddled with the table lamp beside his chair until it threw light on the photograph from the optimum angle, Jeremy Kelling tried Brooks's magnifying glass at various armlengths and at last found one to suit him. "Sarah, I hate to say so, but I believe you're dead right about those masks. I only wish they showed up better. What we ought to do is take this photo to a photographer and have it enlarged to two or three times its present size. Then we'd really be able to see something. What a shame Brooks isn't here; he'd know how to do the work and we shouldn't have to pay him."

Charles put a fist to his mouth and performed one of the genteel semi-coughs that stage butlers are expected to emit when on the verge of communicating something crucial to the plot. "Poddon me, Mr. Jem, but I've assisted Mr. Brooks in the darkroom on numerous occasions. I could do the blowup for you, but it would take some time. As an alternate suggestion, we could pop down to the darkroom right now, put the existing print in the enlarger, and blow it up as big as it will go. That ought to give us a good look at the faces, just so we don't leave the photo under the lamp long enough to fry the evidence. You did say, moddom, that you'd left some others in the LaVerne safe deposit box. Were they all alike?"

"I thought so," Sarah replied, "but I didn't get much chance to look at them because the bank was about to close and the keeper of the vault, or whatever she's called, was dithering for Officer Drummond and me to get out. Let's see what we get with the projector."

What they got was all they needed. The Widows' veils were still a hindrance but the enlargement was good enough to confirm what Sarah had expected to see. The seven faces were definitely masks, all of them exactly alike, all showing the eternally inscrutable Mona Lisa smile.

Having the photograph so much bigger and better-defined gave Sarah a further insight. These masks were too good; by no stretch of the imagination the kind of soft-rubber caricatures that might be found at a costumer's or a joke shop. For masks of this quality one would have to model a prototype in clay, then cast it in plaster to provide a mold that could be lined with papier-mâché, and finally paint each mask like the original. The maker would have had to be an expert copyist with the skill and patience to produce seven exact likenesses. There seemed only one answer.

Had the masks been a labor of friendship or love, or had this been a matter of money earned by a portrait painter with a touch for a likeness, a slim pocketbook, and the ability to keep her mouth shut if she had to? Was this why Dolores had saved those clippings but refrained from pasting any of them in her scrapbook? Whose idea had it been for her to serve as custodian for LaVonne LaVerne, if there ever had been such a person? Why make such a to-do over a few pieces of evidence that didn't seem particularly damning about seven persons, presumably but not certainly female, who'd got their exploits but not their names in the Boston papers not quite three decades ago?

"Uncle Jem," she said after Charles had shut off the projector and led the way back upstairs to the library, "can you tell Charles and me a little more about the Wicked Widows? Were they really widows, do you think, or housewives working out their fantasies? Or just fans of Franz Lehár who'd got their facts twisted?''

"Many have wondered but nobody's ever found out, so far as I know." The quondam beau of Beacon Hill heaved a sigh of nostalgia for those joyously misspent days that would come no more. "It's been a long time, Sarah. You must bear in mind that I was never one of that sophomoric coterie who got their jollies dashing around from one Happening to another in the occasionally fulfilled but more often vain hope that the Wicked Widows would put in one of their unannounced appearances. I did get to see the Widows a few times, though, and I have to say that I found them rather impressive."

"Why impressive, Uncle Jem? What did they do?"

"Not much, when you come right down to it. They never uttered a sound, they merely exuded an atmosphere. They never broke out of their line, they were never in a hurry but always in motion, twining and twisting and swishing those fishtail skirts in perfect coordination, as though they were one big, black snake. At least that's what they made me think of, and that's how they could act if anybody got too close. They didn't always perform on a stage or in a roped-off area; sometimes they'd be right in among the crowd, weaving in and out but never getting quite close enough to be touched. If anybody committed the folly of getting too close, all fourteen of those black-gloved hands would reach up to those great black hats and out would come the hatpins."

"But surely they didn't go around stabbing people."

"Didn't they, though? I personally witnessed one incident that I still wish I could forget. I don't suppose I ever shall. It was at one of those block-party affairs that the Back Bay seemed to be rife with at that time. One could hardly turn around without falling over some wooden sawhorse with a bunch of balloons tied to it. Wouter Tolbathy was with me, I don't know why we decided to join the festivities. I'm not sure we did decide, actually. I think we just found ourselves in the midst and paused to wonder why. We did have some

thought of buying a large codfish and presenting it to Ed
Ashbroom, I remember, but they didn't have any for sale so
Wouter decided to build him one with a swishy tail on it."

"Is the codfish strictly germane to the subject in question?"
Sarah was beginning to wish she'd never started this. "What
about the Wicked Widows with the hatpins, and the incident
you never will forget? Or have you forgotten?"

"Sarcasm will get you nowhere, young woman. As I was
about to say when you so rudely interrupted, Wouter and I
were just wandering around soaking up the ambience when
suddenly, out of nowhere, these seven veiled females appeared
and went into their usual snake dance, if I may call it so.
Naturally people stopped to watch, most of them from respect-
ful distances because they'd heard about the hatpins. But there
was this one middle-aged chap in a yellow sweatshirt with a
diplodocus on the front—at least Wouter said it was a diplodocus and that was the sort of thing Wouter would know. Where
was I?"

"The chap in the sweatshirt," Sarah suggested.

"Oh, yes. He was nothing out of the ordinary. Overweight,
balding, the sort one might find holding up the far end of the
bar at a pub in a run-down neighborhood. He'd obviously
stoked up for the occasion and seemed to be under the misap-
prehension that this was some kind of outdoor striptease affair.
He started yelling 'Take it off! Take it off!' Naturally the
Widows didn't pay any attention. So what did this deluded
dipsomaniac do but rush up and grab the hindmost of them
by her fishtail."

Jem coughed. "Good Gad, I've run out of juice. Rescue
me, please, Charles."

"Coming right up, Your Dryness."

Mindful of Sarah's disapproving eye, however, Charles
gave the guest more coffee instead of gin. Too wound up in
his narrative to notice, Jem drank it down and went on.

"That was something to see, I can tell you. Up went seven
pairs of arms in unison, covered by slinky black gloves all

the way to their armpits. Out came seven long hatpins. I wondered at the time why those enormous hats didn't fall off, but they didn't."

"They'd have had special combs sewn to the insides of the hats that they could slide into their hair as anchors," Sarah interjected. "Go on, Uncle Jem. What happened next?"

"Plenty. Before you could say, 'Scat,' they'd formed a circle with that poor fathead of a drunk in the middle. Each of the Widows was holding her hatpin waist-high, pointed straight at their victim. We could see the sun glinting on the sharp points and we knew the Widows weren't just playing games. So far, they'd been moving slowly and sinuously as usual; now they started to pick up the pace, gliding in a spiral pattern, edging closer with each round.

"The chap in the center didn't know what to do. He kept spinning around like a teetotum, looking for a way to dodge past those sharp points, but there wasn't one. By that time the circle was pretty tight, it was hard to see around the hats. The women were all facing inward and creeping toward him, an inch at a time, until they were close enough to touch him with the points of their pins. They began picking at that yellow sweatshirt, he must have been feeling those wicked points. He yelped a few times, poor devil, then started to bawl like a baby and did what babies do."

"You mean he—how awful!" Sarah cried. "And you just stood there and let them stick him?"

"We were all mesmerized, I think. Nobody moved. Then it dawned on me that I was standing passively watching a fellow human being tortured. I looked at Wouter, Wouter looked at me, we both started yelling 'Help! Police!' and fighting our way toward the circle. That broke the spell, so to speak. A few others took up the cry, a policeman broke through the mob blowing his whistle, then another. By the time Wouter and I were close enough to do anything, there was only that poor devil huddled on the ground with a few small bloodstains on his diplodocus. Whether he'd dropped dead of a heart attack, fainted from terror, or just felt too ashamed to face the crowd, I never found out."

"What happened to the Wicked Widows?"

"They were nowhere to be seen, they'd simply melted away. God knows how they managed it in those skintight gowns and cartwheel hats. So Wouter looked at me and I looked at Wouter and we went somewhere and had a couple of martinis to take the taste away. And that's the best I can tell you. It does strike me that there was one more really egregious episode after that, then they disappeared from the scene. They must have realized they'd gone too far."

"I should think they might," said Sarah. "And nobody ever found out who they were or what became of them? Charles, you know all the theatrical gossip around Boston. Have you ever heard of the Wicked Widows?"

"I'm inclined to doubt, moddom, that the persons in question ever had anything to do with the theater. From what Mr. Jem's been telling us, they sound more like a bunch of well-heeled amateurs. You know what I mean, the kind who prance in the chorus line at some society benefit, develop a taste for the limelight, and get the bright idea of taking their show on the road. Comes of having too much money and too little to do, generally; but this lot must have been something else. I could ask around, if you like."

Jem shook his head. "I shouldn't, Charles, if I were you. As it happens, I have the misfortune to be slightly acquainted with that Turbot blister who's wangled himself onto the board at the Wilkins under the delusion that he'll make himself somewhat more socially acceptable, which is absurd. He'd already tried to bull his way into the Comrades of the Convivial Codfish, you know. Or perhaps you didn't; but, needless to say, he had no more chance of joining our august assemblage than I have of becoming a Camp Fire girl. Anyway, here he is, with his foot barely inside the door and a respected member of his staff lying murdered among the peacocks. Naturally he's going to hush things up as best he can, and God help anybody who doesn't go along with him. Don't you agree, Sarah?"

"I certainly do. Furthermore, he's going to start badgering me about Dolores's will as soon as he twigs on that I'm her executrix, and I'm not going to tell him till Max gets home because I don't like him."

"Isn't Redfern supposed to take care of all that nonsense?" Jeremy Kelling, noting that his martini glass was still dry and nobody appeared disposed to refill it, bowed to the inevitable. "Well, I expect I ought to be wending my way. You don't have to come with me, Charles."

Charles knew an injured tone when he heard one. What could he say? "It will be an honor and a privilege to escort you to your domicile, Mr. Jem. Will Egbert be there by the time you arrive?"

"No, confound it, he won't. Didn't I tell you that the scurvy knave's deserted me for Guinevere? She's bought a greenhouse somewhere in the wilderness where she raises deadly nightshade and poisonous mushrooms."

"How long does Egbert plan to stay away, Mr. Jem?"

"That will depend on whether she feeds him on something out of the greenhouse, I expect. One can only hope for the best and get braced for the worst. Have you ever thought of changing your employer, Charles?"

"Never, Mr. Jem. Rather than leave you to pine alone and desolate, however, may I so embolden myself as to suggest that you spend the night here? If it's okay with the moddom, that is."

"I think it's an excellent idea," Sarah agreed. "You can borrow Brooks's spare razor and one of his nightshirts, Uncle Jem. Since you hate climbing stairs, I'll move to the second floor and you can have what used to be the drawing room. Tomorrow, if you decide you want to stay here until Egbert gets back, Charles can help you collect some of your own things and bring them over. I doubt if any of the clan will be back here before the end of the week, so there's plenty of room. You might even be of some help."

"Naturally I'd pull my own weight. When did I ever not?"

"Good question. Find him what he needs, Charles, since this was your bright idea. I'm going to take my belongings upstairs. You won't forget about my new skirt?"

"It's all sponged, I'll press it first thing tomorrow morning. When is your appointment with Mr. Redfern?"

"I'm not even sure I have one. My thought was simply to pop in and leave Dolores Tawne's will with Miss Tremblay if Mr. Redfern's too busy to see me. Then I need to talk with Wasserman's about what to do with Dolores. It's in her will that she wants to be cremated, which will make things simpler."

Thanks to Cousin Anne, Sarah thought she wouldn't go into that. "You might like to come with me, Uncle Jem. It would make Miss Tremblay's day, you know she adores you."

"As why wouldn't she? Off to bed with you, then. Charles and I have matters of moment to discuss."

"I'm sure you do. Don't let him keep you up all night, Charles."

Sarah didn't wait to hear her uncle's diatribe on nagging women. She collected what she'd need from the bedroom she'd slept in last night, debated with herself whether to be a good hostess and do something about the bed linen or leave it to Charles, and started upstairs with her armload.

She was almost to the top when it occurred to her that, between her own near miss from being run over, Jem's hair-raising story about the Wicked Widows, and the experiment with Brooks's projector, she still hadn't got around to examining that envelope she'd taken from the LaVerne box. Sarah finished her climb, tossed the few necessities that she'd brought upstairs on the bed that had been hers for a while between husbands and was now shared by Brooks and Theonia, and prodded herself into going back downstairs for the letter. She'd left it on the lamp table next to where she'd been sitting, Charles hadn't tidied it away. She picked up the envelope and put it in the pocket of her robe.

"Sorry to interrupt. I've been meaning all evening to read what's in here and forgot to take it up with me."

"That must be because you don't really want to know what's in it," said Charles. "The subconscious mind knows your inner feelings better than the conscious does, you know."

"How clever of it. You could be right, Charles. I just hope there won't be another horror story in this; I seem to be in trouble enough with my subconscious mind already."

She went back upstairs, performed her ablutions as she'd been taught by her first governess, and settled herself in the big double bed, which the late Caroline Kelling had equipped sumptuously with embroidered pillows and satin comforters. Theonia was too thrifty to waste such lovely stuff and too much the grande dame not to revel in it; Brooks was too fond of his wife to balk at her small enjoyments.

This was no night for a down comforter, but it was chilly enough to make a light blanket feel good. Sarah snuggled into a nest of pillows and pulled warm merino wool up around her before she took out what was in the envelope. It turned out to be just four sheets, handwritten on ordinary white paper. This writing was unmistakably Dolores Tawne's, essentially commonplace but meticulously formed and given force by an aggressive forward slant and some sharp angles among the connectives. Dolores seemed not to have been writing to anybody in particular; there was no salutation or word of introduction.

> I don't know why I am writing this, I just feel as if I ought to say something to explain my own part in what has been happening, which I performed in perfect innocence and good faith. I did not know what LaVonne LaVerne, as she called herself on the telephone, was driving at when she told me about the Wicked Widows. I got the impression that it was

something to do with waltzing. I thought that making seven authentic Mona Lisa masks was a wonderful idea and right up my alley even though I had never made a mask before. But I knew I could do it and welcomed the chance. I agreed to handle the whole job by myself and never breathe a word of it to anybody, which I would do and have done because I do not ever betray a confidence no matter what, as I told her flat out.

I told her it would be expensive and would take a little time but she said that was all right because she and her friends had to rehearse, so she would send me $500 in cash as a down payment to show that they were able to pay for the materials and were serious about the masks, and another $500 when I sent them the first completed mask and it was exactly what they wanted, which it was, and $2000 more when they got the other six, also in cash, which sounded very good to me at the time, and I have to say they lived up to their bargain and paid right on the dot which is more than I can say for some of the clients I have done portraits of.

I was never trained in sculpture but I went ahead and modeled the face in clay from a photograph of the original painting, making it a little bit bigger than the real Mona Lisa as she didn't have much of a chin and I thought I should allow for some leeway because faces vary so much and it came out very well if I do say so. Once the clay model was dry enough I coated it with Vaseline and made a plaster mold. I had never made a mold before; it came out very well also. After that I had no trouble making the masks from the mold and painting them all exactly like the photograph. I doubt if any other portrait artist could have done the job so well if at all and so did my mysterious patron. My orders were to destroy the clay model and the plaster mold, which I did after the masks were all paid for.

I cannot help wondering what will become of the masks. I suspect they may already have been destroyed although it would be a terrible shame after all the work I put in. But there is no way I would ever dare to claim them back even if I got the chance which is very unlikely.

It was part of the agreement from the beginning that I would never go to any of their performances in order to protect my anonymity as well as theirs or to mention them in any way to anybody. I have stuck to my bargain faithfully although I could not avoid hearing about them sometimes because the Wicked Widows were literally the talk of the town for quite a while. I was surprised to hear somebody say that they were really men instead of women which was why they wore heavy veils and false bosoms but I refused to believe it on principle although I may be wrong as I never saw them and am probably safer that I did not.

The only name I ever heard was LaVonne LaVerne which was what the one who spoke to me on the phone used when she called me about the masks but according to the news that was the name all seven of them gave when the police were fighting with the reporters to get them arrested properly. I could not believe my eyes when I turned on the news and saw them being hustled into the police wagon or whatever they call it now. That was the only time I ever got any kind of a look at them and it was disappointing because I could not see the masks at all but only the veils and those fishtail skirts from behind.

It was even worse on the late news after the police wagon had been found over in Franklin Park behind the aviary with three dead policemen in the back and a fourth, the driver, dead at the wheel without any sign of what killed them and the Wicked Widows all disappeared. There is a major hunt out and warrants for their arrest on a charge of homicide but I doubt if any of them will be caught because nobody saw their faces except maybe the policemen before they died and nobody knew them by any name except LaVonne LaVerne which they either stole from somebody else or made up for reasons of their own. I have sometimes wondered if the one who talked to me on the phone and sent the money might kill the others if they try to break the vow of secrecy because she struck me as sounding rather strange. But she has played square with me and knows that I am completely honest and reliable and will never let it be known as long as I live that I had any hand in the matter.

Why I rented this box was that today out of the blue she sent me a package by UPS with six of the hatpins in it and a few photographs of her and her friends that I had never before been supposed to see but could hardly have avoided seeing them in the papers and on the television because it made such a stir as she must have realized. The photographs do not show the masks as well as I would have liked but I thought it was nice of her to think of me at such a time even though I do not hold with what happened in the police van. I think she may have meant me to get rid of the hatpins but I was not sure and had no way of asking so I thought a safe deposit box would be the best way in case she wants them back sometime. The reason I think she might want to use her own hatpin again if somebody gets out of line is that there were only six in the package she sent. It will mean my having to pay the rent on the box but that won't be much and she has been really nice to me in spite of what is being said these days, most of which is likely true but a promise is a promise. So I will take the box in her name and sign my own like all the rest.

LaVonne LaVerne

# Chapter 16

If this wasn't typical of Dolores! Sarah didn't know whether to burst into hysterical laughter or cram one of Theonia's silken pillows over her mouth and scream into it for all she was worth. So what if the Wicked Widows had turned out to be murderers? They had at least been civil enough to recognize Dolores Agnew Tawne as an artist of incomparable talent, to wear her superbly executed masks before an admiring public—admiring, anyway, until the hatpins came out—and finally, when the show had come to a bloodcurdling end, to grant her the custody of their hatpins.

Sarah did not suppose that Dolores had ever once thought of going to the police with what little information they might have found helpful, not even after the cold-blooded slaughter of those four policemen. In fairness, though, what could she have told them? All her contact with the Wicked Widows had been one or perhaps two calls—Dolores had not been clear about that—from a voice on the telephone that might have been disguised, and three deliveries of cash in exchange for masks by a messenger who presumably had not paused to chat. Dolores must have realized that she'd have been in serious trouble with those seven harpies if she'd ever broken so much as a syllable of her promise not to talk.

What had become of the Wicked Widows after they'd carried their act too far? Why had Dolores, despite that terrible denouement, chosen to affiliate herself with a gang of murderers by dubbing herself yet another LaVonne LaVerne? Could the bellicose manner that Dolores had displayed around the museum when things didn't go her way have been a means of working off hostilities that must be kept under control? Could she herself have nursed a secret hankering to drive one of those demonstrably lethal hatpins through the base of somebody's brain? Was that the real reason why she'd kept them locked up for so many years, never once opening the safe deposit box but knowing where to get a deadly weapon should the urge become too strong?

Sarah thought it more likely that Dolores had kept the hatpins not for the weak-kneed reason she'd adduced in her written statement but because having them in her sole custody had given her a sense of importance. Whichever of the seven LaVonnes had made that first telephone call must have known in advance the artist's insatiable thirst for accolades and been careful to slather on plenty of the best butter before opening negotiations. That statement Dolores had left in the box indicated that she'd been both paid well and praised well.

Being also made privy to a secret that must be kept forever dark would have given Dolores's ever-hungry ego more food to feast on in dutiful silence long after the Wicked Widows' enormities had been dragged into the newspapers and across the television screens. The artist's own hands had been clean. She had done what was asked of her in good faith and with consummate skill. She had held steadfast to her vow of secrecy. Angels could have done no more.

The statement that Sarah had just finished reading and was by now wondering what, if anything, she ought to do about, reeked of self-satisfaction. All those first-person singular pronouns marching across the pages were like drumsticks thumping "Look at me! Look at me!" But they gave no clue as to who had stabbed Dolores to death with the last of the seven hatpins on Sunday afternoon.

Sarah would have liked to talk with some of the older guards
such as Vieuxchamp and Melanson, but her own position was
too precarious just now. Anyway, Vieuxchamp didn't much
care for either her or Max because they made him feel inferior,
as in fact he was, insofar as his work at the Wilkins was
concerned. Sarah knew nothing of his private life and didn't
want to. As for Melanson, he'd be too busy worrying to
engage in anything like rational conversation.

She could probably get more out of the scrapbook that
Dolores had kept in her bottom drawer. It was filled with
letters, photographs, and clippings related to persons whose
portraits Dolores had painted, most of them chief executive
officers of companies that produced things like blow-molded
plastic bubble-bath bottles shaped like penguins and croco-
diles. Whether the clippings were from big urban newspapers,
small-town giveaways, or merely company newsletters, they
invariably contained a photograph of the distinguished artist,
Dolores Agnew Tawne, shaking hands with her subject,
assuming he or she was still alive, or else with the heirs and
assigns of the deceased. Sometimes the artist and the model
were shown by themselves, sometimes with a retinue of vice
presidents and perhaps a few lesser dignitaries. Quite often
the executive's wife and perhaps a dear old mother, a son
fated to follow in the paternal footsteps, or a daughter checking
out the junior executives as potential escorts completed the
ensemble.

Whatever the setting, Dolores Agnew Tawne's expression
of smug self-satisfaction could never have been missed by
anybody with eyes to see. Suppose, Sarah thought, that during
one of those presentation ceremonies a wife or daughter—
more likely a wife—had realized how completely self-
absorbed the artist was. Suppose she'd had enough art courses
at her expensive finishing school to recognize Dolores's work
as being highly competent if not at all creative, and had made
a note for future reference.

Captains of industry do not always make exciting husbands.

A bored wife, particularly one of those youngish wives who had supplanted an older and dowdier spouse at the time of some tycoon's midlife crisis, might, as Charles had suggested, have engaged in amateur theatricals for one worthy cause or other, got bitten by the acting bug, decided it might be more fun to cut higher jinks for baser reasons, and persuaded a few of her equally bored friends to join her.

Just how an investigator might be able to winnow out a possible starter from among Dolores's outdated assemblage of minor titans and their families, employees, golfing buddies, friends, enemies, and casual droppers-in was more than Sarah cared to hypothesize after the kind of day she'd had. Her knee was giving her fits, now that she had leisure to think about it. She ought to get up and take something for the pain.

If Max were here, he'd give her some aspirin, with a little tender loving care on the side. Gradually, through the pain, she was watching a vague recollection form of a newspaper that some man had been reading at the coffee shop. At the time, she'd been too distraught to pay it any attention but now her hyperactive subconscious was bringing up words like "Argentine pampas" and "bloodless coup." Charles had been buying newspapers to see if there was anything in them about Dolores. Sarah had noticed a neatly folded late-afternoon edition lying unread on the coffee table when she'd tried to relax after her horrendous day. Why hadn't she thought to bring it upstairs with her?

Thus ensued one of those arguments between self and self that never get anywhere. She couldn't keep on popping in and out of bed or she'd never get any sleep. Argentina was a big country, stretching all the way down from Bolivia to Tierra del Fuego. Why shouldn't Max be in some part of it that wasn't having a coup? But if the area wasn't in political straits, why weren't its telephones working? Surely Max must know that she'd be worrying, after the way they'd got cut off on Sunday.

Her knee was throbbing, she ought to stay off it. Nevertheless, Sarah flung off the blanket, fumbled around with her toes until she'd managed to get her slippers on the proper feet, struggled back into her housecoat, limped to the bathroom, took two aspirin, and hobbled to the top of the stairs.

Women of good breeding did not shout down the stairwell at their butlers. Sarah shouted anyway. "Charles, would you bring me up the evening paper?"

Normally Charles loved to fetch and carry, this time he waffled. "Er—um—it's not available, moddom."

"Why not? It was still on the coffee table when I came upstairs."

Sudden muttering at the other end meant that a colloquy was being held. After too long a pause, Charles called up the stairs, "Mr. Jem spilled his drink on it."

"Nonsense! Uncle Jem never spilled a drink in his life, except down his own throat. Bring me that paper, Charles."

"Yes'm."

A person might have thought from the misery in his voice and the obvious reluctance with which he dragged one foot after the other up the stairs that Charles was only marking time until the tumbrel rattled up to carry him off to the guillotine. He presented the still rolled-up paper on a silver tray as stage protocol demanded and made a fast break for the door.

Sarah wasn't having any of that. "Charles, come back here! What is it that you two are so desperate not to let me see?"

The butler cleared his throat. "It's a bit—ah—upsetting."

"What is?"

Before he could answer, the telephone that Brooks had installed beside the bed started to peal. This was one too many; Sarah boiled over.

"See who that is, Charles. I'm not at home to anybody unless it's Max or one of the Rivkins."

"As you wish, moddom."

Conscious that the show must go on but looking as though he'd begun to wonder why, Charles picked up the phone and informed the mouthpiece that the caller had been connected with the Kelling residence. The caller was not taking the information in good heart. Charles was being given a hard time.

"I cannot say, moddom," he managed to get in at last.

The caller found his reply unsatisfactory. Sarah mouthed the words "Uncle Jem" and pointed downward. Charles fell gratefully upon her suggestion.

"Mr. Jeremy Kelling is available. If you would care to hold the line a moment, I will apprise him of your desire to communicate."

He cupped his hand over the mouthpiece. "It's Mrs. Boadicea Kelling."

Aunt Bodie was absolutely the last straw. Sarah groaned. "Charles, I'm going underground. Tell Uncle Jem to say that no information can be given out about anything until Max can be reached, and that he's now in Argentina with the lines down."

"I'll be delighted."

Hanging up on Aunt Bodie was infinitely preferable to listening to Aunt Bodie. Nevertheless, Sarah felt a qualm of conscience. Boadicea Kelling was never one to chat on the phone for no worthwhile purpose, and particularly not after the hour of eight in the evening. It being by now almost a quarter to ten, all Sarah could think of was that some Kelling or other must have died. She laid the receiver on the bedside table so that she could hear when Uncle Jem came on the line, picked up the *Globe*, trying not to rustle the pages, and found the obituaries.

Here it was, close to the top of the list and very short. "Mrs. Sara Biterman of Ireson Town died early today of injuries sustained when she stepped in front of an oncoming vehicle. No funeral plans have yet been announced."

Sarah did not hang up. Bodie was on the telephone now, demanding that Jem explain to her why she hadn't been notified at once. So this was why Charles had tried to keep Jem's niece from seeing the paper. How had the notice got into the paper so fast? Was this some bizarre practical joke, or had the driver of the gray Toyota been so sure of killing the woman he'd come after that he'd put in the notice beforehand to save himself the bother of doing it later?

Boadicea Kelling sounded genuinely upset. This was the oddest part of all, Bodie was almost never upset. Sarah couldn't make out whether her aunt's perturbation was due to the fact that the obituary notice had not been written in accordance with family protocol or because the paper had spelled Sarah's name wrong. Bodie seemed to have been the only relative who'd decoded the misspelling and taken the trouble to make sure there was in fact no Mrs. Sara Biterman in Ireson Town.

The misspelling must have been inadvertent, it matched the envelope that had come to the office with the deadly hatpin inside. That the sender had had to use the office address and that the obituary gave Ireson Town instead of Ireson's Landing as a home address indicated that the would-be murderer or murderers didn't really know much about her and were too lazy, too stupid, or too self-assured to bother finding out.

Either they'd had Sarah Bittersohn pointed out to them in the flesh or else they'd had a clear photograph to go by. Either the hit-and-run driver was a stranger to her or was disguised as one. Either he truly believed he'd killed her or knew for a fact that he'd missed. If this had been the pair who'd harassed her on Sunday, the one who wasn't driving could have acted as lookout to make sure the job was done and had instead seen the intended victim being dragged up on the sidewalk and assisted into the coffee shop by a uniformed policeman.

There were too many alternative possibilities here; all Sarah knew was that she had a husband and a child to live for, not to mention her multifarious connections. She'd been half asleep and not really thinking when she'd told Charles she was going underground, but why shouldn't she do just that? Truly, what alternative did she have?

She'd need some backup, but that wouldn't be hard with

two ingenious rogues like Charles and Uncle Jem in the house. She'd have to let Lieutenant Harris know so that he wouldn't waste time chasing down false clues. She'd have to get in touch with Ira Rivkin and persuade him to lend her a car. She couldn't risk using her own and having the number plate traced. How she was going to manage with a banged-up knee would have to be worked out in the morning.

Uncle Jem would think of something. Right now he was playing Boadicea like a ukulele, pretending to be a good deal more squiffed than he was, spinning a tangled web of non sequiturs that Bodie's logic-oriented tunnel vision couldn't begin to cope with. When he suggested that Bodie phone loopy old Aunt Appollonia to get the facts straight, she gave up in disgust, having learned nothing except that it was high time Jem Kelling got packed off to a sanatorium.

Sarah hung up the extension phone feeling as though she'd got her head caught in Cousin Anne's blender. It had been far from pleasant to see her own name in print on the obituary pages even though, as Mark Twain had cogently remarked in a similar circumstance, the report of her death was greatly exaggerated. And misspelled, to boot. The aspirin she'd taken was making her feel woozy. She turned out the bedside light and let her subconscious carry her wherever it chose to go.

She must have needed the sleep, she didn't wake up until the phone by her bedside rang and she heard Charles saying good morning to Miriam Rivkin. She broke in, still not quite awake.

"Hello, Miriam. Is Davy all right?"

"Yes, he's fine. What's the matter, Sarah? You sound like the morning after the night before."

"Oh, I had a stupid accident yesterday. I fell on the curb in Kenmore Square and gave my knee a whack. It was hurting, so I took some aspirin and I'm still groggy from it."

"What were you doing in Kenmore Square?"

"Looking for a place to eat. I told you that I'm the executrix of Dolores Tawne's will, didn't I?"

"Yes, and you were pretty sore about it."

"I still am. Are you expecting company today?"

"Not that I know of," said Miriam. "Why?"

"Because I'm in a jam and I need some help. Is Ira there?"

"Right here drinking his orange juice. Ira, Sarah has a problem."

"Okay, so what did they pinch you for?" That was Ira, six foot three and chipper as a chipmunk.

"Nothing, yet," Sarah replied. "I need a car. Not for long, I hope. I don't want to go through a rental agency, I don't want anything new or showy, and I don't want to use my own car because it might be recognized."

"That all? How soon do you need it?"

"Sometime today if that's possible. What I'd love to do is spend a little time at the lake and try to get my head straight. I'll have to disguise myself one way or another, so don't be surprised if some old crone with a limp and a false mustache hobbles in."

"We're never surprised. How were you planning to get here?"

"Good question. Charles might be able to borrow his friend's car. If not, I'll ride the T as far as I can and call you or Miriam to pick me up. Will you be around all day, Ira?"

"Depends on how soon I can steal you a car. We have one at the shop getting an overhaul that the owner won't need for a while because he's gone on a cruise; I'll see if it's ready to roll. Anyway, either Miriam or I will be here with Davy. Want me to put him on?"

"No, just tell him Mummy will be coming later. I have some things to do before I can leave."

"Got the directions all right?"

"Oh yes, I can find you. I might even stay the night if you and Miriam have room for me."

"We always have room for you, you know that," said Ira. "Then we'll see you when you get here."

Charles must have been waiting outside the door. Sarah had

barely hung up the phone before he made a proper Jeevesian entrance with a tea service for one and a note on the tray.

"Lieutenant Harris is desirous to speak with you, moddom. That's his number on the note. Shall I dial it for you?"

"No, give me time to drink my tea. Is Uncle Jem up yet?"

"Oddly enough, yes, and in fine fettle."

"Good. Don't either of you go anywhere, we need to talk. I'll be down when I've finished with Harris."

"Roger. Temporarily over and out. May I take your order for pancakes à la Charles, or would you prefer fried salami and eggs?"

"You and Jem have what you please, I'll boil myself an egg when I come down. Dismissed, Charles."

Harris's voice, when she got around to returning his call, was courteous with the kind of exasperated forbearance that afflicts busy policemen who have been kept waiting longer than they consider reasonable. The lieutenant had gone over the report that Officer Drummond had filed yesterday and wondered if Mrs. Bittersohn would mind answering a few questions.

Sarah poured her second cup of tea and braced herself for the long haul, but it wasn't so bad. Drummond's report had been concise and accurate. There was little she could add and less to amend, except when she offered to read Dolores's account of her involvement with the Wicked Widows. Harris seemed not to find it relevant.

"Okay, Mrs. Bittersohn, I don't think we need to spend much time on that angle. Anything else you want to talk about? You have no idea where Mrs. Tawne got all those fancy stickpins?"

"Would you settle for a wild guess?"

"I'll take whatever I can get."

"All right, then. As you of course know, Dolores Tawne made perfect copies of the more important paintings in the Wilkins Collection. She thought she was doing them as a way of preserving the originals, in fact they were being used to cover up a long run of piracy during which the originals were sold for large sums, though probably less than they'd have brought on the open market. Since the looting was uncovered and the originals gradually being returned to the museum, Dolores had been getting her copies back with no strings attached. She'd had a terribly raw deal, you know, and this was the least she deserved.''

''So she'd been selling her copies, is that it?''

''She or somebody, I assume. When Officer Drummond and I went to her studio yesterday, I noticed that she'd hung a few of her copies, but those were only a small fraction of the ones she'd got back. I looked for the rest, but found only some old canvases that had been given a fresh ground but hadn't been painted over.''

''Indicating that Mrs. Tawne was planning to paint some more fakes?''

''She wouldn't have called them that. Dolores was remarkably gifted in her way, you know. Anyway, it did cross my mind just before you called that she may have been taken in by another snake-oil salesman who offered to market her work for her. Otherwise I can't see where she'd been putting the copies that my husband had returned to her as soon as he'd got the originals back at the museum.''

''But where do the stickpins come in?''

''Right where they are. Unless I'm sadly mistaken, they're stolen property that somebody had to find a safe hiding place for in a hurry. My guess is that they might have been offered ostensibly as surety for the paintings that her new agent was planning to market, along with others that she hadn't yet got around to doing. When I visited her studio yesterday, it looked to me as if she'd been getting set to start working there again, which she hadn't done since the grand fiasco seven years ago.''

The letter that Dolores had left in the LaVerne box was still on the bedside table. Sarah picked it up and read a snatch or two to Harris. ''That's the sort of person she was, you see.

She'd believe almost anything, provided it put her in a good light."

"Assuming you're somewhere near the mark, Mrs. Bittersohn, would you have any idea who this new partner of hers might be?"

"No, not a glimmer. Which is particularly frustrating because she'd been planning to come here for tea Sunday at five; she might actually have been on her way out of the museum when she got stabbed."

"How long before that had you invited her?"

"I didn't invite her at all, she'd simply phoned and told Charles she was coming. She'd do that; I shouldn't be surprised if she'd intended to tell me all about her wonderful new agent."

"Let's just hope she didn't tell him about you," Harris grunted. "You're the sole executrix, right?"

"Yes."

"Which means nobody except yourself can open that box with the stickpins in it, right?"

"Oh, my God! I hadn't thought of that. You don't suppose Dolores's death had anything to do with my almost getting killed yesterday?"

"Never happened before, did it?"

"Not with a car. But even if they had succeeded in squashing me, they still wouldn't have been able to open the box. Would they?"

"Might take a little organizing, but there's always a missing heir available if you know where to look. Not to spoil your breakfast, Mrs. Bittersohn, but you might be well advised to join your husband in Argentina."

"He's probably on the way home by now. Anyway, a person with a list of relatives as long as mine can always find a hole to hide in."

There was a pause so long that Sarah thought she'd been cut off. "Are you still there, Lieutenant Harris?"

"Uh—yes."

"Then I just want to say that some thought should be given to Dolores's involvement with the Wicked Widows. I know it's been a long time, but the fact that she was still paying the rent on that LaVerne box suggests that she must have kept up some kind of connection with whichever of the troupe is left."

"So?"

"So I want to know what became of them. My uncle Jeremy Kelling is staying here with me just now. He's told me about a performance where the Widows did something abominable to one of the spectators, then melted quietly away while Uncle Jem and the friend he was with were yelling for the police and trying to force their way through the crowd. And surely you must know about the seven women all in black who murdered four policemen with their hatpins in the van that was supposed to be taking them to jail. That case has never been solved, has it?"

"Not to my knowledge. It doesn't get talked about around the station. I guess we cops don't like to advertise our failures any more than the rest of the world. Then what's the bottom line, Mrs. Bittersohn?"

"Pins, I suppose. You saw the way Dolores Tawne was killed; doesn't it suggest to you that at least one of the Wicked Widows is still alive and up to her old tricks? Or his. They might have been men in drag, for all I know. I brought one of the photographs from the LaVerne box back with me yesterday; it shows the seven Widows with black gloves clear up to their armpits, long fitted gowns with fishtails, those Mona Lisa masks that Dolores made for them, the widows' veils, the cartwheel hats. There was really nothing exposed but the bosoms, which could easily have been false."

"I know," said Harris. "Did you see those clippings in Mrs. Tawne's bottom drawer?"

"Yes, and I'd meant to go back for them after Officer Drummond and I had eaten our lunch, but you know what happened. I doubt if they can tell us as much as Uncle Jem can, anyway. I do wish, and this probably sounds crazy, that we could somehow find out whether there are still any LaVonne LaVernes around the Boston area. I have a hunch that we'd have more luck chasing down their death certificates. There were six hatpins in the LaVerne box and that seventh one you're holding at the station is in bad condition, as you know. I shouldn't be surprised if the wickedest of the Wicked Widows had used hers to kill the other six before she got around to Dolores Tawne."

"For God's sake! Why would she have done a thing like that?"

"Either to save her own skin or because she thought it would be fun to bury all her sister Widows under the same alias. She'd have to be totally insane, of course. Anyway, one has to start somewhere, and so far those pins are the best lead, as far as I can see. You understand that I'm interested on purely selfish grounds. Somebody is out to kill me and I don't want to be killed."

"But why pick you as a target?"

"I can only assume that it has something to do with Dolores Tawne's murder and possibly with my having lunch on Sunday with the Wilkins's new chairman of trustees. It was after I'd left the Turbots with my cousins and stopped at their house to pick up my own car that those two cutups in the gray Toyota began harassing me. They could have followed me from the Turbots', though I can't think why. When I got to Tulip Street, Charles told me Dolores had invited herself to tea, but she never turned up and we learned that she was dead. Whether she was killed to keep us from getting together sounds awfully far-fetched, but by now I'm prepared to believe just about anything."

What was she spinning out this conversation for? Here it was, the jumping-off place. "And now I'm going to ring off and disappear. Either Charles, Uncle Jem, or his man Egbert will be here to take messages. One way or another, I'll keep in touch. Au revoir, Lieutenant."

"Just a second, Mrs. Bittersohn. There was a late bulletin on the car that tried to run you down. It was registered in the name of Dolores Agnew Tawne at the Fenway Studio Building on Ipswich Street."

"But that's absurd! Dolores never owned a car, she couldn't even drive. At least she said she couldn't, apparently I didn't know her at all. And now I'm responsible as executrix for the car that almost killed me, is that it?"

"No, that's one worry you can forget about. The car was found wrecked and set on fire in a South Boston parking lot at two twenty-four this morning. Au revoir, Mrs. Bittersohn."

# Chapter 17

"I'm sorry that call took so long," Sarah half-apologized as she cracked open the two eggs that Charles had, after all, boiled for her. She was still in her robe because she didn't know yet what to do about a disguise; but otherwise ready for action and hungry for her breakfast. "Toast, please, Uncle Jem. You'd better take Dolores Tawne's will to Mr. Redfern at ten o'clock sharp. That's when he usually gets to his office. Make it plain that you're a very busy man. You can't stay to chat with Miss Tremblay, you must have the will submitted for probate as soon as possible. Don't forget to take the will with you, by the way. Charles, make sure he puts it in his inside pocket."

"Yes, moddom," replied the admirable Charles.

"Bah, humbug," snarled Jeremy Kelling. "When did I ever forget anything?"

"No comment," said Sarah. "If either Miss Tremblay or Mr. Redfern happens to bring up that obituary notice, just say you have an urgent appointment with some bigwig or other so you've got to rush off, which you then proceed to do. Have you got all that?"

"If you mean, 'Do you understand what I am trying to say only I'm talking garbled English?' the answer is in the affirmative," Jem replied nastily. "Then I nip down to the stock exchange and corner the market in black-crepe arm-bands, right?"

"What a delightful idea, Uncle Jem! Save a band for me because one never knows, does one? Now, Charles, how are you going to make me unrecognizable? Is there anything in the house that we can use?"

"Good question. Do you have a definite self-image in mind or shall we just wing it?"

"Well, let's see. I'm bound to look like a Kelling no matter what you do, so how about something along the lines of Great-Aunt Matilda? Since I'm limping anyway, I can use that gold-handled blackthorn cane she used to carry when her arthritis got bad."

"The one that unscrews to hold a tot of brandy in the handle?"

"Why not? One never knows. As for clothes, that dark-gray flannel suit I just bought might do if we can antique it a little."

"Piece of cake. We dust the top-floor bedrooms with the jacket, roll the skirt up in a ball, and let Mr. Jem sit on it for a while."

"Yes, that would help. And I could wear those awful gray lisle stockings like the ones Great-Aunt Matilda wore, if we could find any. Do you think it would be tacky to sprinkle my hair with flour to make it look gray?"

"Very. You'd look like a case of galloping dandruff."

"Well, I've got to do something. I do wish I could borrow that Queen Mary toque of Aunt Bodie's."

Charles was aghast. "Nobody in the world but Mrs. Boadi-cea Kelling could ever get away with a hat like that one. We can do better."

"How, for instance?"

"The way will be shown. Have you any really beat-up old walking shoes? Or, better still, a pair of dirty sneakers with a hole in the toe?"

"Yes, Charles, as a matter of fact I do. I keep them in the

trunk of my car in case Davy and I take a notion to walk out on the mudflats or into the woods. I think I washed off the leaf mold the last time I used them, but I'm not sure.''

"No matter. I can pick up some of that whitener stuff if they're too ooky. But we probably won't need it. Are we taking your car?"

"I'm wondering about that. Ira's lining up a car for me but I don't want him driving to Boston in it."

"Then why don't I get the sneakers out of your trunk and work a deal with a friend of mine who owns a 1975 Dodge sport coupe with racing stripes. You can be the little old lady who only drove it to church on Sundays. Now you've hurt your knee and can't drive yourself, so I'm doing a good deed and taking you to stay with relatives. Okay, moddom?"

"Magnificent. Then why don't you nip down to Charles Street and see what you can find at the thrift shop? They know you're an actor, don't they?"

"They do, they're greatly impressed by me. Let's see, we mustn't do you as a freak. The object is to turn you into one of those elderly persons whom one sees but does not notice. It bodes fair to be an interesting challenge."

"Just so you don't get so caught up in your art that you forget what it's for," Sarah reminded him. "As a suggestion, you might look for a tired-looking silk blouse in some fairly revolting color, a hat with a brim that I can pull down to shade my face, and a pair of sunglasses. Perhaps a bar pin or an imitation cameo brooch, something old enough to be called a collectible. You'll know. Will you be able to give me some wrinkles?"

"No problem. Then I'll be off. Hasta la vista. Hey! Why can't you just dress in some of Mariposa's clothes and speak Spanish?"

"Because, Charles, in the first place Mariposa's clothes wouldn't fit me. In the second, I can't speak Spanish any better than you can, and in the third I just don't have what it takes to be Mariposa. I'm fairly sure I can act the part of an elderly woman from Beacon Hill and that's as far as I'm prepared to go. Here, take fifty dollars in case you find something. Now scoot, I'll clear up the breakfast dishes while I'm waiting for you to come back."

Charles whizzed off, Sarah turned to Jem, who was sitting dutifully on her new flannel suit. "Oh dear, I've just had an awful thought. What am I to do about Anne? I suppose I'll just have to stop at Ireson's Landing and tell her."

"Tell her what?" Jem squirmed around a little on his flannel perch to accelerate the process of antiquing, since he would soon have to go home to Pinckney Street for the clean white shirt and suitably mournful tie that Egbert had damned well better have ready for Jem's in-and-out visit to Redfern's office. Having dutifully dropped off the original Tawne will and avoided having to make up any lies with regard to his niece's alleged demise, assuming that either Miss Tremblay or Redfern had seen and deciphered the false obituary, he would then come back to Tulip Street to be the firm hand at the helm and make sure there was enough gin aboard to weather the storm.

In the meantime, Egbert would be sorting out some clothes of Jem's to bring to Tulip Street and gearing up to pitch in wherever he was most needed. All this organizing was not helping Sarah decide what to do about Cousin Anne and the chrysanthemums. Jem's too-pertinent question was still unanswered; it would be most improper for Sarah to leave Anne and Mr. Lomax hanging.

"I've just got to tell her that I'm alive and trying to stay that way. I realize it's putting a burden on you all, having to make ambiguous noises as to whether or not people should send condolences, but I do hope we can keep it in the family. Anne will have to tell Percy, of course, but Percy adores being inscrutable, so those two at least shouldn't present any problem. I just hope this situation won't drag on, I'd hate for Max to come home and find himself bombarded with questions about my funeral. Anyway, you'd better go do what you have to and I'll hide under the bed until you get back here.''

If Jem thought she was being funny, he was dead wrong. Sarah tried to work off her nerves on the house, which had got decidedly scruffy under bachelor management. She'd made an impression of sorts on the downstairs and was wondering what to do about beds when Egbert arrived with a packed suitcase in his left hand and a couple of Jem's suits in a plastic cleaning bag over the right arm. He deposited his cargo in the downstairs bedroom that Jem was using and gently but firmly took charge of the housekeeping. Sarah was beginning to feel redundant when Charles dashed back from the thrift shop, lugging a recycled paper bag of the large size.

''By George, we've got it! How's this for class?''

He delved into the bagful and hauled out a dejected, high-necked silk blouse in a blotchy pattern that wavered between blueberry and pomegranate, a few unlovely trinkets, two pairs of gray lisle stockings still hermetically sealed inside a brittle cellophane wrapping that must have lain for too many years in somebody's grandmother's bureau drawer, the sunglasses that Sarah had stipulated, and a faded purple felt hat that clashed just enough with the dyspeptic blouse to set one's teeth on edge.

''Magnificent, Charles, you couldn't have done better. But what about my hair? Weren't you planning to go to Fuzz-leys'?''

''No, I've had an epiphany. Remember that long gray beard I wore as Noah in that 'Back to the Ark' skit at the Children's Theater? All we need to do is—hang on, I'll show you.''

Charles adored beards with a passion. He bounded up from his basement lair carrying a wild mass of gray false hair, turned it upside down, fitted it around Sarah's face, anchored it there with a stretchy black bandeau—probably a pair of Mariposa's bikini panties, Sarah thought hysterically—and stood back to appraise the result.

''Not bad. Now do we cut or do we pug?''

"Oh, dear! I hate to spoil Noah's beard."

"Fear not, milady. No sacrifice is too great."

"If you say so, then. I vote for cutting, mainly because I don't have the right kind of hairpins to pug with. You'd better spread some newspapers under my chair before you begin snipping, Egbert just finished mopping the floor."

Presumably all the wearables at the thrift shop had been cleaned before they were put out for sale, Sarah was in no position to quibble. She excused herself long enough to put on the dejected blouse and the skirt that Jem had so kindly antiqued, then came back to take the chair under which Charles had spread yesterday's newspaper as directed.

"All right, Charles, go ahead. Do your worst."

Charles's worst was remarkably good. Having swathed his patroness in a tablecloth to keep the clippings from falling down inside the blouse, which hung a little too loosely on Sarah's delicate frame, he went to work. In a matter of minutes, he had hacked off just enough of Noah's beard to achieve the fashionable blue-jay's-nest effect that Great-Aunt Matilda had been wont to produce for herself with one of Great-Uncle Frederick's pearl-handled cutthroat razors and a misplaced faith in her own skill at barbering, rather than squander a few dollars at the hairdresser's three or four times a year.

And now for the makeup. Here was where Charles really shone and Sarah did not. By the time his sticks of greasepaint had done their unlovely job, he had obliterated the roses from her cheeks, dimmed the sparkle in her eyes, and, while not actually manufacturing wrinkles, managed to create an illusion that wrinkles were there. Even Max Bittersohn might not have recognized this haggard crone as his wife, or wanted to.

The gray lisle stockings had presented a problem. Like most women of her generation, Sarah had gone directly from socks to panty hose. She knew little of garter belts, less of girdles; she had, however, seen some John Held drawings of jazz-age flappers with their stockings rolled just above or just below the knees. After a brief period of experimentation and with the help of two sturdy elastic bands, she was able to master the principle well enough for the purpose.

The fact that the stockings bagged was in this case an asset. Great-Aunt Matilda's had always bagged, so did Aunt Appie's and dear old Anora Protheroe's. Not Aunt Emma's, of course; that gracious lady was still the essence of chic and would probably faint on the spot if she were to walk in just now and see what was happening to her favorite niece.

Having wrecked her face, Charles was smearing horrible yellowish greasepaint on the backs of her hands, picking out the veins in an unwholesome blueish shade and adding brown liver spots here and there as the whimsy took him. Sarah wondered how she'd be able to wash her hands without ruining the effect, then she remembered a pair of plum-colored nylon gloves that Theonia used to wear with her bag-lady disguise. These could be taken along for emergency use, they would go quite nicely with the hat and the blouse, although they might seem a trifle on the dressy side for the muddy sneakers with the hole in the toe.

No matter. The persona that Sarah had adopted was too old, too lame, and far too cranky to give a rap what she looked like. She tried on the jacket to her gray suit, decided it could use a little more antiquing, and asked Egbert if he'd mind walking over the lapels a few times. As always, he performed capably and added a few specks of lint from the dry mop for good measure.

The strategy was all worked out, the forces deployed, there was nothing for Sarah to do but go. She didn't want to be recognized by any of the Tulip Street neighbors, so she slipped out the basement door carrying her black Boston bag and Great-Aunt Matilda's cane, and meandered through alleys and byways until she got to Park Street by the circuitous route that Aunt Caroline had worked out many years before and took the subway to North Station.

Her timing was just about perfect. She joined a scattering of other people waiting to be picked up with their belongings and had just enough time to start looking impatient when Charles drove up in his borrowed car, sprang out to take her bag, and assisted her into the back seat where she could ease the wounded knee that was throbbing from her longish walk and the subway stairs that she'd had to climb.

It would be lovely to see Davy. Sarah wondered if he'd recognize her under the makeup; she hoped he wouldn't find her disguise too frightening. If he did, she'd just have to wash her face, thus destroying Charles's artistry but keeping her son's tender psyche intact. Actually she shouldn't have much trouble putting her face back on if she had to; Charles had made up a package of cosmetics and a list of instructions on how to use them for the proper effect.

"You wanted Ireson's Landing first, right?" Charles said as he nosed his friend's car out into the much-reviled Boston traffic.

"Yes, Charles. I haven't called Anne but she's sure to be there. I just want to see how the plantings are coming along and explain why I'm wearing this Halloween outfit. Then you can take me on to the lake. Miriam Rivkin will give us something to eat, after that you'll be free to go back to Boston and get rid of this car. There's no reason why you shouldn't use mine while I'm away, I just didn't want to be seen with you for your own protection. I'll call the house if I need a ride."

It would be perfectly safe for Sarah to telephone to the Tulip Street house. At one time, the library had been bugged, but that would not happen again. Brooks Kelling had taken care of any such attempts by installing a tape on which he had tastefully combined the buzz of the bumblebee, the whine of the mosquito, and the stridulating of the industrious cricket, all of these amplified to eardrum-shattering level. Anybody who tried any tricks on the historic Kelling brownstone—and there was no doubt that such things had been attempted at various times—would have got back his bugs a thousandfold, and an earache to boot.

Now that they were across the Tobin Bridge and heading toward the north shore, Sarah could feel herself beginning to relax. She took off her left sneaker and propped up her aching leg with a couple of pillows that Charles's friend must have left in the back seat. They weren't particularly inviting but she was in no state to be picky. She pulled her faded hat brim farther down over her eyes and wondered how, or whether, she could make Anne understand why she'd been forced to masquerade as some long-forgotten chip off the old Kelling block.

By the time they reached Ireson's Landing, Sarah had a nice little speech all thought out. And Anne was present to hear it. Her car was parked at the top of the drive, she was standing not far from it with a cream-colored chrysanthemum plant in one hand and a pale-yellow one in the other. Mr. Lomax's truck was not to be seen, but a pervading odor of fish indicated that he hadn't been gone long.

Enough plants were already in the ground to show what was being created here. Instead of trying to impose her own will on the rough, stony hillside, Anne was working along with the terrain, letting a narrow gulley become a path leading to an expertly blended tapestry of bloom around a weather-worn boulder, pulling the eye to a clump of young birches among which a random setting of bronzy chrysanthemums blazed in startling contrast to the slim white trunks. Nothing was too overdone or too sparse, neither too flamboyant nor too subdued. Really, the woman was a wonder. Sarah put the sneaker back on, straightened her wrinkled skirt, and waited for Charles to help her out.

It wasn't until Charles slammed the car door after Sarah that Anne roused herself from her reverie and walked over to see who had arrived. "Oh, how do you do? I'm sorry, I wasn't expecting anyone but the man who brings the fishheads. You're—wait, it's been so long, but I'd know a Kelling face anywhere. Ah, I have it! You're Aunt Calpurnia from Virgin Gorda. What a lovely surprise, I do wish Cousin Sarah were here. This is her house, you know, they tore down the old one. I'm Percy's wife, Anne; I'm sure you don't remember me."

Sarah cleared her throat and spoke in her own voice. "Oh yes, I remember you well, Anne. Don't you know me?"

"You're not Aunt Calpurnia?"

"No, just me."

"Sarah! I can't believe it. You fooled me completely. Wait till I tell Aunt Bodie."

"You mustn't! Sorry to be so abrupt, but—" Sarah couldn't remember one word of her carefully worked-out speech. "Let's go in and sit down, we need to talk. But first I have to tell you what a positively breathtaking job you're doing here. I wouldn't have believed our scrubby old hillside could look like this. Come on, you must be ready for a cup of tea. You did recognize Charles, surely?"

"No, I didn't, not a bit. My goodness, Charles, what have you done to yourself?"

"Merely added a red wig and a pair of sideburns. If you ladies want to talk, would you mind my strolling down on the beach for a little while?"

"Not at all," said Sarah. "Just don't go too far from the house, we'll need to get on the road again fairly soon."

They watched him down the long flight of wooden steps that led from the top of the cliff to the rocky strand far below.

"Should we have offered him some tea first?"

Anne was stripping off her gardening gloves and canvas apron, looking wistfully at the plants that she'd been about to dig in among the fishheads, then eagerly back to this intriguing chameleon of a cousin.

"No," said Sarah. "Charles ate a huge breakfast. He'll be fine until we get to the Rivkins', you know how Miriam is about food. They're keeping Davy for me, which is what I have to talk about. Part of it, anyway. Is the house unlocked?"

"Yes, I always open a few windows when I come, you know how a place gets when it isn't aired regularly."

"Really, Anne, you are a marvel. I gather Mrs. Blufert's still under the weather."

"Apparently so. Mr. Lomax says it's malaria that Mrs. Blufert picked up when she was stationed in the Philippines as a navy nurse. She comes down with a bout of it regularly once a year."

"My goodness," said Sarah, "you know more about this place than I do. I'm glad to have found you alone, Anne, because I'm in some rather serious trouble. Charles put this getup together for me because I had to see you and didn't dare show myself as I really am. The thing of it is, you see, that I'm supposed to be dead."

"Sarah, you can't mean it!"

"I know, it sounds crazy, but there it is. Fill the kettle, will you? I'll see what there is to eat, if anything."

"Please don't fuss for me, Sarah. I've brought my lunch, it's in the fridge. We could split an egg sandwich."

"Thanks, Anne. I had eggs for breakfast, but I wouldn't mind snitching a piece of your stuffed celery. You don't take milk in your tea, I hope; there doesn't seem to be any."

"Oh, that's all right. I drink it plain more often than not."

Poor Anne, Sarah could see that her cousin-in-law was having a hard time bracing herself for a life-and-death secret. If this were a case of white fly or black spot or even cabbage worm, Anne would have faced the crisis without batting an eyelid, but the prospect of drinking tea with a dead relative was something else again. One could hardly blame her for clinging to inconsequentials.

"I'm sorry I startled you, Anne," Sarah apologized. "Here, try some of this havarti cheese, I just bought it Saturday morning. The crackers should be fresh enough. One has to keep them in a tin, you know, living so close to the water."

The kettle began to sing, the cups were set out, the teapot filled. Sarah decided it was safe to get down to business.

"I didn't dare just leave you hanging, Anne. Aunt Bodie's already seen an obituary notice that somebody put in the

*Globe* and is champing at the bit to get on with the funeral.
Luckily Uncle Jem was at Tulip Street when she phoned, and
rose to the occasion beautifully. He rambled on about how
nothing could be done until Max came home and made her
so furious that she hung up on him. You know Uncle Jem,
one has to laugh when he puts on one of his performances.
I do have to admit it was a trifle unnerving to look in the
paper and read that I'd been jaywalking and got run over.
Fortunately, whoever put it in spelled my name wrong and put
Ireson Town instead of Ireson's Landing, so I don't suppose
anybody except Aunt Bodie made the connection."

Anne was outraged. "What a detestable thing to do! I do
hate practical jokes, they're neither practical nor funny. Who
do you think it was?"

"Whoever is trying to kill me. Not to spoil your lunch, but
just look at this."

Sarah pulled up her rumpled skirt and rolled her gray stocking down to the ankle. "I don't want to take the bandage off
my knee because it's trying to scab over, but you can see from
the state of my shin that this was no joke. I was deliberately run
down in Kenmore Square yesterday about one o'clock by a
couple of fellows who'd already tried to harass me Sunday
afternoon, when I was on my way from your house, in the
same car with the same number plate. A Boston policeman
grabbed me just in time or I'd have been under the wheels.
There were other witnesses, I can get you a signed affidavit
if you don't believe me."

"Of course I believe you, Sarah. It's just that one doesn't
expect—"

"I know, I wasn't expecting it either."

"But what was the point? You said you were harassed after
you'd left our house. Surely you don't think it was anybody
we know?"

"I doubt that very much. It's more likely that we'd been
followed back from the Turbots' because of something related
to Mr. Turbot's being made the new head of trustees. Anyway,

I'm quite sure I ditched the car that had been tailing me. But when I got to Tulip Street, Charles told me that Mrs. Tawne had called to say she was coming to tea at five o'clock. You've met Dolores Tawne.''

''Oh yes, the one who used to be so good with the peacocks and so bossy with people. I'd wondered how she and Elwyn were going to get along. Of course, now that she's dead it doesn't matter. You never did tell me exactly *how* she died.''

''Well, you can stop worrying. Dolores never showed up for tea, which bothered Charles and me very much because she'd always been punctual to the dot. Then, about half past five, one of the security guards called from the museum to say that Dolores was lying dead in the courtyard.''

''Were the flowers badly mashed?''

Who but Anne could have thought of that? Dire as the situation was, Sarah had to fight with herself not to laugh.

''I don't know, Anne. The guards who found her body were in such a state that they hadn't even thought to call the police. I explained what they ought to do and they did it; at the time it appeared that she must have had a heart attack or something of that sort. So they carted her off, poor thing. The police got her keys out of her handbag and went to her studio in the Fenway building. Her will was there and, would you believe, she'd appointed me as her executrix.''

''You mean she hadn't asked you first?''

''No, she had not.'' And Sarah was still none too happy about it. ''But what can one do? Dolores was more an old acquaintance than a real friend; still, she was a human being and there doesn't seem to be anyone else. I suppose I'd brought it on myself, actually. After her brother died a few years ago, she'd asked me where she could find a lawyer who'd draw up a will for her. I mentioned Mr. Redfern mainly because he was handy.''

''And honest,'' Anne added. ''Percy says Redfern's an old stick, but at least he can be trusted. So what did you do, Sarah?''

Sarah told her tale yet once again. As she'd expected, Anne focused on the hatpin.

"Oh, my! I hadn't thought of those hatpins in years, they were like skewers. Cousin Phoebe and I used to swipe Grannie Ba's. Not her best ones, of course. There was one with a little celadon mouse on top that I just loved. I think it went to Cousin Harriet, I must ask Aunt Bodie; she'll know. Anyway, Phoebe and I would sneak one out of the bandbox where Grannie Ba kept her rainy-day hat and her spare switch, and poke marshmallows onto it and toast them over a lighted candle. I don't quite know why, they got all sooty and sticky and tasted of candle smoke, but we thought it was fun."

Sarah wasn't in the mood for childhood reminiscences; she'd better get out of here and leave Anne to her landscaping. "I'm so glad I've had the chance to see what marvelous things you're doing here," she said, "but I do have to go on to the lake so that Charles can get back to Boston in time to fix dinner for Jem and Egbert."

"I hate to see you in such a predicament, Sarah. I wish there were some way I could help."

"Anne dear, you're already helping. It's been such a relief, having this quiet chat with you in my own house and seeing you taking such wonderful care of the place. I do want to emphasize again, though I'm sure you understand, that I'm not talking through this awful hat. I'm just trying to lie low and not get killed until Max gets home. Naturally you'll want to tell Percy. That's fine with me, he's the soul of discretion. I strongly suggest that neither of you say anything about me to anybody; particularly the Turbots. Don't even mention my name if you can help it. Mr. Turbot has troubles enough already, though he may not know it yet."

"Oh, he knows it," Anne assured her. "Elwyn phoned Percy at the office late yesterday afternoon, he was raving mad over some big fiscal mess he's discovered at the museum. He seemed to think it was Percy's fault, somehow. Percy made it plain from the start that he'd never been in any way involved with the Wilkins until Elwyn dragged him into it, but Elwyn went right on shouting. Percy claims Elwyn was just blowing off steam. Percy does tell me things in confidence, you know. We're like you and Max.''

Sarah let that one pass. Anne was still holding the floor. ''Elwyn does have a pretty wild temper when he gets going. I can picture him charging around among the statues and the bibelots like a buffalo in a china shop. Or do I mean bison? Not that it matters, I don't suppose. But anyway, Elwyn certainly gave Percy an earful. He doesn't yet know what's been going on, but he's bound and determined to get to the bottom of it, and heaven help those poor old trustees. Elwyn says he's going to sweep the whole bunch of them straight out the door, he claims they're all in cahoots with one of the guards. Melanson, I believe Percy said. You must know who he is.''

''Yes, I do, but it can't be Melanson. Nobody with half a brain would pick on poor old Milky. That's what the other guards call him; he wouldn't say boo to a mouse, much less a goose.''

Anne shook her head. ''I don't know, Sarah. Percy always says it's the mousy ones you have to watch. And Percy does have this perfectly maddening habit of being right.''

# Chapter 18

Knowing that Charles was a city boy born and bred, Sarah didn't waste any time looking for him clambering joyously among the rocks down below the cliff or even out in front of the house admiring Anne's miraculous landscaping. He was just where she'd expected, stretched out in a comfortable lounge chair on the ocean side of the deck that ran all around the house, watching a seagull try to open a clam but not offering it any help. Sarah refreshed the sickly lavender-colored lipstick that made her look like Dracula's mother, adjusted her awful hat to an even more unbecoming angle, and pronounced herself ready to travel. Charles was more than willing to get back on the road.

The Kellings were not a huggy and kissy family, but Sarah hugged Anne anyway. Anne took it quite well, considering.

"I do hate to see you go, Sarah."

"I hate to leave, but I am anxious about Davy. I'll be in touch with you, Anne. If it should become necessary to reach me for any reason, all you need do is telephone the Tulip Street house. You have the number and somebody will be there to take a message. Tell Percy the phone line has been bug-proofed, if it makes him feel any better. Good-bye for now, and thanks for everything."

Charles assisted his passenger into the car with a little extra panache, no doubt regretting inwardly that he didn't have a buffalo robe to spread over the moddom's afflicted limb and show Mrs. Percy how classy a chauffeur could be. Then they were off. Once safely down the steep drive, he glanced back over his shoulder.

"How are we for time?"

"Slightly pressed. I hope you're not too hungry. You needn't spare the horses, as I believe Great-Aunt Matilda used to say before Great-Uncle Frederick sold the team to an iceman and bought the Hupmobile, but I'd rather we didn't get caught for speeding."

"You and I both, moddom. The chap I borrowed this hack from tends to wax a trifle sniffy if anybody lands him with a summons when he wasn't even in the car."

"Surely you'd never do a thing like that, Charles."

"Not I. Such presumption would bespeak a lack of couth, which is something to which I do not stoop."

This was pretty much the end of their conversation. Charles concentrated on his driving. Sarah couldn't seem to concentrate on anything for long, there were too many different bits and pieces demanding her attention all at once. That Elwyn Turbot was chewing nails and spitting tacks over the sad state of the Wilkins's finances was only to be expected, but why hadn't the silly oaf asked to see the books before he took on the trusteeship?

As for Melanson's having been an undercover knave all these years, that was just plain ridiculous. Granted that worms did turn on occasion, why should meek old Milky finally have got around to doing what he might have done years ago if he'd been so inclined? Particularly just after a fire-eating new head of trustees had replaced the sweet but ineffectual nonagenarian who, until his not-so-recent death, had occupied a position on the board that he'd never wanted and had known himself to be incapable of filling.

All those years of standing watch over Madam Wilkins's more blatant mistakes might have taught a guard to sleep on his feet without getting caught, and probably had. That would have been the extent of Melanson's derelictions, though, if such they could have been called. Turbot had been looking for a scapegoat because he was that sort of man, as Sarah herself had reason to know. His attempt to bully her had fizzled; this time he'd been careful to pick a victim who was obviously not going to fight back.

An hour or two of being browbeaten, threatened, and accused of crimes that would never have entered the wretched Melanson's head would have left him in such a state that he'd have confessed to anything rather than endure any more of Turbot's hectoring. If this was the way Turbot intended to run the Wilkins, then the Wilkins was in even worse trouble than it had been before that roaring windbag assumed the trusteeship.

Back at Ireson's Landing, Sarah had had all she could do not to come straight out and tell Anne what she thought of Percy's important client. But that would only have made Anne unhappy and Percy annoyed at Sarah's presuming to pass a judgment which might be prejudicial to whatever devious, though no doubt strictly lawful, game Percy himself was playing. She decided to think about something else.

Such as what? Had Uncle Jem dredged up any further revelations about the Wicked Widows? Was the manager at the Fenway Studio Building clamoring for the inexperienced executrix to get the late Mrs. Tawne's meager effects out of the studio she'd occupied for so many all-too-fruitful years so that a new tenant could be installed? Had some long-lost Agnew or Tawne shown up in quest of dear Dolores's hypothetical jewels and stock certificates? Had Max telephoned, or sent a carrier pigeon, or, please God, got on an airplane headed for Boston with his Watteaus tucked underneath his arm?

Not Max's Watteaus, of course, but the Wilkins's. It was downright frightening to realize what a vast amount of wealth remained in the Madam's pink palazzo despite the pillage that had gone on for so many years, despite the fact that too many of the alleged Old Masters were still Tawnes, despite the tenuous network of threads by which so solid-looking an edifice was now being held together. Turbot didn't have the ghost of a notion as to what he ought to be doing. Dolores Tawne was not alive to tell him. Vieuxchamp was too slender a reed to lean on for any responsibility. None of the newer guards was worth a pinch of salt because Dolores had not wanted anybody around who might challenge her authority. And that nonsensical charge about poor old Milky Melanson was absolutely the outside limit.

Her mind wasn't helping a bit, it always came back to the Wilkins. Sarah was so glad when they got to the Rivkins' rented cottage that she might have knelt and kissed the sandy soil if it weren't for her sore knee and her suspicion that Charles would consider the gesture uncouth. Besides, Kellings didn't do such things. What would Davy think? Would he recognize his mother in this getup? Would he be frightened? Bored? Amused? Would he run away howling?

Sarah was winding up to panic when Miriam rushed out of the cottage in sawed-off jeans and one of Ira's old work shirts. Ira himself scrambled up from the lake in bathing trunks and a yellow T-shirt with a camel silk-screened on the front. Beside him was a small boy in another of Ira's T-shirts that came down almost to his ankles and had a platypus on it. At least Sarah thought the creature must be a platypus because she couldn't think what else it might be.

When Ira caught sight of the aged crone in the impossible hat, he stopped short and began to grin. Davy had eyes only for his friend Charles. It was not until he'd told Charles all about the big blue bird with the long beak that went wading in the lake with him that Davy happened to notice the woman who was talking with Aunt Mimi. He gave her a thorough going-over without uttering a word, took one hesitant step forward, then hurled himself into his mother's arms.

"Mummy got a dirty face."

The grown-ups began to laugh, Sarah most joyfully of all.

"Yes, dear, I have. Don't I look silly? How did you know me?"

"Because you're Mummy. Come on, I wash your face. My turn this time."

"Yes, dear, it's your turn." Sarah had her face buried in the wavy blond hair that her son had inherited from his father; Miriam said it would turn dark brown when he got into his twenties, as Max's had. "Wasn't I naughty to get my face so dirty?"

"Mummies don't be naughty, just boys. And girls," Davy added quickly, knowing that Aunt Mimi had strong views on chauvinism. It was merely that mothers came in a special category. "Come on, Mummy, it won't hurt."

"Sorry to spoil your handiwork, Charles, but you know how it is."

Sarah let her son tug her along to the cottage's one reasonably adequate bathroom and submitted to as vigorous a scrubbing as a child not yet three could reasonably manage. Then she shed the hideous silk blouse, which had got thoroughly drenched in the scrubbing, took off the improvised wig because her own hair wasn't dirty and she didn't want Davy's idea of a shampoo, and put on one of Ira's clean T-shirts that she happened to find on the chest in Davy's room. It was blue with a design of two lovebirds wearing Uncle Sam hats, acrimoniously engaged in a feather-pulling political argument.

"I hope you don't mind my swiping your shirt, Ira," she said. "It seemed the thing to do."

"Be my guest. Everybody wears my shirts but me, I have to steal Mike's. Where the hell did you get hold of that outfit you were wearing in the car?"

"We have our methods. It's rather a long story. Charles has to get back to Boston and he hasn't had lunch."

"What about you?"

"I had a bite of Cousin Anne's stuffed celery. You must see what she's doing with our front slope. It's a burning shame that Percy's such a prune about woman's place being in the home, Anne would be a flaming success as a landscape gardener. Mr. Lomax is teaching her the mystique of fertilizing with fishheads and she's happy as a clam at high water. Be sure to drop by Ireson's Landing when you get home from the lake.''

"We may not go home at all," Miriam put in. "We like it here, don't we, Davy."

"Mummy stay?"

"I hope so, dear," said Sarah. "For a while, anyway. You must show me how to catch a minnow."

"Okay. Then we put it back and it goes home to its mummy and daddy. Right, Uncle Ira?"

"Couldn't be righter, big fella. Want to show your mother how you help Aunt Mimi set the table?"

"Allow me," said Charles, "I'm trained for the job. Come along, Dave, show me where they hide the forks and spoons."

The cottage that Miriam and Ira had rented was nothing special except for a good-sized screened porch that overlooked the lake and was equipped with a redwood picnic table and benches. There could hardly have been a pleasanter place to sit and eat the good food that Miriam loved to provide. A big salad, a platter of sliced turkey and roast beef left over from the weekend, a heaped cheese board, and real, non-squishy rye bread to build sandwiches with were paradise now. There was lemonade made with real lemons to drink, unless anybody preferred milk, iced tea, hot coffee, or something in a can with a diplodocus on the label that Mike had bought in a spirit of gastronomical research. Nobody felt inclined to venture on the diplodocus juice just then, which was probably a good thing.

"Now what's all this about the Ashcan Annie getup and you needing a car?" Ira wanted to know after they'd finished their meal and got Charles on the road with warm good-byes from the Rivkins and a sleepy wave from Davy, who was still having afternoon naps. Fortunately the child had dropped off quickly, wearing his mother's ugly hat and clinging to the stuffed llama that he'd named for Uncle Dolph Kelling. Sarah seized the moment and got down to business.

"I've told this story to Anne and I'm telling it to you two because Max isn't here and I have Davy to think of. The gist of it is that somebody apparently wants to kill me."

"For God's sake," barked Ira. "What for?"

"Good question. All I can tell you is that it started Sunday afternoon. Cousin Anne had called me up quite unexpectedly on Sunday morning and asked me to lunch with her and Percy at the Turbots'. They're clients of Percy's; the reason I was invited is that Elwyn Fleesom Turbot—that's his real name— has just been elected chairman of trustees at the Wilkins Museum. As you of course know, Max and I have been involved with the Wilkins ever since before we were married. In fact, he's evidently nailed down those two Watteaus he was after; I spoke to him early on Sunday, but the line went dead in the midst of our conversation and I haven't heard a yip from him since. Anyway, I was there by myself feeling bereft when Anne called. I'll admit I was curious to meet the new chairman, so I got dressed and went."

"Do you think Turbot's going to be any good?" asked Miriam.

"Yes, no, and maybe. Take your pick. He doesn't know beans about art, but Percy seems to think he's pretty sound on the fiscal side, which is more than can be said for the museum's finances right now. Anyway, we got through the meal, which was fairly depressing, but that's beside the point. Then, all of a sudden, Turbot lit into me about Max's being in breach of contract with the Wilkins. That was nonsense, because we've never had a contract. I told him so and he went up in flames. He's the sort of chest-beating he-man who doesn't take kindly to being lectured by females who know more than he does; which wouldn't have to be much, I can tell you. And I must say I don't like being called a dumb little cutie-pants."

"So that's why Turbot tried to kill you?"

"Oh, no. What I think is that somebody's out to get Turbot because there's still some kind of racket going on at the Wilkins and whoever's running it doesn't want a real, live go-get-it executive heading the board. As for myself, I'd say it's most likely a case of being in the wrong place at the wrong time. I'm guessing that ever since Turbot was formally elected to the board last Thursday, there's been a stakeout at his cattle farm. He raises incredibly pedigreed polled Herefords but they don't taste all that good, at least not the way his cook, if they have one, hacked up the meat into what they seemed to think was boeuf bourguignon."

Miriam was horrified. "What a dreadful waste, unless they were just using up some odds and ends. Stewing in wine, which is essentially what the bourguignon comes to, is simply a way of tenderizing tough beef. If I had a lovely big, expensive cut from a pedigreed steer, I'd just cut off any excess fat, shove it in the roasting pan with a pinch of this and a dollop of that, and let nature take its course. Or I could lather it with chopped liver and make a beef Wellington if I wanted to be fancy and knew how to make a decent pastry to wrap it in. Or just cut some steaks and grill them. She must be nuts."

"She who?" said Ira.

"Good question. Mrs. Turbot, I suppose, if there is one."

"Oh, there is," Sarah assured her sister-in-law. "They call her Lala and she comes gift-wrapped in gold. Rings on her fingers and bells on her toes, bangle bracelets all the way up to her armpits and a designer-model pantsuit creation that made me want to cry with envy because it matched her toenails so beautifully."

"Is the color of Lala Turbot's toenails germane to the issue at hand, Sarah?" Ira put in. "I ask because we've only got the cottage for another two weeks and I'd like to get to the point of this discussion before we go home."

"Ira, that's not funny," Miriam expostulated. "Sarah has

come to us for help. The least we can do is let her tell her
story at her own pace.''

''I'll try not to be too tedious, but thank you both for your
interest,'' Sarah replied. ''At this point I have no idea whether
Lala Turbot's toenails are germane to the issue or not. All I
know is that two people I assume to be young men, though
I can't be sure, tried to run me down on the way to Boston.
I'd left my car in Anne and Percy's driveway and ridden to
the Turbots' with them. It wasn't until I'd picked up my own
car and got out on the Boston road that these two fellows
showed up and started pulling their tricks. I ditched them
easily enough because I've been over that road ever since
Alexander taught me to drive in the old Studebaker.''

''So you got to Boston all right,'' said Miriam. ''You didn't
go into that underground garage by yourself, I hope.''

''Oh no,'' Sarah reassured her. ''By some miracle, there
was an open parking space on Tulip Street, almost in front
of the house. Charles must have been waiting for me at the
window, he galloped out to open the door and told me that
Dolores Tawne had invited herself to tea at five o'clock. She'd
do that every once in a while. He had everything ready but
Dolores never showed up, which was not at all like her. About
half past five, one of the Wilkins's security guards called up
in a dreadful tizzy, howling for Brooks. He and the only other
guard left in the place had found Dolores lying dead in the
courtyard, contrary to museum protocol, and didn't know what
to do with her. They really are a pack of idiots over there.''

Sarah went on, describing in more detail than she'd done
with Anne how she'd become personally involved in the situation by learning that Dolores had taken the far greater liberty
of naming Sarah her executrix; and that an old-fashioned steel
hatpin had turned Dolores's apparently natural death into a
case of murder. She described her own hairbreadth escape
from a hit-and-run death in busy Kenmore Square, the staggering surprise that had turned up in one of Dolores's safe

deposit boxes, and the weird imbroglio of the second box and the Wicked Widows.

"So you see what a mess I've been landed in. I'm far more concerned for Max than I am for myself; but there's nothing I can do for him here except try to keep the ship afloat and trust that you'll take care of Davy if anything happens to me before he gets back. Please understand that I'm doing all I can to stay alive, even if it means wearing that outfit Charles dug out of the thrift shop. You had to know what's going on, but I don't want to drag you in any farther than I can help. I'll disappear right now if you feel uncomfortable about my being here."

Miriam's answer was brusque. "Don't be silly. Stick your leg up on the bench, I want to look at that knee."

"I put a fresh bandage on it this morning."

"Sure you did. Get me a basin of warm water, Ira. And the peroxide. And the first-aid kit."

"And a stretcher and an ambulance and a snifter of brandy in case she faints on us?"

"If she faints, how can she drink the brandy, nudnick?"

"The brandy's for me, in case *I* faint." Ira stooped and planted a kiss on the top of his wife's head. "Gesund auf deine käppele, I'll be right back."

Miriam got down to business, her touch was far gentler than her tongue. How lovely it was to be cosseted, to feel a sure hand applying an ice pack to one's bruised shin, dabbing fizzy, cleansing, healing peroxide on one's lacerated kneecap, drying off the trickles, smoothing on a healing salve, laying on a fresh dressing with a touch no harsher than the brush of a moth's wing.

Then Miriam gathered up her scissors, her medicaments, her first-aid kit, carried them out of the room, and came back a few minutes later with something in a mug that smelled odd but not at all unpleasant. "Here, Sarah, you'd better drink this, it's supposed to help you relax. What you need right now is rest. I was going to add 'and peace of mind,' but that won't come till the bad guys are rounded up and Max comes home, so you might as well get some sleep while you have a chance. I'd better warn you that we're not wholly immune from droppers-in, though we do our best to discourage them from coming.''

Miriam's matter-of-fact common sense was the best medicine of all. Sarah even managed to smile. ''I'll keep them off. I'll paint my face dead white from some of the ghastly makeup Charles left and wander around in a bedsheet moaning 'Unclean! Unclean!' You can say I'm on compassionate leave from the leprosarium if you think sterner tactics would help.''

''No, the makeup would probably do it. Get some sleep. Davy will be waking up soon and I'll take him down with me for a swim; I haven't had mine yet today. We usually take some whole wheat biscuits or a little fruit for after he comes out of the water. He carries it down in his lunch bucket and has a picnic on the beach with his friend the heron. Actually the heron keeps a pretty good distance between them, which is just as well. Ira told Davy that herons are like airplanes, they need a long runway so they can work up enough speed to lift them out of the water. He may be right, for all I know. Sweet dreams.''

''Thanks, Miriam, I can use some.''

Oddly enough, that herb potion Miriam had given her to drink seemed to be having an effect. Sarah closed her eyes as an experiment, and didn't open them again until she heard a child's voice beside her saying, ''Are you awake yet, Mummy? I caught you a minnow.''

# Chapter 19

Sarah would have enjoyed a swim in that warm, calm water but she didn't want to give Miriam the bother of bandaging her knee again. Besides, she hadn't brought what most of her Kelling aunts would still refer to as a bathing suit. Miriam's would be too big for her and Sarah was definitely not about to borrow those barely visible scraps of cloth and bits of string that Mike's girlfriend had left at the cottage. She'd had her nap wearing Ira's T-shirt, she kept it on and padded barefoot with Davy down to the water's edge, where he poured the minnow carefully out of his pail and told it to swim straight home like a good fish because its mother was waiting.

Whether the minnow obeyed Davy's instruction they didn't get to find out; the blue heron chose that moment to take off. That was a sight to see, the great bird with its long neck bent into a flattened S-curve, its long legs trailing out behind like a pair of ski poles, its enormous wings dipping and rising with a ponderous, unhurried beat as it made its leisurely way out over the lake toward whatever it might find on the other side.

"He waved good-bye to me!"

Davy waved back until the heron's gray-blue color merged with the mist that had begun to gather and Ira came down to tell Sarah that Jem Kelling was on the phone and did she want to talk to him or not?

"Thanks, Ira. I'd better see what he's calling about."

Sarah did wish that Uncle Jem could have waited another hour or two, it was a shame to go indoors at this magical time. But she went.

"Yes, Uncle Jem. What's up?"

"Lieutenant Harris phoned just before he went off duty. He wants to know when you'll be back, he has some new bee in his bonnet about the Wicked Widows. He also mentioned that Melanson, the guard who was arrested yesterday, tried to commit suicide this afternoon. I suppose that proves he's guilty of killing your friend Mrs. Tawne."

"Then you suppose quite wrongly," Sarah snapped back. "All right, Uncle Jem, did he mention what time tomorrow morning he'd be available?"

"No, he left a number for you to call him tonight. He seems to be hot on the trail."

"He seems to have his head stuffed with peach fuzz." Sarah was furious. "What's the number?"

Jem gave it to her, then revved up to tell her a number of other things that had no relevance to the matter at hand. She did the only sensible thing and lied. "I'll have to get back to you later, Uncle Jem. Ira's making faces at me, I think he's trying to tell me that Miriam wants us to come to the table."

That wasn't a real lie, hardly a fib. If Miriam wasn't ready to serve, she soon would be. At the moment, she was putting the finishing touches on a low-fat, vitamin-rich, delectable-looking meal that would strike a neat balance between Ira's need to lose some weight and Miriam's need to nourish her man. Sarah broke the connection with Jem but kept the phone in her hand.

"Do you mind if I make a call to Boston? Lieutenant Harris wants to talk with me, and I want to speak my piece to him. The halfwit's gone and arrested that nice Mr. Melanson. And Melanson's tried to commit suicide, don't ask me how. Something futile, no doubt, like holding his breath and trying to turn blue."

"Jem told me Melanson's confessed to killing Mrs. Tawne." Ira was digging green olives out of a skinny glass jar; they were supposed to be for Miriam's salad but he was absentmindedly eating most of them himself. "Doesn't that tell you something?"

"It certainly does," Sarah snapped back. "It tells me that the great Elwyn Fleesom Turbot was determined to hang Dolores's murder on somebody or other to show what a hotshot administrator he is, and picked on Melanson because he was the easiest target. Anybody with even the vestige of a brain should have known that Melanson would have confessed to anything from arson to witchcraft after an hour or so of Turbot's bellowing. That Turbot is absolutely the most obnoxious bully I've ever come across, even counting Great-Uncle Frederick. I don't know why I'm railing at you when I could be screaming at Harris instead."

Ira swallowed the last olive. "Need the phone book?"

"No, thanks. Uncle Jem gave me Harris's number."

Sarah dialed, and spoke to the woman who answered. "I hope this isn't a bad time to call. My name is Sarah Bittersohn, I had a message that Lieutenant Harris wanted me to get in touch with him."

"Yes, Mrs. Bittersohn, John's expecting your call. Just a second, he's out in the yard throwing sticks for the dog."

Oh, rats! How was one supposed to maintain a suitably belligerent posture against an off-duty policeman who threw sticks for his dog? Sarah waited, trying to picture the lieutenant as a householder and wondering what breed of dog it was. Either a doberman or a bloodhound, she surmised until she heard a high-pitched yapping that sounded more like a sheltie or a peke. When Harris came on the line, she couldn't help asking.

"What sort of dog is it?"

"Oh, hi, Mrs. Bittersohn. He's a toy poodle. Our kids

named him Looie for Lieutenant, but I renamed him Captain. I figured one of us ought to get a promotion, and it probably won't be me. Thanks for calling back, how's the undercover act playing?"

"All right so far, thank you. I'm still alive, as you've no doubt deduced. What's this nonsense about arresting one of the Wilkins guards?"

"Um, Mr. Turbot, the chairman of trustees, presented evidence—"

"That he'd browbeaten poor old Melanson into confessing to the murder of Dolores Tawne, which wouldn't have taken very long because Melanson has no more spine than a boiled noodle, right?"

"Um—"

"Didn't Vieuxchamp have the decency to stand up for his partner? They've worked together for years and years."

"Um—"

"No, I didn't expect he would. Vieuxchamp wants to keep on Turbot's good side, if there is one. Melanson doesn't play politics. He takes his job seriously, never puts a foot wrong, but is always in a panic for fear that some day he might."

"Might kill somebody, you mean? In case you haven't heard, Melanson signed a confession."

"Does that surprise you? A loud voice is fully as effective as a rubber hose on a middle-aged neurotic who's been staggering all his life under a burden of free-floating guilt. I don't care what Turbot bullied Melanson into confessing, Lieutenant Harris; you ought to have known better. Turbot's been head of trustees for less than a week, this was only his second visit to the museum, as far as I know. My husband and I have been closely associated with the place for seven years, and my cousin Brooks Kelling worked there for some time before that. Brooks knows Melanson inside out, I wish he were here. He'd tell you that if you've booked Milky Melanson on a charge of murder you've made a mistake which will lead to a suit for false arrest, assuming that your victim lives to bring it."

"Milky? Is that what you call him?"

"It's what Vieuxchamp calls him. I believe it's from an old comic strip called *The Timid Soul*, about a man named Caspar Milquetoast. One can't help using the nickname because it fits Melanson so aptly."

"So you really think he's getting a raw deal?" Harris was beginning to sound less sure of himself.

"Of course I do," Sarah fumed, "or I wouldn't be talking like this. I'm worried about Melanson, he's just not built for this sort of treatment. Turbot's an interfering old poop. He knows nothing about the museum or the people who work there. He just wanted to stage a melodrama with himself as the star, and you—"

"I've booked Melanson as a material witness. Does that make you feel any better?"

"No, it does not. If he isn't out of jail by eight o'clock this evening, I'll meet you there with a lawyer. If bail is needed, I'll see that it's provided, but you really must turn Melanson loose before he tries again to kill himself. What Turbot's done to that man is unconscionable; it's a wonder Melanson didn't drop dead from the shock of being accused. Where is he now?"

"Charles Street jail."

"I'll see you there at eight on the dot."

Sarah cupped a hand over the mouthpiece and turned to Miriam. "Where's Uncle Jake?"

"In Boston, luckily. There's some kind of lawyers' dinner at the Copley; I'll call the hotel about seven o'clock and have him paged. He'll be glad of an excuse to miss the speeches. Supper's just about ready; you are going to stay, I hope."

"If there's time. Did you find me a car, Ira?"

"Yes, but I'll be driving it. You're not prowling around

Cambridge Circle alone after dark, not after what you've been telling us. Let me talk to Harris."

Sarah relinquished the phone to Ira and put her arms around Miriam. "I was so hoping we'd have a nice, peaceful evening together, but there's no telling what may happen to Melanson if the pressure isn't relieved very soon. I know perfectly well that he had nothing to do with Dolores's death except to find her body in the courtyard and telephone to Tulip Street, hoping Brooks would be there to tell him and Vieuxchamp what to do. Actually Vieuxchamp should have done the calling and it should have been to the police instead of Brooks, but Melanson didn't have the gumption for that and Vieuxchamp never does anything at all if he can palm it off on somebody else."

"Then why didn't Turbot go after Vieuxchamp instead of Melanson?" Miriam wanted to know.

"Because Vieuxchamp's a big, robust fellow with a cocksure manner and a ready tongue," Sarah told her. "He looks too much like the type who'd fight back, which I'm sure he would if his own neck was in danger. In some ways he's like Turbot, except that Vieuxchamp smarms where Turbot would bellow."

"You seem to know a lot about this Turbot, considering that you only met him Sunday."

"That was enough, believe me. I cannot for the life of me understand why the other trustees were foolish enough to vote him in, though I'll grant you that half of them are too deaf to hear what's going on and the rest too gaga to run an ant farm, let alone an art museum. If those two are planning to gab all night, I may as well go and change."

Ira and Lieutenant Harris had arrived at some kind of gentlemen's agreement about Melanson and gone on to the funny noise in Mrs. Harris's transmission. Sarah went and changed back into her revolting silk blouse and the flannel skirt that she'd absentmindedly put on a hanger instead of leaving it in a heap, the result being that the damp lakeside air had eased out most of the wrinkles Jem and Egbert had put in. With Noah's beard and a scarf of Miriam's covering her hair and a light film of Charles's makeup doing odd things to her by now slightly sunburned complexion, she could have been any middle-aged woman who'd rushed up from the beach on a humanitarian mission, forgetting to change out of her holey sneakers; not that anybody bothered much about such trifles nowadays.

Just as Miriam had set out a platter of steaming corn on the cob, and was beginning to steam herself, Ira hung up the phone and charged over to the table. "So where's the grub?"

"Right in front of you, Sherlock. I didn't want to interrupt what might have been the start of something beautiful. Pass Sarah the corn and cut her some chicken. Davy, do you want to eat your corn on the cob like Uncle Ira, or shall I cut it off for you?"

"Here's a tender little ear that's just your size, Davy. You can nibble it like a mouse." Sarah was feeling contrary twinges, one of gratitude for the exquisite care Miriam was taking of her son and the other a pang of what might possibly be resentment that Miriam was doing it so well.

A fine homemaker Sarah Kelling Bittersohn had turned out to be. There was Miriam here raising Sarah's child, Anne over at Sarah's house landscaping her grounds, Davy's father off in Argentina and Davy's mother not even home to take Max's phone call, if it ever came, because she was about to tear off to jail on behalf of an elderly basket case whom, when one came down to it, she hardly even knew.

What a crazy life for a not quite three-year-old! Yet what a happy little boy Davy was, ready to be friends with a minnow or a heron or anybody who really wanted to be friends with him. Already he could sniff out the ones who were only pretending. He wouldn't need a silly old mother to show him the ropes, and then what could a mother do? Sarah hoped to heaven she wouldn't wind up like Great-Uncle Frederick, running drives to put diapers on the Boston Common pigeons in the interests of a cleaner environment.

But somebody had to do something about Melanson, and who else was there? Dolores was dead. The only one with any power at the Wilkins now was Turbot, and Turbot had done this terrible thing to an innoffensive man who had meekly and faithfully served the museum for most of his life. And Turbot had done it, moreover, for no reason except to swell up like a bullfrog and croak his greatness to a largely uninterested world.

Sarah wondered whether Lala had been told of her husband's coup, and what she'd said about it. Nothing complimentary, Sarah hoped, not that she had much time for Lala either. That seemed an odd marriage, but then marriages did tend to be. She rather wished she'd asked Anne a little more about the Turbots, just out of curiosity. Well, there'd be time for that; she'd better eat.

The meal was wonderful, as Miriam's meals always were. Sarah would have liked to stay for dessert but she and Ira had a fairish drive ahead of them and it would hardly do to leave Harris twiddling his handcuffs at the jail when she herself had been so peremptory about setting the time. She pushed back her chair and took Davy in her arms.

"Give me a good-night kiss, darling. Uncle Ira and I have to go now."

"Will you be coming back tonight?" Miriam asked her.

"I'd love to, if it's possible. I don't know, Miriam. I've never bailed anybody before, I have no idea how long it might take. Maybe Ira had better just drop me off at the jail and come straight back here by himself. I can always phone Tulip Street and have Charles pick me up."

"Nothing doing," said Ira. "Mim, you and Davy will be all right by yourselves, won't you? We can call Mike to come and keep you company, he won't mind."

"Huh," snorted his wife. "Then Mike will show up with Tracy and you two will come back ten minutes later and there won't be enough beds. Which wouldn't bother Mike and Tracy, I don't suppose, but it bothers me. What I think is that Sarah had better stay as far away from Tulip Street as she can get and come back here with you, no matter if it's three o'clock in the morning. Just phone if it's late so I'll know. Okay?"

"Okay." Ira kissed his wife with efficiency and thoroughness. "I'll give you a buzz when we get to the jail. I believe we'll be allowed one phone call."

"That's only if you've been pinched."

"So I'll commit a misdemeanor. You going to be warm enough in that thin jacket, Sarah? It gets chilly once the sun's gone down."

As always, Miriam had what was needed. "Why don't you take my blue shawl, Sarah, the one Mother Rivkin knitted for me when Mike was on the way. It's showing its age, but that's what you want, isn't it? You'll look like somebody's mother."

"Well, I am, you know," Sarah reminded her sister-in-law gently. "Take good care of Aunt Mimi, Davy. I'll be back but you'll be asleep. Tomorrow we can go to see the heron. Maybe he'll show us how to flap our wings so we can fly down to get Daddy."

Moments later, Sarah and Ira were in the borrowed car, a mid-sized sedan of no impressive pedigree but reasonable power and comfort. Sarah offered to drive but Ira demurred. Since this was not his car, he preferred to take the responsibility of driving it, which was understandable enough. Having said his piece, he switched on the radio to a classical-music station and they listened to Brahms and Beethoven most of the way to Boston.

Neither of them talked much. Ira must have been wondering what he'd let himself in for, and so was Sarah. Both took it as a good omen when, as they were crawling toward the jail and wondering where it might be possible to park, a taxi rolled up and Jacob Bittersohn rolled out.

Sarah rolled down her window and stuck out her head.

"Uncle Jake! How dear of you to come. Here, let me pay for the cab."

"Don't be meshugge." Lawyer Bittersohn walked over and opened the car door for Sarah to get out. "We're here on behalf of one Joseph Herbert Melanson, security guard at the Wilkins Museum since April 14, 1965, right? Booked as a material witness to the murder of one Dolores Agnew Tawne, right?"

"If you say so. I didn't know his first name was Joseph," Sarah confessed.

"So you didn't do your homework. Come on, take that foolishness off your head so you won't scare the guards, and give Ira a chance to park the car so he doesn't land in the jug himself. We'll see you inside, Ira. With any luck, we'll see you outside as well."

Since he was double-parked outside a jail, Ira was only too willing to move on. Sarah and her uncle-in-law went inside, where they were met by two guards and a small, thin man with a briefcase who walked like Groucho Marx and resembled him too. This must be the bail bondsman. Jacob Bittersohn greeted him affably by name and insisted on introducing him to Sarah, who was in no mood for socializing. She found him somewhat unnerving. Having disposed of her improvised wig and wiped the unbecoming makeup off her face, she got down to business.

"As far as I can make out, this whole debacle started merely because the Wilkins's new head of trustees wanted to play Perry Mason. Having been subjected to one of Elwyn Fleesom Turbot's totally unfounded harangues this past Sunday myself, I know how devastating it must have been for Mr. Melanson to be yelled at and berated and bullied into confessing that he'd murdered a colleague whom in fact he wouldn't have dared to touch with a ten-foot pole. Mr. Melanson's a very timid middle-aged bachelor, compulsively afraid of putting a foot wrong and easily cowed by practically anybody. I'm told he's already tried to commit suicide and I'm not surprised, not because he's guilty of anything but because he's been mistreated to the point where he just couldn't handle the stress. We'll have to bring suit, Uncle Jake."

"So? How do you know about the suicide?"

"Uncle Jem told me over the phone, while Miriam was getting supper. He said Lieutenant Harris wanted to talk to me. I'm afraid I did most of the talking. Harris was supposed to meet us here on the dot of eight, blast him. I don't want to spend the night twiddling my thumbs, either bring Melanson out or show me where to find him."

"Oy, such a *macher*." Lawyer Bittersohn gazed upon this embattled niece-in-law with wonderment and delight. "How come Miriam didn't join the war?"

"She had to stay and baby-sit my child for me, which is another thing I'm cross about. Never mind that now, it's Melanson I want to talk to. Where do I find him?"

One of the guards made the mistake of trying to placate her. "I don't think he'd want to see you. He's clammed up."

"More likely he's slipped into a catatonic fit," she snapped back. "Has he been seen by a doctor?"

"Well, no."

"Please make a note of that, Uncle Jake. We may have to sue his jailers also. Come along, all of you. I want to see Joseph Melanson right now, no matter what state he's in."

"Hi, Mrs. Bittersohn." By now the voice was familiar. "Am I late?"

"Yes," snapped Sarah. "Oh, Lieutenant Harris, do you know my husband's uncle, Attorney Jacob Bittersohn? He's going to arrange about bail, should that prove necessary. In the meantime, I'm going to see Mr. Melanson."

"You said something about a doctor," one of the guards ventured.

"We can't wait for a doctor. Just seeing one might be enough to push him over the edge, if he's in the kind of shape

I suspect he is. He knows me, I'm not at all a threatening person."

"You couldn't prove it by me," murmured Lieutenant Harris. "Okay, Mrs. Bittersohn. This way, please."

# Chapter 20

Sarah saw Melanson through the bars. He looked just about as she'd expected to see him, a gray wraith sitting slumped over on the edge of an iron cot, his head bowed down by weight of woe, hands hanging loose between his knees, his eyes seeing nothing. Even when the guard opened the cell door, he didn't move a muscle.

"Thank you," Sarah told the guard. "I'll go in alone. Please move back where he won't be able to see you."

"Doesn't look to me as if he's seeing anything," the guard replied.

"Yes, that's our big problem, isn't it. You'll need to lock the door, I expect."

"With you in there? He's a murderer!"

"Oh, I don't think so. I'll call you if I need you."

Shaking his head slowly from side to side, the guard turned his key in the lock and backed away. Sarah sat down on the cot beside Melanson and, with the same delicate touch she'd have used if she were trying to pat a field mouse, felt for a pulse in his wrist.

"I'm so sorry, Mr. Melanson." She tried to keep her voice as gentle as her touch. "You've been given a bad time, haven't you? You know me, I'm Brooks Kelling's cousin Sarah, you've seen me at the Wilkins lots of times. Brooks is away on vacation just now, but he'll want to see you as soon as he gets back. So will my husband, Max Bittersohn. Max has always liked you."

She could barely feel the pulse, a faint thread of life; she tried harder to rouse him. "Do you remember the day when poor old Joe Witherspoon fell over the balcony? All the other guards left their stations, which they shouldn't have done, but you stayed right where you belonged. You always do the right thing, Mr. Melanson. You were the one who noticed those two paintings that had been changed around. Do you remember that? That's how we found out that the museum was being robbed and Dolores's copies hung in place of the old masters."

It hadn't been that simple, but no matter. "Nobody ever tried to steal anything from your station, did they? You have the longest and best record of any guard the Wilkins ever had. You know that, don't you?"

Sarah felt a small tremor in the wrist she was touching. Melanson turned his head a tiny fraction, slowly, carefully, like a rabbit wondering whether it was safe to move. Sarah froze. He put out the tip of his tongue and ran it around his parched lips. Sarah went and beckoned through the bars to the guard.

"Mr. Melanson is thirsty. Could you bring him a drink of water, please?"

The guard went down the hall a short way and came back with a small paper cup. It wasn't much, but it was something. Sarah took the cup from him and held it to Melanson's lips. He took a tiny sip, then another, then emptied the cup. "Thank you," he whispered.

"Would you like something to eat, Mr. Melanson?"

"I—I—"

"I know, this is all strange to you. Let's see what we can do."

Sarah signaled through the bars again. "Mr. Melanson thanks you for the water. Do you think you could find him something to eat?"

"He had his supper but he wouldn't eat it. Just sat there and wasted good food." The guard was, however, human. "There's hot coffee in the guards' room. I guess it would be okay to give him a cup."

"That would be splendid. Cream and sugar in the coffee, don't you think? Luckily I've brought a sandwich. It's chicken, Mr. Melanson. My sister-in-law made it for you in case you might be hungry. Ah, here's your coffee, and here's the sandwich, you'll feel better when you've got something inside you. Just take your time. Your lawyer is outside with a bail bondsman. As soon as the formalities have been dealt with, we're going to get you out of here."

Out, that was the magic word. The prisoner accepted the sandwich, took an avid bite and chewed. And chewed and chewed. Thirty chews, Sarah counted. At least this compulsive mastication gave the coffee time to cool. Another bite, another thirty chews. A vague hint of animation was starting to show in Melanson's face, but the pulse still felt awfully weak to Sarah. He took another sip of coffee, another bite from the sandwich. It was slow going; at least he was back among the living. He finished the first half. That was as much as he could manage, he closed his eyes and flopped over on the cot.

"Guard!" Sarah thought Melanson's collapse was most likely plain exhaustion, but this was no time to take chances. "We must get him to the hospital."

"You're the one that gave him the sandwich."

"What's that supposed to mean? Call my lawyer, he's with the clerk of the court. Now!"

Sarah spent some anguished moments alone in that cell with a body that looked like a waxwork. She kept her finger on Melanson's pulse, she couldn't feel that it was any stronger but it wasn't any worse. The hospital, thank God, was just next door. Uncle Jake would know what to do. If he didn't come right away, she'd scream until he did. She was pumping up to wake the whole jail if she had to when both Jake and

Ira came thundering down the concrete, the guard running a poor third.

"What's the matter?" panted Jake.

"I think he's just been through more than he could handle. He was in a stupor when I got here. I talked to him a bit, he rallied enough to drink some coffee and eat half a chicken sandwich that Miriam sent, then he passed out. He looks to me now as if he's merely asleep, but his pulse is still weak and he's barely said a word. Hadn't we better get him into the hospital?"

"Yes."

Jacob Bittersohn was gone as fast as he'd arrived; he was back in a blessedly few minutes with an intern, an orderly and a gurney. The intern listened to Melanson's heart, raised an eyebrow, injected something into one flaccid arm, helped the orderly to get him on the gurney, and ate the other half of Miriam's excellent sandwich.

"Nothing wrong with the food," was her verdict. "I think the guy's just plain pooped. Has he been through a particularly bad time lately?"

"He certainly has," said Sarah. "He's been falsely accused of murder and summarily fired from a job that he'd held for over thirty years by a bullying half-wit who's about to get slapped with a lawsuit. Right, Uncle Jake?"

"Right, Sadele."

"When did this happen?" the intern asked.

"Just this afternoon," Sarah answered. "Is Lieutenant Harris still around, Ira? He's the one who booked Melanson as a material witness, whatever that's supposed to mean. Melanson is one of those compulsive neurotics who are perennially afraid of doing the wrong thing. Unfortunately it was he who spotted the body of that woman who was killed with a hatpin Sunday afternoon at the Wilkins Museum, where they both worked. He's been carrying that around; and today the new head of trustees, who knows nothing whatever about Melanson's long record as a thoroughly reliable employee, jumped on him simply because he's the type who wouldn't dare fight back. Is that enough for you?"

"Plenty. I don't like the sound of his heart. He'll probably have to be kept under observation for a day or two anyway. Come on, Bill, let's move him out. What about bail?"

"Everything's arranged," Attorney Bittersohn assured the intern. "I'll handle the paperwork while you get him settled. Sarah, you'd better go back with Ira and get some sleep."

"Yes, Uncle Jake." Sarah turned to the intern. "I'm the one who gave him the coffee and sandwich. It didn't hurt him, did it?"

"Might have saved his life. It sure saved mine tonight, I never got time for supper."

Feeling a good deal better, Sarah followed the gurney down the drafty corridor. Under observation was exactly where she'd have wanted Melanson to be. She'd been thinking of asking Lieutenant Harris about a special officer to keep watch over him, but the intensive-care unit would be even safer. She doubted whether the patient would be allowed any visitors for a day or so; she needn't feel guilty if she didn't get to see him right away.

"What happened to Lieutenant Harris?" she asked Ira, who happened to be next to her.

"He went home. He lives in Dorchester, he told me he hadn't had an evening at home for the past three weeks."

"Then I'm sorry I was snippy to him; but how was I to know?"

Sarah didn't apologize for having taken up Ira's evening. He and Miriam were night owls; Miriam was no doubt thinking up some tantalizing midnight snack about now. But it wasn't midnight, or anywhere near. Sarah was surprised to see from the clock on the wall that it wasn't even ten o'clock yet; she felt as if she'd been here for ages on the deep.

It was curious, now that she thought of it, that she'd been born and reared so close to this old building and never once until tonight got so much as a peek inside. She wondered whether any of her relatives ever had been there, and thought it unlikely. Any malefactions they or their acquaintances might have committed would have been the sort that didn't get punished. Renting rat-infested hovels to poor people who'd have had to scrape for pennies to pay the rent collector or find themselves out on the sidewalk would have counted as business, not exploitation. Naturally it would have been the rent collector who got the curses and the complaints, and the absent landlord who ignored them and kept the money.

Kellings had been shipowners during the days of the China clippers. No doubt some of their captains had managed to circumvent the Chinese officials' herculean efforts to keep opium from being smuggled in through their ports by this new lot of foreign devils who were, with true Yankee zeal, emulating their British counterparts who had plied the opium trade so long and so successfully. Should his lucrative sideline have been discovered, the resourceful captain would have been more apt to get an extra bonus than a reprimand.

Sarah was sure that none of her ancestors had ever gone blackbirding; she was not sure their refusal had been entirely on humanitarian grounds. The slave trade had been economically unsound. Human cattle took up too much cargo space, even when crammed together in the noisome holds as tight as they could fit. Too many of them died on the long voyages and had to be thrown overboard at considerable loss of profit. It was altogether a chancy business, and Kellings seldom left anything to chance if they could help it.

Furthermore, slavery as it was known and practiced in the South before Lincoln signed the Emancipation Proclamation was not well-adapted to the northern way of life. Why should it have been? There were always plenty of green immigrants coming off the boats and finding themselves compelled by circumstances to labor long hours for wages hardly sufficient to keep body and soul together. Instead of being whipped for laziness or insubordination, they got docked or fired with no redress until, after long and bitter fighting between the workers and the bosses, the unions came into being.

These were topics that did not, as a rule, get discussed among the Kellings. Sarah had learned a great deal since she'd stepped out from under the family umbrella, perhaps all those conflicting ideas had contributed to her urge to rescue lame ducks and all-but-gone geese. No wonder Walter Kelling had had such a rough time trying to write the truth about his forebears without running afoul of his chauvinistic relatives. It was a lot to think about; Sarah didn't feel up to thinking.

Ira noticed her silence. "Long day, eh?"

"Oh, today was a picnic compared to yesterday." She was trying to be airy but a yawn got in the way. "I can't tell you what a relief it is not having to drive myself back to the lake. It's too bad poor old Milky's heart's started acting up—Milky is what the other guards at the museum call him—but he's surely better off in the hospital than having to be pent up in that dreary little cell. And it's all wrong, somehow."

"What do you mean?"

"I don't know, Ira. I just have this uncomfortable feeling that I'm holding the wrong end of the stick. Perhaps my head will be clearer in the morning, I couldn't be more befuddled than I am now. You know, I completely forgot to ask Melanson if he has anybody who ought to be notified. If Dolores were alive, she'd know, of course; but with her gone, there just doesn't seem to be anyone who knows anything."

"Well," Ira replied sensibly, "if he has a wife or a mother or anybody, they'll have called the museum, don't you think?"

"It closes at five. There always used to be a night guard, but I doubt if he'll have been told about what happened this afternoon, assuming he hasn't been laid off. Surely the last place any connection of Melanson's might call would be the Charles Street jail. They'd phone the hospitals, or ask the police to. So that's a relief of sorts."

Sarah emitted a ladylike snort. "I don't know why I say

that. The problem is that I keep thinking I ought to be doing something and I can't think what to do."

"You've done more than enough tonight, Sarah. That poor slob was about ready to cash in his chips. He'd probably be dead by now if you hadn't intervened. You won't try to see him tomorrow, will you?"

"I doubt very much if they'd let me, since I'm not a family member or even a close friend. I'll call and see how he's doing, naturally; I can do that from my own house. I thought I'd drive over to Ireson's Landing in the morning and spend a little time with Anne. But I don't know about taking Davy with me. I'll have to keep up my disguise and I can't risk involving him."

"That's a relief," said Ira. "I was afraid you were planning to take him with you, and I'd promised to teach him how to call a minnow in Yiddish."

That got a giggle out of Sarah. "How do you call a minnow in Yiddish?"

"You go 'Fisch-e-le! Fisch-e-le!' "

"Oy!" Sarah was not at all surprised to feel tears running down her cheeks. Fischele, "little fish," was one of Max's pet names for her. If only he would call! All she had for a possible connection was the number of that bistro, or whatever they called their taverns in Argentina, and she had no idea whether it would be open at this hour. She didn't even know what hour it might be down there now. She tried to pretend she wasn't crying, but Ira had sensed her mood.

"Then you won't be needing my shirt tomorrow?"

"No, you can wear it this time." At least she could put on a decent pretense of cheerfulness. "One reason I want to go to my own house, if you really want to know, is that I need to collect some fresh underwear. Furthermore, I'm afraid I just won't be able to stand that awful getup of Charles's another day. I'm thinking seriously of pretending to be Aunt Bodie. Did I mention to you that the wig Charles fixed up for me is what remains of the beard in which he played Noah?"

"As in the ark?"

"The very same. Greater love hath no actor than that he sacrifice his beard to a fellow thespian. At least I'm trying to think of myself as a thespian, but it doesn't seem to be working all that well. I did fool Anne, she thought I was Aunt Calpurnia, who lives in Virgin Gorda and sails a sloop. But then Anne's better at flowers than she is at people. Getting back to Aunt Bodie, I might even drop in on her for a few minutes, just to let her know that she needn't bother attending my funeral. Uncle Jem said she was quite wrought up about it when she talked with him after that stupid obituary turned up in the paper. Goodness, I'm tired."

"I should think you might be. Put your hand down between your seat and the door. Can you feel a lever?"

"I think so. I can feel something metal sticking up."

"Good girl. Push it forward."

"I can't, it seems to be stuck."

"Then pull it back."

"Done it!"

Sarah found herself semi-recumbent and somewhat more comfortable than she'd felt sitting up. She shut her eyes and left Ira to play with the radio. When they got to the lake, Ira had to wake her up and walk her inside the cottage.

# Chapter 21

It was a halcyon morning. Sarah had meant to sleep late, but how could she with the breeze so soft and the songbirds so loud and Davy tugging at her hand and wonderful smells coming from the part of the cottage that had been more or less partitioned off for cooking and eating purposes? Luckily she'd had enough presence of mind to tuck a nightgown and a short cotton robe into her tote bag; she wore them to breakfast. Since the cottage was in an isolated spot, she kept them on afterward and wandered barefoot to the lake, wishing again that she'd brought a swimsuit.

But what did it matter? One could always wade, if one didn't mind the schools of minnows swishing against one's ankles and taking tiny sharp nips at one's toes. One didn't mind a bit, of course, particularly when one's small son was getting such a kick out of using his mother for bait to entice them into his minnow net. The heron was not around just now, but an American bittern was, harder to spot among the reeds because its neck was so much shorter and its drab-brownish camouflage so effective, but a sight worth seeing for all that.

The bittern was somewhere between two and three feet tall. There were touches of black on its wingtips and the end of its beak, and a V-shaped black necklace under the place where its chin would have been if birds had chins. But they didn't, and Davy wanted to know why. The best that Sarah could suggest was to ask Uncle Brooks when he and Aunt Theonia came home, as she fervently hoped they would. She was still tired and the bruises on her leg had turned into something the Museum of Modern Art might have liked to exhibit, but the knee was less bothersome. Checking her own problems, Sarah was reminded of Melanson's. When Ira came out to see the bittern, Sarah asked if he'd mind keeping an eye on Davy while she telephoned the intensive-care unit. She got an affirmative answer, as she'd confidently expected, and went inside to dial.

The report was nowhere near so positive as she'd hoped but less dire than she'd feared. Visits by members of the family, had there been any family, would have been discouraged. Visits by mere acquaintances were not to be thought of. So Sarah had the day off. She came back outdoors and stretched out in one of the old-style folding canvas deck chairs that the cottage provided and watched her son make sand castles. Miriam sat beside her under a beach umbrella that had seen its best days but still offered shade enough for practical purposes, and worked out a list of how many Rivkin relatives to invite in case Mike and Tracy ever got around to naming the fateful day.

"Sarah, you didn't really mean that about visiting your aunt Bodie, did you? My God, Tracy's mother's going to have fits when she sees this list. Hadn't you better lie low while you have the chance?"

"I am lying low." Sarah was in fact waving her wounded leg around in the air, trying a few careful knee bends. "I do think I ought to drop over and see Cousin Anne. Didn't you say Tracy's mother was coming to lunch?"

"Yes, and she's bringing her sister from Rehoboth, I should be so lucky. Jeanne's a doll, but I have to say I'm glad Iphigenia or whatever she calls herself—Imogene, Iolanthe, Ish Kabibble, who cares?—lives too far away to be dropping in. Not that she would because we're not classy enough. I was going to suggest that you might like to come down with a migraine about half past eleven, but having lunch with Anne is a much better idea. You could take some of that chicken we had last night."

"Oh, Miriam, I meant to tell you the sandwich I took to Melanson last night may have saved his life. That's what the intern said. He hadn't been able to eat anything until I managed to get him soothed down a bit, then he went after it like a starving wolf. He said thank you. That's about all he did say before he passed out. Well, if I'm going to Ireson's Landing, I suppose I'd better stir my stumps. I'll try to see Melanson tomorrow but I'll have to go as myself. He's had shocks enough already. I don't know what's to become of that poor soul if Turbot stays on the board and won't give him back his job."

"You really think Turbot could be that mean?"

"Oh yes," Sarah assured her sister-in-law. "He's mean enough for anything, he's proved that already, but he's cutting his own throat. With Melanson gone, there's nobody on the staff who actually knows how the museum should be run. Vieuxchamp's a cipher and the rest are all zombies."

"You don't suppose that's the real reason why Turbot fired Melanson?"

"Good heavens, Miriam, I hadn't thought of that angle. It seems bizarre that anybody could ever see Melanson as a threat, but everything's crazy about this situation. I do wish I could take Davy home with me, but Anne's not much interested in children and I'm feeling awfully skittish about letting anyone see him and me together, as you must be sick of hearing by now. He's having the time of his life here with you—oh, look, quick. The bittern is flying. I must fly too."

"I'll make you and Anne a little lunch while you're getting dressed. I've got to fix something for Jeanne and Her Highness anyway. You're not wearing that god-awful blouse again, are you?"

"I have to stay in costume, but I do think I'll put on a less depressing blouse and my old walking shoes instead of those holey sneakers. I might as well stick with the hat, it's no uglier than the one Aunt Bodie's been wearing for the past umpty-million years."

"Do you need help with your bandage?"

"No, the knee's pretty well scabbed over by now, a Band-Aid or two should serve the purpose. I'm going to wear those gray stockings again, I wish I'd had sense enough last night to wash them."

"That's okay, I rinsed them out and dried them in front of the oven. They're on your bed."

"Oh, bless you!"

Sarah took a quick and chilly shower, the plumbing in the cottage being adequate but only just, and put on the by now thoroughly antiqued gray flannel suit. She didn't try to do much about her face, the hat brim and the sunglasses would hide most of it. She'd got away just in time; as she switched on her blinker for the turn onto the highway, she spied a far grander car than the one she was driving, waiting to make the turn into the narrow road that led to the lake. In it were Miriam's likeable sister-in-law-to-be, whom Sarah had met once or twice, and a regally upright blonde with an impressive hairdo and a hoity-toity expression.

Thanks to Davy's early rising call, she'd had time to do the things she'd wanted and still make it to Ireson's Landing within a reasonable span for a picnic lunch. As she'd expected, Anne was right out there among the chrysanthemums, wearing the relatively new blue jeans that she'd bought after having donated her old ones to the unfortunate man in the rhubarb leaf. She had this pair pretty well broken in by now; after a few good soakings in detergent and bleach she might even be able to get the smell of fish entrails out of them.

Hearing the car come up the drive, Anne stripped off her canvas gloves and came over to Sarah. "How nice, I was hoping you'd come again. What would you think of massing white, yellow, and rust-colored mums in separate little free-form plots among those birch saplings down by the road? Just a sort of natural effect, but enough color to make a statement."

"What a marvelous idea!" Sarah replied. "If you keep on at this rate, we'll have tourists lining up to buy tickets. I hope you haven't eaten your lunch yet, Miriam packed us a basket."

"How kind of her. It's too bad she wasn't able to come with you."

Anne didn't mean what she said, she was just being polite. Miriam was too intellectual and far too liberal for Anne; neither of them actively disliked the other but they had virtually nothing in common. Miriam was not a whit interested in horticulture but wouldn't have minded talking about cooking as a fine art. To Anne, food was merely fertilizer for the human plant. All one had to do was administer the correct amounts of the proper mixtures at appropriate times. How the mixtures tasted was a matter of no great importance.

Anne did not balk, however, at eating the lioness's share of Miriam's excellent chicken salad, enhanced with chopped apples, celery, walnut meats, and Miriam's own special hand-whisked mayonnaise dressing, the recipe for which she intended to give Tracy as a wedding present. The corn muffins were from a mix, but Miriam allowed herself some latitude when on vacation.

They ate out on the deck overlooking the ocean. Even here, Sarah kept on her wig, her purple hat, and her sunglasses in case somebody might wander around behind the house; she didn't even want Mr. Lomax to know she'd been home. She was wearing the heavy old walking shoes that she'd got thoroughly banged up walking along the stony beach; she'd dropped the horrible blouse in the hamper, put on a cotton shirt that buttoned up almost to her chin, and added a scarf to hide the fact that her neck wasn't wrinkled.

Sarah even had Theonia's purple gloves handy to put on if anybody came, but nobody did. The cousins lingered over their meal, ate the sweet grapes that Miriam had put in for dessert, and drank big glasses of iced tea instead of hot, the day having turned out warmer than the weatherperson had predicted. Even Anne was in no hurry to get back to her chrysanthemums.

"I must remember to put in some mint for you, Sarah. Perhaps down by the carriage house. Mint's awfully grabby about nutrients, though. Maybe Mr. Lomax wouldn't mind bringing us a few more fishheads."

A person might have thought Anne was drinking something other than tea; this sudden burst of sociability was going to her head. Sarah wondered how Percy was taking it, then decided he wouldn't mind, particularly if Max should prove amenable to signing on with Kelling, Kelling, and Kelling as a client. Which brought her, by a somewhat circuitous route, to Elwyn Fleesom Turbot. She chose the obvious opening.

"Those stodgy flower beds of the Turbots' would look awfully sick beside what you're doing here. I don't suppose you've ever tried to drop a hint that there are better ways."

"Oh, no, I wouldn't dream of it." Anne was deadly serious. "Elwyn would go up like a rocket if anybody ever criticized anything he'd done, no matter how stupid it was."

"Lala must have a hard life of it then. Though she certainly didn't act afraid, from the way she was talking to him."

Anne permitted herself a chuckle. "I don't think Lala's afraid of anything, she's been through too much of that. Her first husband committed suicide. He told her he was going to kill himself, then deliberately ran his car into an abutment and smashed it all to pieces, himself with it. A brand-new Porsche; Lala was dreadfully upset for a long time. She told me the insurance company was quite nasty about settling, she never understood why. But they finally came through after she'd got a really mean lawyer, so she went on a round-the-world cruise and met this nice older man who owned a chain of furniture stores. Jules, his name was. They got married aboard the ship in Yokohama Harbor and just traveled around wherever they felt like going until one night in Venice when he'd had a little too much to drink and decided he'd go out for a walk to clear his head."

"Good heavens!"

"As they say, every street is Canal Street in Venice. I suppose the servant who opened the door thought Jules was just going to sit on the steps and have a smoke or hail a gondola or something. Jules was always inclined to be impetuous, Lala said. His real name was Julius, but she thought that was too stodgy for a man like him. Lala told me what attracted her to Elwyn was that he reminded her of Jules, but she didn't know then about the polled Herefords."

"How long has Lala been married to Mr. Turbot?" Sarah asked, not that she really wanted to know.

"About three years, I believe. Lala confessed to me in private that she'd had one or two little flings on the side when she was between husbands. I suspect it may have been more than one or two but there's no sense in trying to be judgmental these days, is there? Of course I'd never mention Lala's little flings to Percy, particularly since she doesn't seem to have got much of anything out of the extras. She made out very well with her settlements from Lambert and Jules, but she's inclined to be extravagant. You did notice all that gold jewelry, I expect, Sarah."

"How could I not? She was clanking like Marley's Ghost every time she moved her arms. Which she did very gracefully, I noticed. I wonder if perhaps she's been a model or a showgirl somewhere along the line."

Anne shook her head. "Nothing would surprise me about Lala. What did you think of that outfit she had on?"

"I thought it must have cost old Elwyn a pretty penny, since you asked. It did seem a bit much for a luncheon in the country; you looked just right in that daisy-print dress, Anne. But then, you always do."

"Why, thank you, Sarah. Percy told me so too. At least he said he was glad I didn't have foolish notions about dressing up like a circus horse to go and look at some cows. Percy can be quite witty, you know, though he doesn't care to have it mentioned outside the family. One knows what to expect with Percy, which is a great comfort. Can you imagine what it must be like for Lala, having to train one husband after another—oh, Sarah, please forgive me. I'd forgotten about poor darling Alexander.''

"That's all right, Anne. Aunt Caroline had Alexander trained long before he married me." Not that theirs had been much of a marriage, but Sarah was not about to go into that. "And Max didn't need any training, it's been more a case of his training me. But getting back to Lala, can that be her right name?"

"Now that you ask, I have no idea," Anne confessed. "We don't see a great deal of each other, actually, and when we do get together she never mentions her family. I have the impression that she comes from around here somewhere even though she looks and acts so New Yorky, and I know darned well she's a lot older than she lets on. Even Percy admits that. To tell the truth, he's not exactly crazy about Lala and I can't say I am, either. She's—oh, it's hard to say. Different. I shouldn't be talking like this about a client of Percy's, but I know you won't repeat a word to anybody and I must say it's a relief to let one's hair down once in a while."

"I'm glad you mentioned her age, I was wondering too. I'm also wondering how much longer that marriage is going to last. Have you any thoughts on the subject?"

"Why, I really can't say, I've never thought about it. I'm so used to people who stay married, you see. I don't recall a single one of the Kellings ever getting divorced. Even that silly business of Cousin Lionel's wife and that crazy woman she paired up with petered out fast enough once he'd made it clear that Vare wasn't going to get another cent of his money as long as she stayed with—Eeyore, was it?"

"No, Tigger," said Sarah. "Tigger's in a mental health care facility now and Vare's helping Lionel and their ghastly children spend Aunt Appie's fortune. Getting back to other people's marriages, what about Elwyn Turbot? Surely he must have had a previous marriage if he and Lala have only been together for three years. I can't picture him not wanting somebody around to browbeat."

Anne was giggling again. "I don't think Elwyn browbeats Lala much. I do remember Percy saying something about the first Mrs. Turbot's being drowned, but he didn't elaborate and I wasn't all that interested anyway. It wasn't as if I'd ever known her. If I remember correctly, she'd been dead awhile before Percy got the Turbot account."

"How long ago was that?"

"I'd have to ask Percy. I'm a National Landscape Judge for the Federation, you know, and have had to do quite a lot of traveling from time to time. What with that and trying to keep our own garden in some kind of shape and Percy in clean shirts and socks and underwear, not to mention Emily's two youngest having all those visits to the orthodontist, I've never given much thought to what was happening at the office. I mean, Percy doesn't come and help me judge the gardens, so why should I interfere with his adding machines? He understands. I can't say he's thrilled about coming home to an empty house and a TV dinner sometimes two or three nights in a row, but he does understand. Emily's good about inviting him over to dinner once a week or so, and Percy enjoys his grandchildren, in small doses."

"But you're not judging this year?" Sarah asked her. "I hope you didn't give it up for me."

"Oh no. I've done a little, mostly at flower shows. I do prefer to judge the landscaping but it takes a lot more out of one, so I thought I'd let some of the other judges fill in for a while. I wonder who'll get to judge this place."

Anne cast a wistful glance at some flats of barely opened mums that needed to be got into the ground. Sarah took the hint.

"I must be getting back to the lake, Anne. It should be

safe enough now, the ladies from Rehoboth will be on their way home. That's quite a drive, you know, almost to Fall River. And I do want to get in some more time with Davy because I'll probably have to go back to Boston tomorrow. Oh, one thing I forgot to ask. Who was that young fellow in the colonial getup who served the luncheon on Sunday? He wasn't the cook, was he?"

"No, the cook is his twin brother, if you can believe it. Tommy and Timmy, I think they're called. They tend Elwyn's precious cows and pinch-hit as household help when they have to, though they don't seem to like it much. They're some kind of relations of Elwyn's. Or Lala's, I've never been quite sure. Most likely Elwyn's, because of the cows. Between you and me, Percy thinks they've been in some kind of trouble and are out on parole, lying low. He also suspects they're Elwyn's own sons, resulting from what one might call extra-curricular activities either before or after the first Mrs. Turbot died."

"How old are they?"

"I can't say for sure. Twenty-five or thereabout; Percy might know. Lala doesn't like having them in the house; they have to sleep in the barn, which isn't so bad as it sounds. Elwyn's had a couple of rooms partitioned off with a bathroom and space heater and all that. Lala has housecleaners during the week but they won't come on weekends because that's the only time they can be with their families and all go to church together, which I think is rather nice. I don't see why the Turbots have to entertain at home on Sundays, Lala looks like the type who'd much rather be taken out to a good restaurant. That's what Percy would do. Percy's not a bit mean, you know, just careful."

"Yes, I've noticed," said Sarah. "Speaking of careful, you know that odd little episode I had on Sunday with the gray Toyota after I'd picked up my car at your house—and, by the way, I don't know if I ever thanked you properly for that lovely bouquet, what with all the to-do about Dolores Tawne's turning up dead. Well, I had noticed at the Turbots' that the twin who served us was not at all happy about having to do it. I'm wondering now if those fellows might have been the twins working off a bit of spite against the one member of the party they thought would be the most vulnerable."

"I wouldn't put it past them. Shall I ask Percy what he thinks?"

"Please do. He might know what sort of car they drive, assuming they haven't lost their licenses. He may even remember the registration, he has such a phenomenal head for figures. Maybe Percy wouldn't mind phoning me at the lake this evening. I did give you the number, didn't I? Have him reverse the charges, of course."

Sarah gave Anne a peck on the cheek, made sure she hadn't left any of the bright plastic plates and cups or the bamboo-handled cutlery out of Miriam's elegant picnic basket, let her gray stockings bag a little more, and got back on the road.

# Chapter 22

"Telephone, Sarah."

"Thank you, Ira."

Sarah would far rather have stayed down by the lake and watched a heron catch its supper, but this must be Percy calling collect. She turned Davy over to his uncle and ran back to the cottage.

"Hello, Percy, how good of you to call. Yes, we had a lovely time together, I had no idea what an accomplished landscaper Anne is. No, I quite agree, Max would feel the same. I don't know when he'll be back, Percy, but I hope it will be soon. What a lovely idea, we'll make a real celebration of it."

Since Percy wasn't paying for the call, he was quite willing to wax loquacious. Sarah had a bit of a struggle getting him around to the one thing she needed to know.

"Percy, can you tell me if the Turbots' two cowboys drive a gray Toyota, and if so, do you know the year and the registration number? It's important, or I wouldn't be asking."

Percy knew, and he told. Sarah couldn't remember afterward whether she'd thanked him. Percy need not be sworn to secrecy; far would it be from him to squeal on an important client's illegitimate sons, or whatever they were, unless he had to. However, Sarah lost no time putting in a call to the

Boston police, who promised to call the Foxford police, who in turn telephoned the cottage to let its temporary residents know that they were scooping up the twins on a charge of attempted vehicular homicide. They sounded happy to do so; they'd been trying for some time to pin those unprintable persons on a major offense, and were pressing for a denial of bail, which they would get on the strength of the malefactors' previous records.

Sarah went to bed a good deal easier in her mind than she'd felt since Sunday morning. With her would-be murderers safely locked up, she would not have to go through that distasteful dressing-up performance again tomorrow morning. She could even take Davy back to Ireson's Landing and resume their normal life, though she hated to separate him from his new friends the minnows and the herons.

But there was still the problem of the Wicked Widows and Dolores Tawne's death by hatpin, not to mention all those hypothetical stickpins in Dolores's safe deposit box. As executrix, Sarah had a responsibility to see this enigma through to a resolution. Now there was also Joseph Melanson to be considered; she'd phone the hospital in the morning and find out whether he was sufficiently recovered to be allowed a visitor.

Sarah had always been an early bird, Davy must take after her side of the family. He was up with the sun, tugging at her to come and see the pretty bird with the funny hat on. Sarah recognized a kingfisher, nattily dressed in its white clerical collar and russet-banded white waistcoat, its touseled crest and back exactly the right shade of blue. As she and Davy watched, the kingfisher swooped down over the water and came up with a minnow. Sarah hoped its prey hadn't been one of her son's special pals.

"Come on, Davy. Let's find ourselves a bite to eat."

Sarah got milk and bread out of the camp-sized refrigerator, fixed herself a cup of tea and a piece of toast and her son a mug of milk and a bread-and-butter sandwich. They took their snack down to the beach. Davy offered a bite of his sandwich to the kingfisher but it wasn't interested. Sarah had to explain that not all birds were like those ducks in the Public Gardens who chased after all comers, demanding largesse with ear-piercing squawks.

Miriam and Ira came wandering down to the lake about half past seven. They all watched the kingfisher awhile, then Miriam scooted them back to the cottage for a proper break-fast. After that, they sat around doing nothing in particular until Ira guessed he'd better phone the garage.

As soon as Ira had been reassured that nobody had walked off with his livelihood, Sarah put in her call to the hospital. Mr. Melanson had been upgraded from acute to merely criti-cal, which she supposed ought to be taken as good news. The police officer who was guarding him had stipulated that nobody except another guard or a Mrs. Sarah Bittersohn was to be admitted. Was this Mrs. Bittersohn speaking? Sarah assured the voice on the other end that she was indeed Mrs. Bittersohn, that she was glad to hear Mr. Melanson was being properly guarded, and that she would come to the hospital between half past ten and eleven o'clock, if the time was acceptable.

Pleasantly surprised to learn that it was, Sarah went to do something about her hair now that she didn't have to wear Noah's beard any longer. The blouse she'd worn back from Ireson's Landing yesterday would do for today with a little touch-up. The gray one that she'd bought with the flannel suit and hardly got to wear was still hanging in the downstairs bedroom closet at Tulip Street; it would come in handy if she couldn't get back from Boston tonight. She pressed out the white blouse and the overworked skirt with an aged electric iron and a damp linen dish towel and was ready to travel.

Fortunately Davy was not the whining kind, a child so young would never have been allowed in the intensive-care unit. She'd have had to park him with Egbert and Uncle Jem, who'd probably have sung him naughty songs and offered him a martini; he was much better off here with the heron. Davy bore his mother's departure with equanimity and presented her with a pure white gull's feather as a going-away present. She stuck it in her lapel and set off for Boston.

The traffic was more incoming than outgoing at this time of day. Sarah entered the sprawling great hospital on the dot of ten-thirty, found the cardiac unit after a few false twists and turns, and saw to her relief that the policeman guarding Melanson was her good friend Officer Drummond.

"Good morning, Officer Drummond, what a nice surprise to find you here. How's the patient doing?"

"He hasn't said. Maybe you can get him to talk."

"I'll try."

Sarah stepped to the patient's bedside, trying not to startle him or trip over any of the paraphernalia that surrounded his bed. He was lying very still but didn't look any worse than he had two nights before. "Hello, Mr. Melanson. I'm glad you wanted to see me, and sorry that I forgot to bring you another chicken sandwich. You don't mind if I pull this chair closer to your bed? Be sure to let me know if I'm tiring you. Or boring you."

"Never. Good to come." Those few words left the patient gasping for breath, but he seemed relieved to have uttered them.

"Not at all," Sarah replied as enthusiastically as she could manage in the presence of so many tubes and bottles and mysterious machines. "What was it you wanted to see me about?"

He took a while remembering. "Oh. Presents."

She didn't quite catch the word, was it presence or presents? She tried the latter. "Do you mean birthday presents, that sort of thing?"

"Christmas presents. Dolores's bag."

"Dolores was doing the Christmas shopping early and had bought a bagful of presents, is that right?"

"Yes, all wrapped. Pretty paper, red ribbons. All the same. Whole bagful."

"Was it a big bag or a small one?"

"Medium. Full of presents."

"They couldn't have been very big presents, then."

"No. Not big. Like medal boxes. I got a medal once. For spelling."

"Good for you. When was it that you saw Dolores with the presents, Mr. Melanson? Can you recall the date?"

"August thirty-first. My birthday. No present for me." The wraith in the bed managed somehow to dredge up a wry attempt at a smile. How long had it been since anybody had remembered this bashful old ditherer's birthday?

Sarah smiled back. "Then we'll have to give you a belated party when you get out of the hospital. You can be thinking about what you'd like for a present. As for Dolores, some people do like to get their Christmas shopping done in the summertime. Did she mention whom her presents were for?"

"Not hers. Keeping them for a friend."

This was interesting. "She didn't happen to mention the friend's name?"

"Ages on the deep. Out of touch. It happens." Melanson fell silent, Sarah waited. He drew a long breath. "Made her happy. Trusted."

"The friend was trusting her to guard the presents but not to open them, was that it? Do you know where Dolores took them?"

"Home? Took them to lunch, came back without them." Melanson was talking less painfully now. "Never mentioned it again. All those pretty presents. Water, please?"

"Let me pour it for you, here's a straw to suck through. No, don't try to raise your head, you might joggle some of those tubes loose. That's a good patient."

He drank, paused, drank again. Sarah gave him a short rest before she asked her next question. "Did Dolores happen to mention her friend's name?"

"Silly name. *V* for victory."

"It wouldn't happen to be LaVonne LaVerne, by any chance?"

"Stupid name. *V* for vulgar."

"Yes, isn't it? Dolores must have been itching to open those presents, don't you think? But she wouldn't have broken her trust, would she?"

"Not poke my nose into other people's business."

Melanson was perking up, attempting to burlesque Dolores Tawne's booming voice. He didn't do it well, but the fact that he'd tried at all was heartening. Sarah laughed, as needs she must. Melanson shrugged as well as he could under his freight of tubes and wires. She could see that he was beginning to wane; she'd better leave.

"I'm so glad we've had this talk, Mr. Melanson, but I think I'd better go now and let you get some rest. I don't want to tire you out."

"Come again?"

"Oh yes, if your nurses will let me. I'll ask on the way out."

"Thank you. Worried. Friends not getting presents. Stupid of me. Dolores didn't want friends. Only slaves."

The sick man shut his eyes and slipped at once into what Sarah hoped was peaceful sleep. She went out to the front desk, where Officer Drummond was having a cozy cup of coffee with the attendant on duty.

"All set, Mrs. Bittersohn?" he asked her. "How did it go?"

"Quite well, I think." She turned to the white-uniformed woman behind the desk. "I'm leaving now. Mr. Melanson asked me to come back. Is that all right?"

"I'd suggest you wait till tomorrow. The patient's in a fragile condition, we don't want to wear him out. Are you his daughter?"

"No, just a friend. Mr. Melanson has no relatives that I

know of, but my husband and I have been acquainted with him for quite some time. Is he going to pull through?"

"We hope so." The attendant had her eyes on the monitors and no time to waste on visitors. "Tomorrow, okay?"

It must be getting on for lunchtime. Sarah could hear the rattling of trays on serving carts. She asked Drummond if he had someone to relieve him at mealtimes.

"Yes, ma'am," he assured her. "As soon as Officer Maule shows up, which should be any minute now, I'm through for the day. Seeing as how I've been on duty here since midnight, I don't mind leaving."

"Then perhaps you'll let me buy you a lunch, with a string attached. Mr. Melanson's just told me something about Dolores Tawne that should be looked into."

"Hey, how about that? What's a twelve-hour shift if I get to play cops and robbers afterward? Where were you planning to eat, Mrs. Bittersohn?"

"Wherever you say. I did think we might go back to that café in Kenmore Square, then drop in on Mrs. Fortune. By the way, have you heard that those two young fiends who tried to run me over are now in the county prison without the option of bail because they have such awful previous records? I'll tell you about it over lunch; would you mind if we went in my car? It's not mine, actually, but that's part of the story."

"No I wouldn't mind a bit," Drummond assured her. "One of the cruisers dropped me off here last night and I was planning to go home on the T. I live in Watertown, so Kenmore Square's on my way. Ah, here's my relief."

Officer Maule was a woman in her middle years. She looked smart and purposeful in her uniform, good nature and common sense showed in her face; Melanson would be in good hands. Sarah nodded to Drummond and they went to get the car.

"There's no special reason why we have to let Lieutenant Harris know in advance what we're planning to do, is there? You're off duty and I'm the executrix."

Sarah knew she was babbling as they neared the car, having

somehow found a parking space quite near the right entrance. She had to keep telling herself that nothing bad was going to happen this time and nothing did; except that after a day or two of Miriam's cooking, the food at the café tasted rather flat. Since Drummond hadn't had anything but a hospital breakfast, he thought it was just the ticket. Sarah urged him to order a second helping, he settled for a banana split on account of the potassium in the banana and ate every bite like a good cop while she dawdled over a cup of coffee and wondered whether she should have phoned Mrs. Fortune for an appointment. Too late now; she paid the check and stood up to go.

# Chapter 23

"Is Mrs. Fortune available? Please tell her Mrs. Bittersohn and Officer Drummond would like to speak with her for just a few minutes."

Luckily Mrs. Fortune was indeed available, and in a somewhat better humor today. "Well, we meet again. Don't tell me you've found the key to another box, Mrs. Bittersohn."

"No, two are quite enough, thank you. I suppose the inventory ought to be next on the agenda, but today I only want to ask you a question. Could you tell me, please, when Mrs. Tawne last visited her box? I believe it would have been August 31 of this year, but I need to have it verified. Were you working that day?"

"Let's see, that was on a Wednesday. Yes, I must have been." She flipped through the back pages of her desk calendar. "Right, she came in just about noontime. I remember because I was planning to meet a friend for lunch at half past twelve and I knew Mrs. Tawne would make a big production out of whatever she'd come for; she always did. This time she had a shopping bag, one of those fancy ones you get at stationery stores. It had a big Santa Claus with a lot of holly and stuff on the sides and was full of Christmas presents. At least I assumed they were, she had them all wrapped up in Christmas paper and tied with narrow red ribbons, the real satin kind with picot edging. It looked to me as though she was rushing the season, but naturally I didn't say anything."

"Did she?" Sarah didn't know why she asked; Dolores would surely have been saying something.

"Oh yes," Mrs. Fortune replied. "She was running on about some old friend of hers who'd come begging her to do a very special errand because she was the only one who could be trusted to do it right, and so forth and so forth. I was impatient for her to give me her box key and let me get on with my part of the job, but she kept rummaging around in that great big leather sack she always carried until I thought I was going to scream. Finally she said, " 'Oh, darn it! I haven't time to make another trip, I'll have to use this one.' "

"Which key was she talking about?"

"Good question. At the time I thought she was just going through one of her usual performances. I have to say it didn't make any sense to me at the time because we always give our box holders duplicate keys, as you probably know. Anyway, she fiddled around a little longer and finally came up with her usual key. I got her box out for her and opened up one of the cubicles. She stuffed herself in with her Santa Claus bag, her box, and her handbag, if that's what you call something the size of a mail carrier's pouch, locked the door and spent far too long to suit me transferring the presents from the bag to the box. At least I assume she did, she came out with an empty bag and the box weighed a lot more when I put it back than it had when I took it out for her. Naturally I missed my luncheon date and she buzzed off without even bothering to say good-bye. I could have—well, I'd better not say what I was thinking by then."

"I understand perfectly," said Sarah. "She affected everybody pretty much the same way, if it's any comfort to you. Thank you so much, Mrs. Fortune, you've been a real help. I'll be back with Mrs. Tawne's lawyer as soon as he sets up an appointment with your people about the inventory, but I'll make very sure it's not scheduled to interfere with your lunch hour. By the way, has anybody shown up yet with a second key for the LaVerne box?''

''No, not yet. But they will, you can bet on that.''

Another box holder claimed Mrs. Fortune's attention; Sarah and her bodyguard took the hint. As they left the bank, Drummond asked, ''Did you get what you came for, Mrs. Bittersohn?''

Sarah shrugged. ''I'm afraid to say yes, but I can't say no. My guess is that whoever sent Dolores that bagful of alleged Christmas presents had instructed her to put them in the LaVerne box, the one that had been sitting unused all these years, quite possibly for just this purpose.''

''That's pretty crazy, isn't it?''

''You just don't know collectors. A really dedicated one might wait half a lifetime or more and resort to incredible dodges to get hold of one particular object that he's set his heart on. But anyway, what I started to say was that Mrs. Tawne, in her excitement over getting another assignment from her old connection, must have forgotten to bring the right key for the LaVerne box. Considering how long ago she'd hidden the key, she might easily have lost track of where she'd put it. She'd have been in a mad rush, as she always was; rather than spend half an hour pawing through that great big sack she always carried or going home to look for the key, she'd have made a snap decision to put the packages in her own box and switch them when she got the chance. But then some new crisis came along, and she forgot about the Christmas packages as she naturally would, being Dolores.''

''Kind of a flake, was she?''

''Not really. It's just that she always took on a little more than she could handle, and the latest job took precedence over the one before. So there they sit, and I don't know what to do about them. And there's poor Dolores, waiting to be reduced to a little heap of ashes, if it hasn't happened already. I must check with the undertaker about that. I suppose whoever murdered her Sunday afternoon was working on the principle of 'kill the messenger.' What do you think, Officer Drummond?''

"I think we'd better get hold of Lieutenant Harris." Drummond's last few words were obscured by an unstemmable yawn. Sarah took pity on him.

"And I think you should go straight home and get some sleep. Catch yourself a Watertown car; I'll talk to the lieutenant. Where's a pay phone that works, I wonder?"

Drummond yawned again and pointed. Sarah fumbled for a quarter and dialed police headquarters. She learned from the desk sergeant that Lieutenant Harris was at the Wilkins Museum; that was fine with her. She kept a quasi-maternal eye on Drummond until she'd seen him safely down the subway stairs and went on to where she'd parked the car Ira had borrowed for her. The car had acquired a parking ticket. Sarah thought of having it framed and presented to Officer Drummond as a memento, but he'd no doubt seen far too many parking tickets already.

There was a for-pay parking lot not far from the museum. She paid her fee like a virtuous citizen and walked over, noting that Harris's car was illegally parked at the entrance. Just behind it was an opulent vehicle that must be Elwyn Fleesom Turbot's; Sarah could hear the head of trustees in full cry even before she'd set foot inside the lobby. Why wasn't Turbot off at some criminal lawyer's office trying to find an attorney bloody-minded enough to act for his villainous twins? She made rather a point of ignoring him.

"Oh, there you are, Lieutenant Harris. I have some information that Officer Drummond thought you should hear as quickly as possible. Is there someplace where we can talk?"

"You can talk in front of me," growled Turbot. "I happen to be the executive in charge here, in case you've forgotten."

This was much too good an opening to ignore. "On the contrary, Mr. Turbot," Sarah replied sweetly. "I seldom forget anything. Right now I'm remembering the lawsuit that Joseph Melanson's lawyer is about to bring against you for criminal harassment. If he fails to recover from the inhuman treatment to which you subjected him, the charge will of course become either manslaughter or first-degree murder."

"What the hell are you talking about? I got a confession out of him, didn't I? Any of the guards will tell you that, they were witnesses. I sent Melanson to jail because he's a goddamn murderer."

"No, you didn't, Mr. Turbot. You sent an innocent man to jail because you're a loud-mouthed bully who needed to show the staff what a big, tough he-man they've got for a boss. You picked Melanson as a target for the sole reason that he was the one you knew would be easiest to intimidate. Anybody with half an eye could have seen that Joseph Melanson is one of those over-conscientious worriers who are afraid of their own shadows. He could no more have killed Dolores Tawne than a mouse could kill a cat."

"The hell he couldn't. He confessed, damn it, right here where I'm standing."

"I know he did. After the way you'd been yelling and browbeating and humiliating him in front of his co-workers, Melanson would have confessed to raping your great-grand-mother, just to get away from the sound of your disgusting voice. I saw him night before last in a prison cell, and so did Lieutenant Harris; he was virtually catatonic. If he'd been left alone in that cell all night without any medical attention, he would very likely have been found dead yesterday morning."

"Ah, you bleeding hearts. The bastard was faking."

"He was not faking. We were both with Mr. Melanson when he collapsed from a heart attack. Fortunately he was near enough to the hospital to be treated in time. I wasn't allowed to see him yesterday, Lieutenant Harris, but I did go this morning."

"How's he doing?"

"So-so. He's in intensive care, of course, and very weak. His heart isn't good, I learned that he'd been getting treatment from his own doctor for some time. He kept digitalis in his locker and took it regularly during his morning and afternoon breaks and at lunchtime, or would have if Mr. Turbot hadn't put on that show of histrionics and kept him from getting at it. It appears to have been a combination of not getting his medicine and the shock of being arrested for a crime he was incapable of committing that triggered Melanson's heart attack. Right now, it's touch and go. I did manage to exchange a few words with him in the hospital."

"Is that what you want to talk with me about?" Harris asked.

"Yes, it is. Maybe we could go up to the chapel, if Mr. Turbot will excuse us. There are seldom many visitors there on a weekday and I'd prefer not to be overheard."

Turbot doggedly refused to be excluded; Sarah decided there was no point in making a scene. The dark-brown paneled walls and heavy chandeliers, in need of a cleaning which they probably wouldn't get now that Dolores was gone, struck the proper note of solemnity. She sat down in one of the carved oaken chairs and motioned for Harris to take the one beside it.

"What I heard from Melanson is about Dolores Tawne. On the Friday before she was killed, she got a phone call from an old acquaintance whom she hadn't heard from for many years. The caller wanted her to do a favor, quite a simple one but something that could only be entrusted to a true and loyal friend. Dolores had always prided herself on her probity, she was only too glad to say yes."

"Damn fool," growled Turbot.

Sarah ignored him. "What it came down to, Lieutenant Harris, was that the friend would send some packages to be kept in a long-unused safe deposit box to which Dolores had the key. A messenger would bring them to the museum before lunchtime. When she got them, she must immediately take the packages to the bank and put them in the empty box.

"Dolores was excited at getting her finger into this interesting new pie, she let Melanson see the bagful of what they both took to be Christmas presents. Melanson thought they were pretty, little boxes all in holiday wrappings and tied with red ribbons. This was on the thirty-first of August, which happened to be Melanson's birthday and gave him a special reason to recall the incident."

"So?" said Harris.

"So it appears that Dolores did not put the packages in the bank at once, as she'd been told to do. It wasn't until lunchtime that she showed up at the bank. And then she couldn't find the key she wanted. According to Mrs. Fortune, who has charge of the safe deposit boxes, Dolores made a great fuss, then decided to use her own box, to which she did have the key."

"Have we come to the punch line yet, Mrs. Bittersohn?"

"Almost, Lieutenant. Do you remember the day I was deliberately run down and nearly killed by somebody driving a gray 1989 Toyota, license number seven-five-three-two KG?"

Sarah thought she saw Turbot wince, but she couldn't be sure. "That was the day Officer Drummond and I went to the bank, after I'd learned that I was Dolores's executrix. You may not remember my telling you about the stickpins in her safe deposit box; you were talking on your car phone and it sounded as if you were being shot at."

"Ah yes, I remember it well," said Harris. "The shooting, that is. You'd better refresh my memory on the stickpin part. You'd already been to Mrs. Tawne's studio, right?"

"Right. That's where I got the safe deposit key that you'd already found, plus a different one that I found under the paper lining in her bottom dresser drawer. The second box turned out to have been rented in the name of LaVonne LaVerne back in the sixties. Dolores Tawne had been paying rent on the box for approximately thirty years, but it had never once in all that time been opened. As executrix, I got to open it, and found nothing inside except six old-fashioned steel hatpins and some photographs of a group of women in fancy dress, whom my uncle Jeremy Kelling identified as the Wicked Widows."

"Oh yeah, you mentioned them before. So what's the story?"

"Knowing Dolores as I did, I surmised that she'd been instructed to put the packages, unopened, in the box which had presumably been kept ready for that particular purpose. Having taken on too many responsibilities at the Wilkins, however, she dashed off to the bank forgetting the key that she'd hidden in the drawer, most likely at the time the box was first rented. She may even have forgotten where she'd left it; she was a great fusser and a demon for getting things done, no matter how. It would have been like her to shove the packages into her own box, meaning to change them over when she found the right key, and race back to the museum on some desperate mission like trimming the peacocks' claws, forgetting all about the mixup she'd left at the bank."

"Mixup? My God! If they're in her box with no identification on them—my God! Don't you realize what she's done, you dumb little half-wit?"

Turbot took a threatening step toward Sarah; Harris forestalled him. "Kindly control yourself, Mr. Turbot. As executrix, Mrs. Bittersohn, you were entitled to open whatever you found in Mrs. Tawne's box. This would include the wrapped packages. Did you open them?"

"I opened some of them," Sarah replied. "They were velvet-covered jewelers' boxes, each containing an antique gold stickpin. One had a cluster of emeralds and opals in an elaborate baroque setting, another a diamond of perhaps ten carats surrounded by alternating sapphires and rubies. I can't tell you what they'd sell for in today's market, even as single pieces. As a collection, which I surmise the packages to be, they might be worth more, assuming the stones are genuine. My husband could give you an estimate, and also tell you who stole them, like as not. Since I can't do that, I thought the sensible course would be to leave the packages just as I found them until Mrs. Tawne's lawyer makes an appointment with me, the bank officer, and somebody from the Treasury Department to open the box and evaluate the contents.''

''The Treasury Department?'' Turbot was past roaring, he sounded as if he were being strangled.

''Oh yes, I believe they always have to be—catch him, Lieutenant, he's having a heart attack.''

Turbot was not having a heart attack. He was simply so engorged with fury that he'd cut off his own breath. Sarah was all for shipping him off to the hospital on general principles, but Harris had encountered this kind of situation before. He performed some arcane variation of the Heimlich maneuver that got the head of trustees back into bellowing condition quite easily. Needless to say, he got no thanks.

''That goddamn woman!'' Turbot bellowed. ''If she were still alive, I'd kill her myself. Can't you get it through your head—''

''If you mean me, I understand you perfectly,'' Sarah replied with her sweetest smile. ''Was there something else you'd like to say, Mr. Turbot?''

What Turbot had to say was not the sort of language that ought to be used in a chapel. Sarah felt a surge of gratitude that Aunt Bodie was not among those present.

''Please don't bother to run Mr. Turbot in on my account,'' she told the lieutenant. ''Mr. Turbot's had such a string of mishaps lately. I realize he's terribly disappointed that those prankish twins of his muffed his instructions to run me over on Monday. No doubt he still feels that Officer Drummond was taking too much upon himself when he pulled me out from under the wheels of that gray 1989 Toyota sedan, registration number seven-five-three-two KG.''

Turbot had not expected this. ''You're lying! It can't have been the twins.''

''There were witnesses, Mr. Turbot. Don't forget this happened right in Kenmore Square, at a busy time of the day. People notice such things, you know. Officer Drummond took down the registration number as soon as he'd snatched me away from the wheels and got me up on the sidewalk. I'd already recognized the car. I'd seen it before, on Sunday afternoon, when I'd left your house and you'd sent your two cowboys to run me off the road because I'd foolishly revealed at the table that I knew too much about stolen paintings in general and the Wilkins Museum in particular."

Sarah was about as angry as she'd ever been. "You shouldn't have been so quick to underestimate a dumb little cutie-pants, Mr. Turbot. You must be upset at having both your sons denied bail because of their terrible police records, but I'm afraid you can't have been a good father to them."

"I'm not a father at all, damn it! How can you call those two hyenas mine? If you think I'd ever—good God, who's that?"

There had never been any electricity installed in Madam Wilkins's palazzo during her lifetime, and according to the terms of her will, there must never be any changes. The only illumination came from gas jets and candles. Here in the chapel, a rack of votive candles was set below and to the left of the altar, but only a few of the cups were alight. Those inside the room could see nothing but a silhouette in the doorway. It was that of a woman who might have been dressed for that sumptuous opening-day blowout when Madam Wilkins first flung wide her doors to the cream of Boston society.

The woman gave an impression of great height, but the illusion may have been created by the huge cartwheel hat that she wore very much to one side. Her face was veiled in a great swath of black net, its ends tossed back over her shoulders. Her gown fitted her tightly down to the mid-thighs, then fanned out in a great pouf that concealed her nether limbs.

Sarah had known for some time that Lydia Ouspenska was going to regild some of the museum's more decrepit frames when she got the chance. It would not have been beyond Lydia to dress for the occasion, as Peter Paul Rubens had been wont to do; but this outfit was something else, and Sarah knew what. She snatched up one of the paper spills that Dolores had always kept handy to light the votive candles with and went quickly down the line, touching off wicks until there were enough of the small flames alight to see by. Even so, the silence, with that startling figure still poised in the doorway, was eerie.

Sarah was in no mood for any more histrionics. "Lieutenant Harris," she said calmly, "may I present you to Miss LaVonne LaVerne, who is, I presume, the last of the Wicked Widows? I know you never talk, Miss LaVerne, but aren't you supposed to flap your veil or something? We'd be delighted to get a better look at that Mona Lisa mask you're wearing. Your old friend Dolores Tawne did a superb job on those masks, didn't she? It's a great shame you felt it necessary to kill her. I marvel that you got those stickpins away from Mr. Turbot without killing him first."

Sarah had no idea why she was so recklessly taunting a murderess who'd killed four Boston policemen, six Wicked Widows, and heaven only knew how many others, not counting the woman who'd been true to her trust and bragged about it. Right now, Dolores ought to be here in the chapel, dusting the altar and scraping wax out of these votive candle holders that were getting so badly smoked up. As Sarah had anticipated, the housekeeping was already going to pot.

Either the Wicked Widow didn't hear or didn't care. Ignoring Sarah, she glided without a sound toward Harris, her black-gloved arms and black-sheathed torso writhing in a sensuous, hypnotic rhythm. The lieutenant stood frozen, his police revolver still in its holster. Turbot was worse than useless, standing there with his mouth agape. For once, no sound was coming out. Sarah stepped out of her shoes, slipped around behind the Wicked Widow, and climbed up on one of the long oaken benches, as close as she could get to Harris and Turbot.

The Widow appeared to be in an ecstatic trance, working her serpentine way closer and closer to those two mesmerized males, sliding away, swooping back, stalking her prey like a cobra. Standing on the bench, Sarah had a bird's eye view of that enormous hat. She could make out the curved backs of the combs that had been sewn inside the brim and anchored in the too-coarse, too-abundant raven hair. A wig, for sure. Good.

Now the Widow was literally chest-to-chest with Harris. He'd be unable to get his gun free of its underarm holster without having to wrestle her for it. Now she was pressing even tighter against him, raising her black-gloved right hand above her head, fishing for the weapon she expected to find there. That was when Sarah shoved the cartwheel hat, wig and all, down over the Mona Lisa mask, grabbed two handfuls of the black mourning veil and crossed them at the back of the Widow's neck, cutting off a howl the likes of which she hoped never to hear again.

"Shut up, Miss LaVerne, or I'll strangle you. Lieutenant, get that mask off her."

Sarah kicked contemptuously at the object which had fallen clear of the wig, a slim blade of polished steel about seven inches long, blunt all around and set into a sphere of black plastic about the size of a golf ball. "Was this the best you could do in lieu of a hatpin, Miss LaVerne? Handcuff her, Lieutenant, and tie her legs with this veil so she can't try to run off. Just to put your mind at ease, Miss LaVerne, we have all seven of your hatpins, the six that Dolores had kept in the bank and the one you'd already used to kill off the rest of the Widows and goodness knows how many others before poor Dolores inadvertently crossed you up about that safe deposit box she'd been paying your rent on all those years. I'm afraid this is the end of the Wicked Widows, Miss LaVerne."

# Chapter 24

Most embarrassingly, the last of the LaVonne LaVernes was also Mrs. Elwyn Fleesom Turbot. And crazy as a coot, which came as no surprise to Sarah Kelling Bittersohn. Once Lala got it through her head that she'd been duly trapped and put out of commission, she began to talk. She talked all the way in the police van, at the station, in the lockup. There was no stopping her short of a bullet or a hatpin.

Sarah didn't get to hear much of Lala's ramblings firsthand. However, Lieutenant Harris was kind enough to stop by the Tulip Street house when at last he could get away from that human talking-machine to take a statement from Sarah and a well-earned drink from Charles.

"That Mrs. Turbot's really something else, I can tell you. The Wicked Widows thing was all her doing. She'd got bored with her husband of the moment—she's a lot older than she looks, in case you hadn't noticed—and talked a few of her girlfriends, who must have been as crazy as she is, into getting an act together. She could talk anybody into anything, it seems; she was like a witch or something. I don't know how many poor slobs she married. I figured it as seven verifiables, five probables, about twenty possibles, and the rest doubtful. Some of them survived the marriages, I don't know how many didn't. There seem to have been a disproportionate number of suicides that will have to be checked out, not that it's going to help the poor guys now."

"What about the twins?" Sarah asked him.

"Oh, Mrs. Turbot's pretty bitter about that pair. They're her own sons and they've done her wrong. They stole her hatpin and brought it to your husband's office because they were afraid she intended to kill their stepfather with it and keep them from inheriting his cattle, of which they seem to be quite fond. They didn't seem to be showing any qualms about having tried to run you down, Mrs. Bittersohn, but their mother's furious with you for having been so discourteous as to survive after they'd gone to the bother of running your obituary in the paper. Somehow or other, Mrs. Turbot's decided this mess was all your fault. She made a big scene in the van about the jewels you and Dolores Tawne allegedly stole from her."

"How so, Lieutenant?"

"This one's straight off the wall. It seems that when she was a young girl, back in the early fifties, she'd heard her father talking about this man Turbot who'd inherited a lot of valuable stickpins. He kept them in some hiding place where nobody ever got to see them, so I don't know what good they'd be to him, but there they were and she wanted them, sight unseen. His people were pretty well-heeled and he stood to inherit the family business, so it looked like a good deal all around to—Laura, was it?"

"Could be," said Sarah. "I've only heard her called Lala. Charles, please cut Lieutenant Harris another sandwich or two and make some coffee. He's had a hard day."

"So have you, Mrs. Bittersohn." Harris reached for a sandwich. "Thanks, Charles. So anyway, the girl never forgot about the stickpins but she never happened to run across the man who had them. That didn't slow her down any, she married two or three or four different guys and organized her Wicked Widows troupe to relieve the monotony. That was how she got involved with Mrs. Tawne. Thinking ahead, she got her to rent a safe deposit box to be held in LaVonne LaVerne's name until such time as she'd need it to hold all those fabulous stickpins she was going to wheedle out of Turbot after she'd got her hooks into him."

"So she just kept on marrying and tossing out the rejects until the big fish came along, is that it?" Jeremy Kelling asked.

"That's it in a nutshell, Mr. Kelling. As you can imagine, she had to be out of the country pretty often on account of her peculiar hobby, but eventually she came back and who should she run into at some charity ball or somewhere but Mr. and Mrs. Elwyn Turbot. So she made sure this was the Turbot with the stickpins and sharpened her own trusty hatpin. Two months later, Turbot was a widower. That was kind of a poignant moment," Harris reflected. "There we all were in the van, her babbling on like a brook and him not saying a word for most of the ride. But when she got to the late Mrs. Turbot, the poor guy lost it. " 'You killed Agnes?' " he bellowed. " 'Damn it, Lala, I *liked* Agnes!' "

# Chapter 25

Whether the twins who had been so effectively brainwashed by their mother could ever be turned into normal human beings had developed into a subject for warm public debate by a covey of psychiatrists. Whether Lala Turbot had ever been or wanted to be anything but a serial killer of a peculiarly seductive type was not even debatable; she had regressed to a howling madwoman, treatable only by heavy sedation and physical restraints.

The death certificates on the six other LaVonne LaVernes that Sarah had suggested Lieutenant Harris look up early in the game were also public property by now and giving the media a prolonged Walpurgisnacht such as the old Hub of the Universe had not experienced since the panic over the Boston Strangler back in the early fifties. Sarah was not interested, she had more important matters on her mind.

Max was home from Argentina, in fine fettle and in time to see the hillside at Ireson's Landing ablaze with autumn color; to hold his wife and his son in his arms again; to show Sarah the rescued Watteaus and get her somewhat expurgated report on the doings at the Wilkins Museum. Brooks, Theonia, and Jesse were back from a tour that had proved to be both informative and lucrative. Jesse had demonstrated himself able and eager to take some of the traveling off Max's shoulders and give him more time with his family.

Miriam and Ira, home from the lake, were revving up for Mike's wedding. Ira's present to the bride and groom would be a 1956 Ford Thunderbird, magnificently restored by his own hands; Miriam's, a wonderful set of high-tech cookware and a file of her own recipes to get the newlyweds off on the right foot, foodwise. The Rivkin and Bittersohn grandparents were clubbing together with Sarah and Max to complete the renovations that had been started some time ago on Sarah's Victorian carriage house. The newlyweds would be at liberty to use the place year-round until such time as they might choose to live elsewhere; which they probably wouldn't because, as Mother Bittersohn sensibly pointed out, why should they?

Having brought back the missing Watteaus, Max Bittersohn had naively expected this to be the end of his connection with the Wilkins. Instead, he found a shambles. The museum's chatelaine had been murdered and its just-elected chairman of trustees forced to resign because of his marital ties to her murderess. Titian's original, unequivocally genuine, *Rape of Lucrece* had been discovered, at the suggestion of Mrs. Sarah Kelling Bittersohn, hidden in Turbot's barn behind a meretricious parody of a farmyard hoedown painted on century-old boards that had deserved better treatment. Turbot was trying to claim that he'd only been storing *Lucrece* as a favor to a friend, but skepticism was rife.

Turbot ran into another snag when Max came up with a detailed monograph on the Turbot stickpin collection, published privately forty-six years ago and bearing a sad little penciled-in postscript giving the date on which the stickpins had been found missing. The great-uncle from whom Turbot claimed to have inherited them was by now long dead; there seemed to be no proof that young Elwyn had actually robbed his own great-grandfather but neither was there anything to show that he hadn't. Max foresaw a family wrangle on the scale of the Eustace Diamonds; he was glad he didn't have to get mixed up in it.

As to the Wilkins Museum's staff, if such it could be called, Vieuxchamp had proven himself a broken reed. The guards whom Dolores had picked were no more capable than he. The only member who knew what to do and how to do it was the self-effacing veteran whom Vieuxchamp and his satellites had scornfully dubbed Milky.

Joseph Melanson had weathered his false arrest and his heart attack, he'd come out of the hospital not quite a new man but certainly a more interesting one. His close brush with death and the concerned support he'd been given had created a fresh incentive to live. With nobody bullying him, his old friend Brooks lending moral support, and the beauteous Theonia cooing at him over the teacups, Melanson was able to overcome his shyness and reel off anecdotes always interesting, often funny, sometimes even a tad risqué about the museum where he'd been for so long a part of the woodwork.

That was all changed now. The enfeebled board of trustees had voted unanimously to give their ablest and most respected employee the position Mr. Fitzroy had held. Now he was Mr. Melanson to everybody except the egregious Vieuxchamp, who called him Joseph to his face and followed him around trying to persuade the other guards that Vieuxchamp was still really the man in charge, which didn't fool them a bit.

Still, the Wilkins lacked a head of trustees. Max Bittersohn was offered the position, or any other position that he might consent to take, but declined. A museum whose exhibits had been acquired almost a century ago and had to be kept exactly where Madam Wilkins had put them offered no enticement to a man in the prime of life with a zest for action. What this museum needed was a curator in the simplest sense of the word, somebody to take full charge over what was already there. Since this can of worms had been handed to Sarah at the beginning, it was only fitting that she should be the one to put the lid on, and she did.

"We're off the hook, Max! I've asked her, and she's willing."

"Who's willing to what?"

"Aunt Bodie, of course. She's the ideal head of trustees. She was a docent at the Museum of Fine Arts for years and years, she's chaired a zillion committees and fund drives. She'll have the Wilkins whipped into shape in a matter of months, she'll keep it running like a trainman's watch. She'll organize a Friends of the Madam's group, give teas for all the society editors, and spearhead a drive that will put the palazzo back in the black in no time flat. You'll see."

Max was unconvinced. "That's a long commute every day for a woman who still drives a beige-and-gray 1946 Daimler."

"It won't be a commute at all. She's planning to sell that great ark of a house which neither of her children nor her children's children will ever want to live in, and move into the palazzo."

"Huh?"

"Like everyone else, you forget about the apartment Madam Wilkins kept for herself on the top floor. It's never been shown to the public and doesn't count as part of the museum, so she can just move in and do as she pleases. Within reason, of course, but Aunt Bodie is never unreasonable. There's a tiny elevator that goes all the way from the cellar to the penthouse, which is another thing nobody remembers; Aunt Bodie's going to have it put back in running order."

"Great, she can give rides at a buck a time for the good of the cause. What sort of shape is the apartment in, or shouldn't I ask?"

"Not too bad. Dolores used to see that it was cleaned every so often. The plumbing's a disaster, that antique Boston fine-thread tubing which hadn't been changed since the palazzo was built is in a state of total collapse, of course—the zinc in the brass alloy rots away and the whole system falls apart if you so much as look at it—but she's planning to install copper tubing all through at her own expense. If Madam Wilkins's ghost drops by to register a protest, she won't get far with Aunt Bodie."

"That I can believe," said Max. "What about the heat and lights? She's not going to electrify the place, is she?"

"Oh no, she'd never do that. She claims she doesn't mind a bit reading by gaslight and keeping the apartment warm with gas logs and coal fires. That will mean heating the whole building enough to keep the pipes from freezing, but Aunt Bodie will underwrite the costs until the museum is solvent again. She's filthy rich, you know, though she doesn't look it."

"So all's well that ends well."

Except that Dolores Agnew Tawne was dead. Sarah didn't quite know how she felt about Dolores, even after the soul-searching she'd done at odd moments when she'd got the chance. There was no question that Dolores would have taken an awful beating from the media if it had ever leaked out that she'd been the master forger who'd made the Wilkins a laughingstock, and also a confederate of the Wicked Widows. And it would have leaked out; Lala LaVonne LaVerne would have seen to that if she hadn't gone too far around the bend. Why were there always willing victims waiting around for the torturer to show up? Sarah decided not to think about that.

"You know, Max, I had to search Dolores's studio. One thing I couldn't understand was what she'd done with so many of the copies you'd given back to her, until Joseph Melanson enlightened me. It turns out that he owns quite a big house in West Roxbury that he inherited from his mother. From some things he said and a few more that he didn't say, I gathered that Mrs. Melanson must have been something special in the blood-sucking line, which may explain why he hid out in the back rooms at the Wilkins all those years. Anyway, Dolores got the bright idea that Joseph should turn his house over to her and refurbish it as a museum where the paintings she'd done for the Wilkins could be permanently on display."

"And what was he supposed to do then? Rent a houseboat?"

"Good question. I don't think she gave much thought to that part of the program. Anyway, Joseph had sense enough not to go for it, but he did hang some of the paintings in his living room to shut her up for the time being. His own idea is that the paintings might be used to teach art appreciation in schools, taking them around a few at a time, giving the teachers information that they could pass on to the pupils in an interesting way, then letting the pictures hang in the classrooms for a while so that the children could get a feeling for real painting instead of stupid television. I think he ought to get together with Aunt Bodie and talk it over, don't you?"

"Sure." Max gathered his wife into his arms. "So you didn't even miss me. Good going, *fischele*. What are you planning to do for an encore?"

Sarah told him. Max was none too happy, but he acquiesced.

Autumn went out in a blaze of glory, the wilted chrysanthemums in the Wilkins's courtyard made way for the holly and the ivy and pots of poinsettia red, pink, and white. Then came the New Year and time to close the museum for its annual three-month shutdown, during which period everything that needed to be done would have been done skimpily or not at all if Boadicea Kelling hadn't been right there wielding a duster with the best of them. After the drab walls had been repainted in their original vibrant colors, the rotten draperies replaced by new fabrics woven to order in the same patterns and shades that Madam Wilkins had picked out, the dulled gilding burnished anew by the skilled hands of Lydia Ouspenska, and all things made as bright and beautiful as they had first been gazed upon by the awestruck guests at Madam Wilkins's opening party, there was to be a gala reopening that would kick off a fund drive such as the Madam had never dreamed of but would surely have applauded.

The work was done and, thanks to Boadicea's formidable powers of persuasion, done on time. Now there were only the fresh plants from the Madam's greenhouse to be set into the redug and replenished flower beds. On the Monday before the Sunday that was to be the grand reopening day, a small group of persons associated in their various ways with the Wilkins Museum gathered at the corner of the courtyard that had been Dolores Tawne's favorite spot.

As they stood around on the mosaic walks, accompanied by a few of Dolores's old friends the peacocks, one of the trustees who had known her the longest delivered a short eulogy and said a little prayer. Then Sarah Kelling Bittersohn stepped forward and opened a small rosewood casket borrowed from one of the exhibits. Reverently and a bit tearfully, she spilled out the contents onto the fertile soil and stepped back. As the gardeners raked what was mortal of their late associate into the place where she had asked to be let lie, Brooks Kelling affixed a small brass plaque to the courtyard wall behind them. It read simply:


DOLORES AGNEW TAWNE

1933–1994

A gifted artist, a dedicated worker,
and a staunch friend of
the Wilkins Museum

*There be of them that have
left a name behind them.*


And that was that. As they walked away, Max asked his wife, "Where did you get the quote?"

"It's from the Apocrypha via Bartlett's," Sarah told him. "I'm not altogether sure what it means, but it seemed to fit the purpose. Did I mention that Aunt Bodie's invited us to tea in her aerie? It's just as well the Madam can't be here, she never did get on with the Kellings. But then neither did lots of other people. Come on, darling, I think the Wilkins owe me a cup of tea."

Welcome to the Island of Morada—getting there is easy, leaving . . . is murder.

Embark on the ultimate, on-line, fantasy vacation with
# MODUS OPERANDI.

Join fellow mystery lovers in the murderously fun MODUS OPERANDI, a unique on-line, multi-player, multi-service, interactive, mystery game launched by The Mysterious Press, Time Warner Electronic Publishing and Simutronics Corporation.

Featuring never-ending foul play by your favorite Mysterious Press authors and editors, MODUS OPERANDI is set on the fictional Caribbean island of Morada. Forget packing, passports and planes, entry to Morada is easy—all you need is a vivid imagination.

Simutronics GameMasters are available in MODUS OPERANDI around the clock, adding new mysteries and puzzles, offering helpful hints, and taking you virtually by the hand through the killer gaming environment as you come in contact with players from on-line services the world over. Mysterious Press writers and editors will also be there to participate in real-time on-line special events or just to throw a few back with you at the pub.

**MODUS OPERANDI is available on-line now.**

Join the mystery and mayhem on:
- America Online® at keyword MODUS
- Genie® at keyword MODUS
- PRODIGY® at jumpword MODUS

**Or call toll-free for sign-up information:**
- America Online® 1 (800) 768-5577
- Genie® 1 (800) 638-9636, use offer code DAF524
- PRODIGY® 1 (800) PRODIGY, use offer code MODO

Or take a tour on the Internet at
http://www. pathfinder.com/twep/games/modop.

**MODUS OPERANDI—It's to die for.**